PRINCESS OF PRIAS

COURTNEY DAVIS

5 Prince Publishing

Published by 5 PRINCE PUBLISHING & BOOKS, LLC

PO Box 865, Arvada, CO 80001

www.5PrinceBooks.com

ISBN digital: 978-1-63112-287-3

ISBN print: 978-1-63112-288-0

Cover Credit: Marianne Nowicki

*To my husband, your belief that I can create worlds is endless
and I couldn't have done it without your support.*

ACKNOWLEDGMENTS

Thank you to the wonderful staff at 5 Prince Publishing for believing in me a second time and helping me to bring the dream of this book to life.

PUBLISHER ACKNOWLEDGEMENTS

Thank you to Cate Byers, Marianne Nowicki, Bernadette Soehner, and Briana Nagler for your assistance in the publication of Princess of Prias by Courtney Davis.

PRINCESS OF PRIAS

PROLOGUE

K dragged her bruised and battered body away from the smoldering wreckage. Once she was sure she was a safe distance away, she laid on her back and took in her strange surroundings. The first thing she noticed was the air, it was breathable and clean, though frigid as it filled her lungs. This gave her a bit of comfort, perhaps all was not lost. The ground beneath her was hard and covered in white stuff that melted where she touched it. Soon moisture was seeping through her thin tunic, chilling her even more. She knew she needed to get somewhere warm and safe, but she wasn't sure she could do anything more than crawl at this point. She needed strength. She looked up, trying to draw strength from the stars, but all she could see was a canopy of green shielding her from what would have been an unfamiliar night sky. She hoped the burning flight pod was similarly covered, undetectable by the Enforcers who were surely out there looking for her, and the others.

She sighed heavily, knowing it wouldn't really matter if they could see it; it was only a matter of time before they tracked her here, her shackle made sure of that.

K lifted her arm and looked at the gold cuff, shuddering at

the reminder of her selfish stupidity. It glared up at her like a beacon, promising vengeance from the Enforcers and Temis. The baby was still safe—still kicking around in her belly—but she knew she didn't have much time. The rest of her plan had to be followed through, tonight.

The first labor pain stabbed across K's stomach, making her curl into a ball. "Just hold on a little longer, baby, Mama's going to make sure you can have a life." Another stabbing pain came and went, then K tried to stand, she had to find shelter.

She made it two steps before another pain, followed by a rush of water, brought her to her knees. She screamed up at the sky, cursing her uncle and calling to her Goddesses to save her child and use it to bring vengeance down upon the head of Temis for the destruction of their utopia.

Her plea was answered. A light flashed in the darkness. "Achromic?" she whispered and waited as the light flashed over her and hurried closer. She soon realized it was no Goddess but something of this planet that approached. She touched the small device in her ear, making sure she'd be able to understand and speak whatever language her savior spoke.

"Oh dear, what happened to you?" The voice was quiet but confident, and so calm.

K knew she was safe; her Goddesses had sent a savior for her child. She lifted her head and saw a small woman with lots of grey hair piled atop her head, kind blue eyes, and weathered skin. She was wearing an odd red gown and large brown boots. Not exactly what she was expecting to see in her savior, but she wasn't about to question it.

"What's your name?"

"K."

"Can you walk, Kay dear?"

"I don't know." K tried, and with the woman's help, she was

able to rise. The woman helped her through the darkness and soon they arrived at a small cottage.

The woman didn't ask K to explain herself or her situation. She led her inside and straight to a bed. As K lay there, letting each rush of pain wash over her and bring her closer to her baby, the woman set about readying for the imminent delivery. K screamed and cursed through the pain when it got too intense, but the woman kept reassuring her.

"There, there, dear, you are doing quite well."

K thought she was crazy. It wasn't supposed to hurt this much, was it?

"Just relax as much as you can between the contractions. Don't worry, Aunt Sara is here to care for you and the little one."

K reached out and grabbed Sara's hand, stilling her. "Yes, the baby, you must take care of it, protect it from them. They will look for it, you have to hide the pod and take care of the baby." K was frantic in her pleading, but the woman just looked at her calmly, reassuring her again that she was going to be fine.

It continued for hours, and just when K didn't think she could possibly take any more, it was over. The baby was delivered with one final push, and she was cradling her screaming baby girl in her arms at last. The baby had a blue mark high on her right arm, a mark of the Goddess Cerulean, daughter of Achromic. They *had* heard her call, answered her, and had given the child their blessing.

K knew she had made the right decision for her people. A familiar tingle rippled up her own arm, reassuring her even more.

"It's a perfect girl," Sara proclaimed enthusiastically.

"L," K said as she gazed into purple eyes exactly like her own. This was the new Princess of Prias, next in line to be queen and blessed by the Goddesses to save their people. So perfect, so beautiful. K's eyes blurred with tears, knowing what she had to do now, before it was too late.

"Elle, what a beautiful name."

"Clean her up please, I must rest." K handed her daughter to Sara and watched them walk away. She blinked back the tears and asked the Goddess Cerulean for courage. She honestly believed her sacrifice would matter, hard as it was. She would make it quick, and as painless as possible. She slid off the bed and before Sara even knew she was up; K had the scissors buried deep in her own chest.

As K lay bleeding out on the floor, staring up into the kind blue eyes of Sara, she saw the blue tinged face of Cerulean floating above, ready to welcome her to the next plane of existence.

"You have to take special care of her, she is the only princess, and she must be queen. The Goddesses have given their blessing and she will save our people. Take my journal, she'll need it and don't let her touch the cuff until she is ready for the fight." Her eyes slid shut. Her chest stopped rising, the cuff opened and fell from her wrist.

The Queen was dead.

ONE

Elle smoothed lotion over her body. As always, her fingers were drawn to her birthmark and lingered there for a moment. A small blue star high on her right arm, it was about the size of a nickel and slightly raised. She had always liked the odd thing and it gave her a kind of comfort to touch it, almost as if it grounded her in her body and out of her head, which is where she spent so much of her life.

She had never seen a birthmark like hers on another person and every doctor she'd ever asked about it, said that although it was something they had never encountered before, it was nothing to worry about; it wasn't cancerous. Like the white streak of hair at her right temple and her deep purple eyes, it was just something about her that was different. She liked to blame these things for why she never found herself surrounded by large groups of great friends, but that was also a side effect of spending too much time in one's own head.

Of course, it didn't help that she was shy. Having been raised in the deep woods of North Idaho by her loving, yet admittedly crazy, Aunt Sara, hadn't exactly prepared her for a social life. She hadn't spent much time with anyone her age until she was old enough to legally drive herself into the tiny town of Bonners Ferry, and even then, it wasn't as if she'd had friends to hang out with. Most of her outings had consisted of a stop at the store and the library; not that there was much else to do in the town. She was home-schooled by her aunt and did as much learning on her own as possible. Books had been her only way of getting outside her safe little world in the woods and she'd lost herself in many. At the age of seventeen she'd made the terrifying decision to leave the safety of her home and go to the closest community college in Coeur d'Alene.

That was ten years ago, now she was Dr. Elle Monroe, Ob-gyn, once again living in Coeur d'Alene, Idaho. Her roommate, Katherine, was her best friend. They'd met in college her first year, and Katherine had taken an instant liking to the awkward girl, making it her hobby to get Elle out of her shell. It had worked a bit, but if she were being honest, Elle knew she was only slightly less awkward than she'd been as a child.

Elle slipped on her t-shirt and running shoes. She would go out to the lake and run off the stress of her day, then return and get ready for her Friday night, which usually consisted of take out and a romance novel, sometimes a movie with Katherine. Tonight however, she had a date with Ryan, an anesthesiologist she often worked with in the delivery room. He had been asking her out since the day they met, and in a moment of insanity, she'd accepted. She was seriously regretting it now and wondering if she could cancel without making work with him awkward from here on out. Of course, a bad date would make things even more awkward in the delivery room, not that the date was going to make things between them terribly comfortable.

It wasn't that he was unattractive, quite the opposite actually, he had shaggy black hair and dark skin, kind brown eyes and a quick smile filled with white teeth. All the nurses were in love with him and envied her chance at a date. The problem was, Elle didn't really date *anyone*. She had just never enjoyed the embarrassing ritual. Awkward dinner trying to make conversation, uncomfortable dark movie theater where he tried to hold your hand or touch your leg without breaking his gaze from the movie that no one is actually paying attention to. Then there was the kiss goodnight, which was by far the worst part, fumbling, bumbling, wet kisses full of grabby hands and bad breath. Rarely did she have a second date, which meant her sex life was nonexistent. She wasn't still a virgin at twenty-seven, but her partners had been few and far between, and utterly forgettable. It had always felt like something was missing, like they just weren't doing it right. Not that she really thought that; she was a doctor, and her job was mostly helping women through pregnancy and delivering babies, she knew the mechanics of how they were made.

Not for the first time, she wondered if it was her. Maybe she was just one of those people who didn't enjoy sex. Except that she was perfectly capable of having a good time by herself, it's just that including anyone else in the situation felt dull and disappointing. Katherine was convinced it was Elle's choice in past partners, Elle couldn't deny that was a real possibility, although the admission still didn't leave her eager to try again.

She just didn't see the appeal of repeating the process very often. But every once in a while, she was so distracted by a pretty face and strong arms that she forgot how dreadful the experience was bound to be. Elle pulled her dark red hair into a ponytail that hung down to her shoulder blades and told herself that she had to give Ryan the benefit of the doubt. *I can't judge him based on my past experiences, blah-blah-blah.* She repeated the mantra Katherine tried drilling in her head on a regular basis, but it didn't make her feel any more optimistic. Quite the opposite actually; it made her think of all her past experiences and how terrible it was going to be to work with Ryan after this failed attempt at romance.

"I hope you don't plan on wearing *that* for your date with Doc Hottie." Katherine was leaning against the doorjamb of Elle's room, still in her scrubs from work, eating low-fat yogurt with an amused look on her face. Katherine was constantly on a diet, even though she was a nurse and knew how unhealthy that was. She just couldn't accept the ample curves God had given her to go along with her short black hair and big blue eyes. She was cute and energetic; just not much fun when that energy was focused in Elle's business.

"I'm going for a run before my, uh..."

"Date?" Katherine supplied around a mouthful of yogurt.

"It's not a date, not really. We are just friends getting together for a meal, that's all." Elle pushed past Katherine and rushed out of the apartment before any more could be said. Katherine tended to make a big deal about this sort of thing, and Elle definitely did not need that kind of pressure.

The afternoon was warm, the lake was beautiful, and by the time Elle was back at her car, she was feeling slightly better about her date. Ryan really was a genuinely nice guy, always a gentleman at work, and attractive. There was no reason to not expect to have a good time; except that her past experiences had conditioned her to expect otherwise.

Elle arrived back at the apartment with plenty of time to get ready. Katherine and her boyfriend, James, were cuddled up on the couch.

"Hey James." James played guitar in a band and tonight he was dressed for a show. All leather and studs, his electric blue hair spiking out all over his head and lots of eye makeup, obviously a Katherine job. "Where are *The Lights* playing tonight?"

"Sherman Park, you going to come watch?"

"James, I told you, Elle has a date tonight," Katherine said, whacking him playfully on the arm.

"Oh yeah, some Dr. Dude, I remember. Well, bring him by. If he's cool, he'll like it."

"Oh yes, I will definitely be judging his *coolness* by how appreciative he is of your music." Elle laughed, she almost wished she didn't have a date tonight, she really did like going to James' concerts. The loud music made it impossible to think and she was always exhausted afterwards and able to sleep dreamlessly. It was a great wind-down after a busy work week.

Elle retreated to her bedroom and got ready for her date. They were going to get some sushi and then head to the local playhouse. A simple but nice evening. One thing she appreciated about Ryan was that he wasn't pretentious. Most doctors were so full of themselves that Elle had never even been tempted to date one.

Elle dressed in a knee length, white, peasant skirt and a yellow, three-quarter sleeve top with a neckline plunging just enough to show off some of her C cup. She braided her hair to the right side, hiding her white streak, and strapped on white sandals. She spun in the mirror and was satisfied enough; casual, cute, not overly sexy, and certainly not trying too hard.

She was just about to leave her room when her cell rang.

She couldn't think of any of her patients that were in danger of going into labor tonight, of course that didn't mean none would. In her experience, it was never an impossibility. She really didn't want to cancel her date, not after she had spent so much time talking herself into keeping it. She crossed her fingers and picked up the phone. It was a Bonners Ferry number, and not one she recognized.

"Hello, this is Dr. Monroe."

"Hello Doctor, this is Shelly Traips down at Boundary

Community Hospital. Your aunt, Sara Monroe, was brought in this afternoon."

Elle's heart shuddered to a momentary halt at the news. "What happened?"

"We think it was a heart attack, I'm sorry Doctor Monroe. Your aunt didn't make it."

Elle let the phone slip from her shaking hand and drop to the floor, her body quickly followed, crumpling with a deep sob.

TWO

Elle looked around the tiny, cluttered cabin that she and Aunt Sara had shared for seventeen years. She ran her hands along the familiar worn fabrics and smooth woods of the furniture, inhaling deeply the scent that was home; the scent that could only come from years of wood stove heat and comfort food cooking.

She closed her eyes and remembered the joy of growing up here. So much freedom being surrounded by state land, able to run about safely, star gazing up at the clear night sky uninterrupted by city lights. She'd had a wonderful childhood, Aunt Sara had made sure of that, albeit a little lonely.

Elle knew that there was no real relation between herself and Sara, but it hadn't mattered. There was plenty of love that came from the heart, no DNA necessary. The fact that neither of them had any other living relative made them all the more important to each other.

Elle sank into Aunt Sara's favorite chair and pulled the old afghan over her body, despite the heat of the day. She huddled underneath it, trying to block out the oppressive loneliness that threatened to overtake her. She was now completely alone in this world.

The tears she had managed to hold in during the small memorial that morning, finally fell. She cried long and silent for the only mother, aunt, grandmother she had ever known.

Sometime later, Elle pushed herself out of the chair and rubbed her face clear of tears, determined to be done with them and to get started on cleaning this place out. She didn't want to wait, the sooner she took care of things here, the sooner she could get back to her life, back to her work. She planned to box everything up and take most of it to the thrift store, then sell the cabin. There were about ten acres here so she knew she would be able to get a fairly good price for it. With the money, she could buy a place of her own if she wanted or take a vacation and a chunk out of her massive student loans.

She knew what her aunt would say. 'Treat yourself to something special, a once in a lifetime experience. Bills will always be there no matter how many you pay off.'

"Goodbye, Aunt Sara," Elle whispered as she started to fill the first box.

Three days and two trips to the thrift store later, Elle had the cabin cleared out. She stood looking around the empty space and her heart ached for her loss. She would never again come here and smell her aunt's home cooked chili and sweet cornbread, never again hear the comforting sounds of her aunt's clicking knitting needles and crackling fire.

"I love you, Aunt Sara, and I will miss you." Elle turned away and shut the door. Just one thing left to do. Elle looked at her watch, 4:45, the realtor was due in about an hour. She had just enough time.

Elle entered the small shed next to the cabin and began

loading her borrowed truck with its contents. She was sweating in her cutoffs and t-shirt, covered in dirt and dust by the time she had the shed cleared out. She stepped back and took one last look, there was something in the far corner of the top shelf. Running her hands along the shelf, her fingers passed through unimaginable years of grime until her fingertips hit a small box just out of reach. She tried jumping and reaching, but no luck. In the end she had to brace her feet precariously on two shelves to reach the box. It seemed to be as far out of reach as it could possibly get. How had Aunt Sara managed to get it there in the first place? Obviously, it wasn't something she had planned on retrieving, maybe ever.

The hair on Elle's arms rose as she grasped the small box and jumped down to the ground. It was an old shoebox, only big enough for baby shoes. She wiped the dirt off the top and saw that *Elle* was scrawled across the lid in Aunt Sara's familiar hand. A strange sense of foreboding ran down Elle's spine and a sharp pain stabbed at her upper right arm.

Elle dropped the box and rubbed at the pain, centered at her birthmark. She knelt down and stared at the box for a moment, not sure she wanted to touch it again. She was not a superstitious person, but some things were undeniably creepy. She refused to be intimidated by a box however, and besides, it had her name on it. Obviously, Aunt Sara had saved it for her, probably just forgot it was up there.

But what could Aunt Sara have possibly put up here so long ago that was hers?

Elle took a deep breath and reached out cautiously to the box, her heart hammering in her chest. A car honking made her jump and scream. She chastised herself for being such a wuss and grabbed the box, then threw it inside the truck before walking over to meet the realtor.

"Hey, you must be Elle Monroe." A young, dark haired,

man emerged from a car advertising Century 21. He wore a short-sleeve pinstripe shirt, blue tie, wranglers with a big belt buckle, and cowboy boots. As he straightened away from the car, he donned a well-worn brown cowboy hat to complete the outfit, and smiled brightly, revealing surprisingly perfect white teeth.

"Yes, and you must be Bobby, the realtor."

"At your service, Ma'am."

He tipped his hat, making Elle smile despite the fact that calling her Ma'am made her feel ancient. She guessed he was only five or six years younger than her though, so she assumed he was just being respectful and professional.

"This is the last load of stuff. I have some people coming out to clean in the morning, then it should be ready to show." Elle called upon all her professionalism to keep the emotion out of her voice. The thought of selling this place was heart-wrenching, but there was just no reason to keep it. She didn't *ever* want to live in this tiny town again and even the thought of coming here for weekend getaways without seeing Aunt Sara was too much.

"I wish I could say it was going to be an easy sell, being so far out here though..." Bobby shook his head with a look of regret on his face. "There is quite a bit of land though, so that will be a selling point."

Elle showed Bobby around and they discussed fair market value before she slid into her borrowed truck and shut the door. He tipped his hat and called her Ma'am again, then got in his car to follow her down the long dirt road.

By the time Elle was back in Coeur d'Alene and returning the truck to her friend, it was nearly eleven and she was exhausted. She had tomorrow off, and she planned to sleep for most of it. She was half asleep already and pulling out of the drive when Anita ran after her with something in her hands. Elle rolled down her passenger window and waited.

"You forgot this," Anita said, tossing the forgotten shoebox onto Elle's passenger seat. "See ya!"

"Yeah," Elle called to her friend, a little late. She was staring at the box, her exhaustion momentarily forgotten.

Elle drove home quickly, anxious to look inside the box. Was it possible that there was something from her mother that Aunt Sara had always meant to give her? Elle had asked Aunt Sara about her mother all the time as a child. She'd always answered the same way. *'Your mother was beautiful, just like you are, and she loved you so much that she gave her life to bring you into this world and trusted me to take great care of you.'* Elle had soon figured out that Aunt Sara had not known her mother and so there was no way for Elle to know anything about her birth family. Of course, she had come up with many wonderful stories as a child about how her mother was a princess hiding from an evil queen and her father was a brave knight who slayed dragons and would one day show up to take her back to the kingdom and claim her rightful place.

She had grown out of that fantasy a long time ago and now realized that her mother was most likely a fugitive or drug addict that was hiding in the woods. Maybe trying to make it across the border to Canada when she went into labor. She stumbled across Aunt Sara's cabin just in time and died after giving birth because of the lack of medical care. Not nearly as nice, but much more likely.

Elle turned the engine off in the apartment parking lot and stared at the small box.

Never in her life had she felt like she fit in, she had never had a history to draw from, or peers she identified with. She had been forced to make herself from scratch, and she always felt like a couple major ingredients were missing, like history and family. In the books she'd read as a child, kids like her grew up to be superheroes and princesses; chosen ones. She'd made herself into something though, and she'd accepted that she'd come from nothing special. Aunt Sara had been an angel, saving her from what might have been a sad existence had she grown up with a drug addicted or fugitive mother.

Elle reached for the box, attributing her sudden chills that ran up and down her body to the air conditioning still coming from the car vents. Her hand touched the box, and she did her best to ignore the stab of pain in her right arm, maybe it *was* a cancerous mole. She made a mental note to check it for color or shape changes soon.

The box was small and light. It couldn't be holding much, but somehow, she knew it held something important.

Elle carefully picked at the tape on either side of the lid. Before she lifted it, she took a deep, steadying breath, her hands were shaking. She chastised herself for being a coward and lifted the lid with one quick movement.

On top of some old, crumpled newspaper, was a small card with *Elle* written on the front in her Aunt Sara's hand. Elle picked it up and bit back the tears that threatened to fall again. She was done crying over her loss, she reminded herself.

She opened the card and read:

My dearest little Elle-

I know that someday you will come upon these, if I don't give them to you first. When I found your mother, Kay, she was so obviously in trouble, running from someone and I worried for the first few weeks that someone would come looking for you and you'd be taken away from me. When no one came after a couple months, I decided you were mine and I knew that these should be put safely away for you to have when you grew. Maybe you'll be able to make sense of them, I never could. I have no doubt your mother wanted you to have them though. She was wearing the

*bracelet when you were born, and the journal was in her pocket.
You cry whenever the bracelet is near, as if you can sense the loss
of its owner, so I am putting it far out of your reach. I love you so
much little Elle, and I count myself blessed to have been given
the chance to raise you.*

Love Always,
Aunt Sara

Elle couldn't help shedding a couple more tears after reading
the note. Aunt Sara had provided so well for her. Elle knew she
couldn't have possibly been more loved had she been raised by
her own troubled mother. She felt like she was betraying Aunt
Sara by feeling so incomplete. She didn't think Aunt Sara would
have judged her for it though, she would have understood the
loneliness, especially now.

Elle took a deep breath; her hands were sweating, and her
heart was beating erratically. She peered into the box.
Newspaper covered what was inside. She reached in and
slipped her hand around the old paper until her fingers hit upon
something cold and smooth. Her heart sped up a bit more as she
pulled out a two-inch-wide gold cuff with some kind of odd
markings on the inside. If it was a language, it was one she had
never seen before.

As she held the cuff in her hands, peering closely at the
strange markings, her right arm began to ache. She ignored the
pain and looked closer, cupping it in her hands, trying to place
the markings among the few languages she had studied in
college. Her body warmed the gold against her skin and the
markings began to glow with an eerily mesmerizing green light.
Pain stabbed so sharply at her arm that she dropped the cuff
back into the box.

"What the fuck was that?" Elle whispered, disbelieving

what she was seeing and feeling. The markings continued to glow for a moment, then the light weakened and finally stopped altogether. Elle rubbed her arm where it pained and felt the slightly raised birthmark where the pain seemed to be radiating from.

She reached in the box again, careful to avoid the cuff, and pulled out a small black leather book. This must be the journal Aunt Sara was talking about. She was shaking as she opened it to see what secrets her mother had left within.

What she found were the same strange markings that were on the bracelet, indecipherable and quite possibly a secret code rather than a foreign language. The characters looked similar to English letters, only slightly different, but in no recognizable order.

With a disappointed sigh, Elle placed the journal back in the box and crushed the lid back on, then shoved it under the seat of her car. She quickly got out and refused to think about any of what had just happened. *I am tired and suffering from a grief-induced hallucination.* She told herself as she made her way to her apartment. Reasoning that her fantasies of otherworldly origins she had entertained as a child were coming back to her in this time of stress. She was a doctor; she knew what kind of crazy could suddenly come over people in stressful situations. She just needed a good night's rest, and that is exactly what she intended to get right now.

Elle showered and crawled into her soft bed, quickly falling into a deep sleep, completely unaware of the blip on two different screens billions of miles away that had briefly alerted others to her existence. Brief though it was, it was still long enough for them to lock on to her general location and give them reason enough to head towards her to investigate, each with their own goal for retrieval.

THREE

A week and a half later, Elle sat in her office, on the phone with her dermatologist.

"What do you mean there is nothing to worry about. Last week I woke up with another birthmark, how is that all right?"

"Elle, I am sorry I don't have a better explanation for you. I will run some more tests, but I am telling you there is nothing wrong with you. Some people just develop skin abnormalities. It's nothing to worry over."

"Blue, star shaped ones, *overnight!*" Elle whispered harshly so as not to alert anyone to the conversation.

"I'm not saying it isn't weird, I am just saying you shouldn't be worried, ok?"

"Yeah, thanks, Trish. Let me know if you find out anything else." Elle hung up the phone and rubbed her arm. The day after she had come home from Aunt Sara's, she'd woken to discover a new blue star on her right arm, identical and adjacent to the other. She had been so freaked out she'd run to her dermatologist right away; but so far, they had not been able to find any reason for it. Elle had a theory of course, but she wasn't about to share that with anyone, she would be sent directly to the loony bin for a nice relaxing vacation if she did.

She pulled the shoebox from her purse, where she had been keeping it, although she hadn't touched the cuff except one other time since the first night. It had warmed to her touch and began to glow, and *two* stabs of pain had shot through her arm! She looked at it and the journal often though, sure they held the answers to all her questions. She was afraid of what those answers might be, she wasn't sure she wanted to know her history anymore.

Elle ran her fingers over the box and thought about putting it on. *What would happen then?* she wondered.

A knock at the door brought her out of her musing. Break time was over, time to see patients. "Darlene, I will be there in just a minute," Elle called and turned to shove the box back into her bag.

"I hope I'm not interrupting your break."

Elle spun around, surprised to find Ryan filling her doorway. She hoped she successfully hid the disappointment. She had been avoiding him since their cancelled date.

"I'm sorry I haven't had a chance to get back to you." Elle didn't kid herself into thinking he was here for any reason but to force her to talk to him. He worked at the hospital and would have had to cross two parking lots and a busy street to get to her office. This was definitely a social call, and that sucked. She was so much more comfortable talking about work.

"I was hoping if I made the trek over here, you would agree to reschedule our date." He gave her his smile that melted most hearts, but only ever left her feeling anxious.

God, what is wrong with me? she wondered with frustration. She should be jumping at the chance to go on a date with this gorgeous doctor. So why wasn't she? "I have been really busy lately, and not feeling up to being good company, I'm sure you can understand." Elle stood and grabbed some charts off her desk, trying to look busy and avoid the inevitable.

"Is that a no on my dinner offer for tonight then?" Ryan looked disappointed, but not surprised. Most of her colleagues knew she rarely dated; they whispered about her being frigid and boring. She ignored it most of the time, she knew she shouldn't care that she didn't fit in, it was nothing new really, but suddenly she did care. She wanted so badly to fit in and belong, especially after the loss of the one person she had always belonged with and the weirdness that was clouding her mind. Normal sounded amazing at the moment.

"I would love to join you for dinner tonight, actually."

Ryan's face lit up with shock and excitement. "Wonderful, I will pick you up about seven?"

"Sounds great, I'll see you then." Elle rushed past him, looking as distracted as she could manage, which wasn't that difficult considering she had just agreed to a horrifying experience. She handed the files to Darlene and asked her to return them to her desk as she hurried to the first examination room. Darlene looked at her like she was nuts, which she probably was, but didn't say anything, just hurried to do as she was instructed.

Elle went through the rest of her day with dread building in her stomach. She did not want to go out with Ryan, not really. It was Thursday and she just wanted to go to bed early. Maybe she would call and cancel after work, tell him she wasn't feeling well. That maybe another time they could get together, of course then he would just keep bugging her for that date. The best thing was to go out with him, get it over with and then they could both move on from the awful experience. She was so back and forth in what she wanted; she really *was* starting to feel sick.

After work she had a voicemail from Ryan asking her to decide where she would like to go for dinner, and he would pick a movie to see after. She hated when guys did that, why not take her on a date that they planned instead of being all fair and making her make half the choices; it was crap. She didn't even want to go on the date, now she was planning half of it.

As she sat at a stoplight on the way home, going through scenarios in her mind that would be adequate excuses for cancelling the date, her arm was suddenly on fire with pain. She nearly doubled over from the intensity of it. She quickly pulled off to the side, not really looking where she was going, and nearly ran into a black SUV filled with big, scowling, blond men. Their sharp blue gazes threw daggers in her direction, and she was thankful for the tinted windows that partially hid her from them; they looked like the kind of people to hold grudges for this sort of thing.

The pain continued and Elle's stomach rolled. She forgot the men and leaned over to rest her head on her steering wheel as she battled a wave of nausea. She breathed in and out, slow, and deep, then, just as suddenly as it had come on, it left.

"What is wrong with me?" She was starting to think she needed to go in for a full cat scan. Maybe she had a brain tumor that was causing phantom pain and keeping her from being able to make up her mind about going on a date with a handsome, successful doctor.

She was feeling perfectly fine now, as if nothing had happened, except for the fact that she was parked on the side of a busy street with people staring as they passed. She rubbed her arm, no pain at all. She didn't understand it, but she was starting to wonder at her sanity.

Elle drove the rest of the short distance to her apartment without incident. She decided she had a good enough excuse to cancel her plans with Ryan, and chicken that she was, she called him from her car so Katherine wouldn't know. Luckily when she told Ryan, he took it well, especially since she rescheduled with him for Friday night.

Elle felt much better as she strolled up to her apartment. She wouldn't feel the crushing panic of the impending Friday night date until this time tomorrow; for now, she was free. Of course, with the thoughts of dating Ryan gone, thoughts of her mysterious pain returned and with them a feeling of unease around the whole situation.

How much stress does it take to push someone over the edge of sanity? she wondered.

Katherine wasn't home yet, so Elle rushed to change into shorts and a tank top, then headed back out for a run. She would hopefully be relaxed when she returned. Otherwise, Katherine would jump on her with questions that Elle did *not* want to answer.

She ran from her apartment to the beach, not wanting to take the time to drive out to the lake path. Her hair swished across her back in a ponytail and nearly hid the streak of white at her temple. She tried to hide it whenever possible, it always made people stare. She told herself she should dye it, but she just couldn't bring herself to do it. Aunt Sara had told her that her mother had the same hair and eyes and so she'd never wanted to get rid of that one link. Somewhere in the back of her mind had always been the thought that perhaps one day someone would recognize her as her mother's daughter, and then she would know something about herself.

Elle lost herself in the feel of her muscles straining, her heart pounding, and her lungs filling deep and even. Physical exhaustion was often the only thing that settled her mind. She was completely unaware of anything outside of her physical body as the adrenaline pumped through her veins, a runner's high; it was a beautiful thing.

FOUR

Locan studied the crowd of people scattered across the beach, ignoring the curious looks he was receiving. He knew he stood out among these people, he was seven feet tall, and his long, dark brown hair hung in one long braid down to his mid-back. His naturally golden-brown skin was even more sun-kissed because of the last planet he had been searching for Prians on, and his muscles bulged in the ill-fitting clothing he had acquired that morning. Upon his arrival, he had realized that he stood out far too well in his traditional clothing, and on a planet where the general population thought it was alone, that was a problem he didn't need.

He shifted uncomfortably in the knee-length, tan pants; how could these men stand having their manhood so tightly bound? He felt like he was trying to castrate himself. Despite the fact that the salesperson had said he looked *scrumptious,* he did not like this Earth attire.

After adjusting himself to a slightly more comfortable position, he leaned against a tree and scanned the section of beach in front of him. *Hopeless,* he grumbled to himself as his eyes traveled over the crowd. He had no idea who he was looking for, or even where to look. He had asked the salesperson at the shop where the best places to spot an old friend were, wherever a crowd gathered he figured was a good place to start looking. She had pointed him toward the beach.

He had been here most of the day and he had seen no one who resembled a Prian. He hadn't seen any of Temis' Enforcers either, which *could* mean he was searching in the wrong spot. Locan fingered the jagged scar on the right side of his neck. He hoped to run into those bastards while he was here. He smiled wickedly, remembering the scar he had left on Jabon. Locan would finish what he started with that man when he got the chance.

A mother rushed her children away from him and he quickly removed the look of murder from his face, replacing it with cool confidence.

"Locan, what the hell is going on down there? Why do I see half naked women all around you? Did you find an orgy? Can I join?" Traylon joked excitedly into Locan's ear, through the nearly invisible receiver.

Traylon was tracking Locan from the ship and could zero in on Locan and his surroundings. The horny bastard was probably salivating at the sight of all the barely-clad women here. Locan was unaffected by the sight, he was on a job, and he didn't have time to think about his physical needs. Besides, he tried to avoid sex with other-worlders, even if they looked normal, you just never knew what kinds of weird sexual habits they might have.

A shiver ran down Locan's spine at the memory of one particular encounter that had ended with him covered in yellow slime and stuck to a wall; and the woman had looked just like a Prian! He shuddered and shook himself back to the present. Not an experience he wanted to repeat.

"I am at a beach, apparently it is where everyone 'hangs out', or so I was told. I haven't had any luck locating the target though. I am going to give it a little more time, then I will try another location. A 'bar' or 'club', is a good place to find people at night apparently."

"Any sign of Enforcers? We don't show a ship in the area, but that doesn't mean they aren't hiding out of range."

"Not yet. I will let you know if I do, then you may join me here to fight."

"Yes, Sir," Traylon said with mock respect.

Locan made a mental note to give him toilet duty on the return trip. That would take some of the humor out of life for him. The man was just too young to take things seriously. He had only been allowed to come on this mission in the first place because he annoyed everyone else, and they had hoped a year with Locan as his commander would calm him down. It had been almost five years now and he hadn't calmed one bit. The man found humor in any situation and the pervert was all about sex with other-worlders. He didn't seem to mind what oddities they had. Traylon was probably itching to come down here and test one of these Earthlings, especially since they so closely resembled Prians.

As a Prian, Locan was able to easily tell them apart. People of Earth—no matter that they looked so similar to Prians—just felt different. When a Prian stood next to a Prian, they could feel a connection. Next to an Earthling there was no such feeling. Prians were joined on a different level by the worship and blessings of their Goddesses. No doubt the people here could tell he was different but were unable to pinpoint exactly why. It would make them avoid him when possible and uncomfortable in his presence.

Locan was once again perusing the people on the beach and in the water, when an undeniable urge took him over. His entire body went on high alert and without knowing what he was rushing towards, he took off at full speed; flat-out running towards whatever it was that called to him. His vision went completely black except for two tiny sparks of blue light in the distance. He raced to them, knowing that whatever it was, he had to get to it fast before it was harmed.

Locan didn't question the sudden compulsion. He embraced it and charged toward the pinpricks of light, cursing the fact that he was weaponless. If there was a fight, he was supposed to call for his backup. That was the plan, but there was such a sense of urgency in him that he didn't dare waste a single moment or ounce of energy in calling for Traylon. He had to take down the threat, now.

Regardless of his lack of weapons, he was a formidable Warrior. As a descendent of a Royal Guard member, he had the ability to make his muscles swell with readiness as he pushed adrenaline through his system, making him nearly twice as large as he normally appeared. The Warrior was a separate, and dangerous, being that shared his body. He tried to never let it out, tried to never acknowledge it and let it gain power. Most embraced this other half that gave them strength. Locan resented it; he knew what it could do.

Locan was nearly upon the lights when his vision returned to normal. He saw four things at once. Dark red hair, white streak at the temple, purple eyes, and blue stars, all running towards him. His heart thudded in his chest and his palms went slick with sweat. "Princess," he whispered. He was about to reach for her when he saw the two Enforcers closing in behind her. Locan wanted to grab her and make a run for it, but he couldn't risk letting the Enforcers alert Jabon to her existence, if they hadn't already.

Locan fisted his hands and charged into the two. He stopped them with an arm to each throat. They were both knocked to the ground, but only momentarily. They quickly jumped to their feet and came at Locan with hatred burning in their pale blue eyes. He heard people gasping around him, but he couldn't care about that now. He threw punches and landed one on the nose, blood spurting out in a satisfying spray. The other he landed on the chin.

He was kicked in the stomach and knee, but barely felt the pain. With his body swelled like it was, he could take almost any impact without a flinch, but he would feel them all later. He managed to fling one Enforcer to the ground, then the other; neither moved to get up. Locan kneeled to check them; still breathing. As much as he would like to snap their necks, he didn't dare risk such an act in public. Hassling with whatever the local law enforcement happened to be was never a good idea for any mission, but this one had just become far more important, and dangerous.

Locan looked around and frowned at the crowd that had gathered to watch the fight, *what is wrong with this world that these people find such violence entertaining rather than frightening?* He wondered, then stood and they all stepped back; finally showing some sense, in his opinion.

He hurried in the direction he had seen her go and they parted for him to pass. He could feel his body returning to normal as he jogged on at a steady pace, and with it, the pain starting to become apparent. It wasn't too bad really; they hadn't been good fighters, probably just recon specialists. Soon they would send out their Warriors, and if Locan was still here, he was sure to meet up with Jabon then.

"Traylon," Locan called, pressing the device in his ear.

"Yep."

"I need you to take care of a couple Enforcers down here."

"Awesome, I am on my way, how many are there?" His voice was so filled with excitement, Locan almost wanted to tell him to forget it and send Leda instead. Locan had to remind himself that for all of Traylon's annoying habits, he was a good man; loyal and discreet.

"There were two, they're unconscious now. I just don't want them to be able to alert anyone else." Locan paused, trying to keep his voice even and detached. "I found her," he whispered, completely failing at the neutral tone he was going for.

"So why didn't you kill them?" Traylon asked, obviously too distracted by the action to realize the most important part of it all.

"Take a look around, there are people everywhere. The last thing we need is the local law asking us questions we won't be able to answer. Don't draw attention, remember, it's like rule number one of interplanetary travel."

"Got it. Clean-up duty." Traylon's spirits seemed to fall only slightly at the news, he still got to leave the ship, and that was exciting.

Locan caught sight of the dark red ponytail ahead and slowed his pace. He had to hold tight to the scraps of material that were left of his short pants. Luckily, they hadn't completely torn off with his change, otherwise he would be forced to chase after her naked. That would have surely caused more of a scene than he wanted. He wasn't sure how he was going to do this, but he knew he didn't want to approach her in public if he didn't have to. As long as he had her in his sights, she was safe enough, and he could figure out the best approach.

Locan's gaze traveled down her slim back to her perfectly flared hips and round butt.

"Why are your vitals going erratic, Locan? Are there more Enforcers?" Leda asked, breaking him out of his dangerous line of thought.

"I am jogging behind the target." He kept his voice purposefully flat, unemotional.

"Oh," Leda said with obvious disdain. No doubt she

guessed the sight he was enjoying and was probably even now zeroing in on him to get a look for herself. He couldn't hold back the urge to raise his hand in a derogatory gesture she was bound to see.

"Same to you, pervert. Just remember what you are there for, and more importantly, *who*. Do you see those stars?"

"Get back to work, Leda. I am sure Traylon will need your help chaining the prisoners when he drags them in."

"She's just jealous, Locan," interrupted Traylon, "and I wasn't able to bring them aboard. The law was already there. Oh, and get this, their law enforcement rides bicycles! How the hell are they supposed to chase down criminals on bicycles when motorized vehicles are so abundant? Anyway, I managed to inject them both discreetly. They will be dead within the hour. Now I can sit back and enjoy the sights."

Traylon's words irritated Locan more than they should have. "Turn off the screen and remember who it is that you're ogling."

"Yes, Sir," came the mocking reply, but Locan knew he was obeyed, and that ensured he wouldn't have to kill Traylon later.

Elle let out a relieved breath when she was leaning against her locked apartment door. Her run had started out great, normal even. When she had neared the beach, her arm had started to hurt, but she decided to power through it and keep going, losing herself in the run. Then out of nowhere the pain had turned into the most unbelievably pleasant tingling sensation. It was almost more disturbing than the pain. She still didn't stop though. She refused to let those, probably imagined, feelings affect her. Some kind of grief-induced psychosis, no doubt.

As she'd continued her run, she had become aware of a sense of being watched, followed even. She hadn't been able to see anything out of the ordinary when she glanced behind her, but she could *feel* the intense presence of someone else. She couldn't explain it, but she was sure her arm tingling and the feeling of being followed were connected.

"I am probably going insane," she grumbled as she threw her keys on the table. "That would be the connection."

"Elle? Are you talking to me?" Katherine popped her head out of her room, her long black hair wrapped up in curlers. In a shiny silver halter top over black capris, she was obviously getting ready for a night out.

"No, just myself. Where are you going tonight?" Elle suddenly didn't want to spend an evening by herself. She almost wished she hadn't cancelled her date with Ryan, *almost*.

"*The Lights* have a gig downtown. Wanna help me cheer them on?" As she spoke, she jiggled her enormous boobs, trying to make Elle laugh. Katherine was always so full of fun and had so much enthusiasm for life. Elle needed that energy right now.

"Sure, but I have to call Ryan and tell him to meet us. If he found out that I went out tonight without him, I'm not sure I would be able to face him in a delivery room ever again."

"Cancelled on him again, did ya?"

Elle huffed, feigning affront. "I *was* feeling ill after work. I feel great after my run however and so I will honor my date, sort of. At least this way it's done, and it won't be uncomfortably intimate."

"Oh yeah, you wouldn't want to get close to Doc Hottie," Katherine said, her voice dripping sarcasm.

"I don't want to," Elle said, childishly defensive. "He is just not my type," she amended with a little more dignity.

"No one is, honey. At least, you don't give anyone the chance to be," Katherine said sadly and retreated to her room.

Elle stomped to her own room and threw herself across her bed. *It's not true that* no one *is my type. Is it?* Elle thought about that for a while, staring up at her ceiling. She admitted that she had never felt a really intense attraction to any of the men she had dated, but what did that mean, really? She just hadn't yet met the man she was meant to spend the rest of her life with. Kind of an old-fashioned way of thinking, perhaps, but it really did seem like more of a bother than anything else when you looked across the table at your date and all you could think about was the hero in the current romance you're reading. That was her type; big, strong, and alpha. So maybe her type didn't exist in reality. That really sucked.

A knock on the front door brought Elle out of her brooding. She called Ryan, determined to give him a real chance, and quickly got ready.

Elle turned in the mirror and admired her quick work. She was ready to go in a pair of jeans that clung lovingly to her curves and a white t-shirt that highlighted her upper body very well. Her hair hung down her back in loose curls and she pulled the side up with a small comb, emphasizing rather than hiding, her streak of white. Her blue stars showed beneath her capped sleeves, and she wore amethysts on her ears and around her neck that matched her eyes. She slipped on a pair of strappy white sandals and sauntered from her room, determined to have a good time.

FIVE

Locan stood in the shadows across from the building he had followed her to. She had gone inside quickly, looking over her shoulder. She had sensed him, no surprise really, even though she was unlikely to know what she was sensing. A Prian born off-planet and raised among other-worlders would not realize what they were recognizing in the presence of another Prian. She had been aware of him following her, though, and she was more than just a Prian. Even now he could feel her pull, which meant the Enforcers might as well, if they got close enough.

He scanned the area but saw no signs of more Enforcers. When she had gone inside, he was about to follow but he had sensed an Enforcer nearby. Luckily, she was out of sight and Locan was able to dispose of the lone Enforcer with no problems. Unfortunately, it wasn't Jabon, and so was less satisfying than it could have been. He'd decided to wait and watch the door, convinced this was her residence. He wasn't sure how best to approach her, though. This wasn't like other rescue missions; she was on a planet that didn't believe in other inhabited worlds, and she was more than just a Prian citizen he wanted to offer a ride home to.

"How do things look from your view, Traylon?"

"Not nearly as good as they did a while ago. She is going to star in my dreams tonight, no doubt."

"Traylon," Locan growled. Anger filled him at Traylon's words. "Get your mind on your work, we *can't* lose this one."

"I don't see anything from here. Are you going in?" Traylon amended his attitude and for that, Locan was thankful. This was complicated, and all team members needed to treat it as such.

"I don't think that will be necessary." The door opened and Locan's entire awareness focused on her. "Damn." She wasn't alone. He slunk back farther into shadow. He would follow from a safe distance until he could get her alone.

She had changed clothes, which confirmed this was her home. At least he would know where to come back to if he managed to lose her. He watched her shiver, rub her arms, and look around, peering into all the shadows. The sun was setting and Locan was confident she wouldn't spot him. Her eyes landed near the spot he was hiding. They stayed there, peering closely, confused. She said something to her friend, and they hurried to a car.

"Damn, damn." Locan cursed, he wouldn't be able to keep up with them on foot. He closed his eyes and tried to invoke whatever had possessed him before to be able to see her light from a distance. He opened his eyes, nothing. Just the back end of her car turning onto the street and his body felt the same. No surge of fighting lust or increased muscle. The brief thought of calling his Warrior floated through his mind and he quickly suppressed it, he could not call to something that would put her in danger. He felt a small tingle in his chest and smiled, here was one thing that would help him find her.

It took him an hour, but he tracked her down. He could feel the pull of her, calling to him for protection and service. All his instincts were shouting at him to give her whatever she wanted, to protect her from all harm. Plus, something more that was strong, and he didn't yet understand. He didn't like whatever it was, but he could appreciate that it helped him find her faster. What he knew of the way the Royal Guard had worked in the city, was a queen who had invoked the power of the mother Goddess Achromic, could command any Royal Guardsman to do almost anything. It was in the guardsman's blood; none could deny it. But even without that invocation, his instincts were to protect the princess from all harm.

He looked around the small dark building that his senses had brought him to. A crowd of people were standing around drinking by a bar, another crowd swayed and writhed to the beat of the music. There were no Enforcers here, he was sure, which meant she wasn't in imminent danger. He almost wished one would show up so he could more easily spot her among the throng. If she were in danger, she would be a brighter beacon to him.

As it was, he could sense her presence, but he couldn't spot her. Locan stood in a far corner where he could see almost the entire room. The woman she had left the building with was close to the band. The man singing with bright blue hair spiked around his head and a collar around his neck was looking at her as he screamed out words to what Locan supposed was a song of love. Locan wasn't sure how these people could stand listening to this, but everyone around him seemed to be enjoying it just fine. Everyone around him had unconsciously moved slightly away. Not enough to make him stand out, but enough that Locan noticed his effect. He was used to this, most people of other planets responded negatively to his Prian energy. They should respond even more significantly to hers, which could be helpful in locating her.

Was he possibly mistaken about where she was? No, Locan

trusted his Warrior instincts. She was here somewhere; he could feel her. Locan closed his eyes and pushed the steady beat of the music out of his mind, picking through all he was sensing, pushing aside even the Prian vibe, and pinpointing her personal draw. It pulled on one particular part of him. He had a loyalty to the royal family as only a Warrior descended from the Royal Guard could have. He reached out with his senses and held onto that draw. When he felt sure of his mental grip, he opened his eyes. The room wasn't black, but it was dulled, and the noise was no more than a slight buzzing in his ears, nothing like the pounding from before. He could actually see the blue-tinted draw of her now, pulsing in time with her heartbeat and reaching through the crowd to him. He still couldn't see her, but he knew that all he had to do was follow that draw and he would be led straight to her.

He'd had plenty of time to think about what he would say to her. He had a few options and would keep trying new ones until she responded to him, maybe not the best plan, but it was the only one he had. He didn't hesitate a moment longer, he started walking through the crowd, which parted to let him easily through.

When Locan spotted her, she was facing away, talking with a dark-haired man who Locan had the unexplainable desire to punch in his pretty face. Not that the man was threatening in any way, he wasn't an Enforcer and although he was broad-shouldered and fit-looking, he was still much slighter in build than Locan. Locan just didn't like the idea of her having a man. He told himself it was because it would make it that much harder to convince her to leave with him. The ones who were attached to their current situation were harder to get away. Locan watched for a moment, assessing their relationship. If necessary, he would remove the obstacle to make it easier for her to leave the planet with him. The man didn't get too close to her. He kept his body separate even when he had to lean in to hear what she was saying. Obviously, they were not lovers.

Good, growled through his mind as if spoken aloud.

Locan stiffened and everything about his surroundings that he had been holding at bay crashed back in on him. The music and conversation filled his mind to the point that he couldn't hear himself, or anyone else, think. He shook his head, trying to calm his racing pulse. Panic tried to grip him, but he shoved it out and concentrated on his mission.

The man she was talking to looked up and met his gaze briefly. The man's eyes showed nothing more than momentary curiosity before they returned attention to her. Locan clenched his fists when he saw the dark-haired man reach out and tuck a piece of hair behind her ear with familiarity. Locan took a deep breath as his vision started to haze.

There is no reason to attack, he thought firmly and took another deep breath. *As long as he doesn't touch her again,* ran through his mind.

Locan took a step back and pressed a finger to his ear. "Traylon, are you trying to talk to me?" he asked, almost hopeful, ignoring the strange looks he got for seemingly talking to himself.

"Locan? I can barely hear you. What is all that noise about?"

Locan frowned. There was no way Traylon had been speaking to him earlier. "Their version of musical entertainment."

"Hm, interesting."

Only Traylon would find this loud annoying beat interesting. There was something wrong with that boy, he went way beyond adventurous.

"So, is she there?"

"She is, but she isn't alone." The last word was a growl and a few people who were close enough to catch it, scurried away from him with a wary look. Locan pressed his lips together in a scowl and ignored Traylon's barrage of questions. He was drawing way too much attention to himself to risk responding.

Locan moved to where he could see her face and watched her for a while, hidden behind enough people not to be too obvious. She smiled and listened politely to the man, but the smiles never reached her eyes and she continuously glanced around as if hoping to find something more interesting. Or perhaps sensing him and wondering what it was all about. Locan couldn't help but hope for the latter; he wanted her to be aware of him the same way he was aware of her. *It will make her more accepting.* He told himself. *Nothing more.*

The man took her empty glass and excused himself. Locan was sure he wouldn't be gone long. He had to take this opportunity to talk to her.

Locan walked through the crowd as she turned around and showed him her back. He was thankful that he had been able to find more comfortable, and less tattered, clothing while following her here. He was currently dressed in a tight black t-shirt and loose-fitting black pants; well, they were looser than the short pants he had busted out of earlier. They were still not comfortable compared to what he usually wore. He fit in, and that was the important thing. She shouldn't suspect anything odd right away. In his experience, if they were scared off immediately it was twice as hard to convince them.

He was directly behind her and about to touch her arm to get her attention when she spun around. Her hair flew across his face, immersing him in the sweet scent of her. He was speechless for a moment, lost in it. Her purple eyes narrowed accusingly at him as she rubbed furiously at her right arm.

"You," she said angrily and pulled Locan out of his stupor. "You have been following me."

"It is imperative that I speak with you, alone." He grabbed her arm, intending to lead her through the crowd and out the large doors opening to the street.

She jerked her arm easily out of his loose grasp and slapped him hard across the face. "I don't know you and I don't intend to go anywhere with you. Why have you been following me?"

"I will explain it all if you will just come with me. I didn't intend to force you, only guide you through this crowd so we may speak easier." Locan reassured her with studied politeness, and it was true, he would never, *could* never, force her to do anything against her will. It would go against every bit of instinct in his body.

She gave him a look that said she wasn't buying any of it. "I don't think so, buddy, find someone else to stalk, okay. I am not that interesting."

"How do you know I have been following you? You have not seen me until now." He felt like he was shouting to be heard over the music, and it felt wrong to be yelling at her, but he had no choice if she wouldn't go out to where it was quieter.

"Ha! So, you admit you have been following me." She crossed her arms under her chest, drawing his gaze down to the luscious display where a purple stone glittered atop creamy flesh. "Eyes up here, creep." She dropped her arms and pointed at her face.

"Is this guy bothering you, Elle?" The man who had been with her earlier, returned and handed her a glass filled with red liquid.

"L, your mother managed to name you before she killed herself?" Perhaps she would know more than many of the others then. That would make things much easier. Perhaps she even activated the tracking device on purpose, wanting to be discovered and taken home. He dared to hope.

The look on her face told him that she was now quite

intrigued with him. "My mother died giving birth to me, she did not kill herself," she whispered the words, but a sudden lull in the music allowed her to be heard clearly.

"Perhaps," Locan knew both were likely possibilities, but if K had been able to name her daughter, then she was well enough to most likely survive. She had been left with the only other option for protecting L, killing herself.

"Elle, do you know this guy?"

"No, but don't worry, Ryan, he is just someone trying to hit on me who can't understand that I am *not* interested. Not a danger to me, just annoying." L turned to face Ryan. "Let's dance, shall we?" She set down her drink and grabbed his hand, pulling him into the throng of people.

Locan watched them go with barely restrained fury. *Ryan* was flirting with death, dancing with Prias' one and only Princess when a Royal Guard member was in the room. Not that anyone was aware of it other than him. He settled back in the crowd where he could watch and reassess his approach.

L bore the mark of the Goddess Cerulean, the blue star. Cerulean was the Goddess of loyalty and wisdom; these were the gifts that L would hold. Locan wondered how he could use that to his advantage. She was intrigued by him, the mention of her mother had almost made her agree to follow him, *almost*. She was cautious, which meant she was also smart, he could appreciate that. It was imperative that she come willingly; he couldn't force her no matter how much easier that would be. His instincts of protection would not allow him to do anything that was not in direct alignment with her wishes, or her safety. If he had the choice, he would throw her over his shoulder and carry her out of this place and have her on his ship before she could so much as open her mouth in protest. Unfortunately, that wasn't an option unless she was in mortal danger at that exact moment and that was the only way to save her. Where was a horde of Enforcers when he needed one?

Locan moved to a vantage where she was clearly visible among the crowd. She was near the stage now, next to the woman she had left her building with. Ryan was trying his best to catch her attention as he danced beside her. The corners of Locan's mouth lifted slightly as he watched L expertly keep him from getting too close. She was definitely not interested in the man. The satisfaction that knowledge brought was very unsettling. Locan straightened away from the wall he had been leaning on and focused his attention on her. Willing her to look up and meet his gaze.

Her head swung around, and purple eyes clashed with green. Her gaze turned curious, and she made a slight move, as if she were going to approach him. Then she hissed in pain, he heard it as clear as if she were next to him and he felt it in his gut, she needed him. He whipped his head around to the direction her gaze had flung, and he saw three white heads pushing their way through the crowd: Enforcers.

Locan cursed himself, he had been so distracted trying to get L's attention he hadn't felt the danger approaching. *She* had actually felt it, even before he had. She definitely had Cerulean's wisdom. If she learned to listen to it, she just might stay safe.

SIX

Elle scanned the crowded bar. Her arm was suddenly burning. *Something is very wrong,* her mind screamed, *I have to get out of here, fast!* She didn't question the sudden intuition, she just jumped into action. She tried to get through the pulsing crowd, but this close to the stage, it was nearly impossible. She got about three steps before the crowd crushed her back to where she had started as *The Lights* began playing a new song. She frantically looked for an easy exit; her entire being telling her that she had to move faster, danger was approaching. The burn in her arm was steadily increasing, as if she were playing a very demented game of hot and cold.

Her eyes landed on three blond heads moving toward her through the crowd, her newfound intuition shouted, *danger!*

"Blond men; bad," she whispered to herself. Trying to remain calm, she turned away from them to try and make an exit out the back.

"Elle, is there something wrong? You don't look well," Katherine asked, drawing Ryan's attention away from the nearby group of twenty-one-year-old drunk chicks, and back to Elle. She would rather have had him keep his attention diverted until she was gone, she did not want to deal with anyone's questions right now.

"She's right, you look upset." Ryan placed an arm around her shoulder, intending comfort, but only managing to annoy her.

Elle shook off his arm, not caring about being polite anymore. "I have to go." Elle started pushing her way through the crowd. Her mind was screaming that she had to get out, *now*. She didn't know who those blond men were, but she was sure they were the cause of her pain. Just as she was sure the very large, very sexy, dark-haired man was the cause of her earlier tingles.

What the hell is wrong *with me?* She wondered as she pushed her way toward the back of the club. *Since when am I given to such fantastical thinking?* Either something really Twilight Zone was going on, or she was graduating in her delusions to full on psychotic episodes.

She didn't stop her forward movement or try and convince herself that she was wrong in her thinking, as skewed as it may be. She was going to trust her sudden inner wisdom; she would question it later.

"Elle, wait up, I'll take you home," Ryan called from behind her. She looked back to see Ryan pushing his way through the crowd, trying to follow her. "Wait up, Elle!"

A sudden, and very unfortunate, lull in the music caused Ryan's shouted request to carry through the crowd. Four heads turned their way, three blond and one chestnut, all four faces wore a look of murderous determination, and all were turning to stalk toward her now. The dark haired one was farther away than the others and no longer playing nice with the crowd. He started shoving people roughly out of his path as he made his way closer to her, purpose in every step.

Run, he mouthed fiercely, then said something that drew

the attention of one of the blonds who turned to him as the other two continued in her direction.

Obviously, they knew each other, and it wasn't friendly judging by the growls they both let loose as they shoved patrons out of the way to get to each other. Her dark-haired man threw the first punch and connected the blond right in the jaw. His head flew back and sprayed nearby onlookers with his blood. The now-bleeding blond recovered quickly and threw a punch that her dark-haired man deflected easily with his arm. All she could think was, *wow, what a man*. He reminded her of a character from one of her romance novels and she started to rethink her assumption that they only existed in fiction.

"Elle let's get out of here, that fight looks rough," Ryan said, coming up beside her. His comment showed clearly that he was not the fighting type, which didn't surprise Elle, but it did add to her resolve that he was not her type. Somehow, she felt a more rugged fighter would be for her, not that she had ever considered that until this moment. Damn but that big, beautiful man was messing with her in so many ways.

Elle shook herself and spotted the other two blonds, they were getting way too close. Thank goodness for the crowd that was now crushing to surround the fight. It made a wall between her and them; albeit not impenetrable, it would slow them down at least.

Elle turned back around and doubled her efforts to get out. She heard a gunshot and people started to yell behind her, then suddenly everyone was trying to leave at once. She was almost to the back door, she knew she could make it, especially with the forward movement of the crowd now rushing her along. She rode the current and when fresh night air was filling her lungs, she plastered herself against the side of the building and out of the way of the spilling crowd. She gave herself a moment to breathe deep and settle her screaming nerves.

Ryan tumbled out the open door and Elle scrunched down; she didn't want him to see her. She didn't want her friends anywhere near her if those men truly wished her harm. Apparently, they were armed, which would make that pretty easy. Elle bit her lip and tried not to imagine her chestnut-haired man suffering a gunshot wound.

"Elle!" Ryan called frantically, and started searching the gathered crowd for her.

Elle heard sirens in the distance. No way was she waiting around to talk with the police. She didn't even understand what had just happened, how could she explain it to someone else? Her arm was still hurting, so she knew she wasn't safe yet. She saw two blond men emerge with a surge through the door and take off in the direction of the fleeing crowd. When they rounded a corner, she hurried in the opposite direction down the alley toward the street her car was parked on. She just wanted to get home so she could try and understand, or better yet, forget, what happened.

She was almost to her car when her phone rang, it was Ryan. She hit ignore and beeped her doors unlocked. She jumped in and quickly locked the doors; her nerves were fried. She started the car with a shaking hand and dialed Katherine as she pulled away from the curb and accelerated down the street.

Katherine's voicemail picked up.

"Hey Katherine, it's me. I just wanted to let you know that I'm okay and am on my way home. I will see you back at the apartment." Elle hung up and gripped the steering wheel with both hands as she navigated the increasingly chaotic streets surrounding the club.

Elle's mind was beyond comprehending, it had shut down and her body was on the verge of following suit. She needed to get home before she completely broke down or shut down. She would text Ryan when she was safe at home, so he didn't worry.

By the time Katherine stumbled into the apartment on the arm of James, Elle was bathed and cuddling in her bathrobe with a cup of hot tea clutched in her hands. She was finally feeling relaxed. Her nerves were settled, and her mind had finally stopped insisting that she should throw herself into the strong arms of a chestnut-haired man like a medieval damsel in distress.

"What a night, huh, and it's only eleven." James said, flopping Katherine and himself onto the couch.

"Yeah, crazy. Was anyone hurt, or arrested?" Elle asked, trying to sound casual, but if either of them had looked, they would have seen her death grip on her coffee cup revealing the fear behind her question.

"No. The two guys who were fighting made an escape before the police arrived, well the one with long brown hair dragged the one with short blond hair outside and then they disappeared into the night," James said, his voice dripping with dramatic emphasis.

"Well, I guess it's good no one was seriously injured." Elle's hands relaxed on her cup. He wasn't sitting in jail, and he wasn't sitting in the hospital. Somehow that did more to calm her nerves than the bath or tea had done.

"Well, I wouldn't go that far. There was blood all over the floor where the two were fighting."

"I thought you said no one was shot!" Elle leaned forward and sloshed tea onto her white robe, her heart palpitating irregularly.

"They weren't. The shot was some idiot cowboy out front who thought he was cool enough to stop the fight. Damn idiot shot a hole in the sign and started a stampede, but the fight didn't break up until sirens were heard."

"Stupid redneck," Katherine added as she cuddled closer to

James and closed her eyes, obviously having drunk way too much tonight.

"Well, I'm off to bed since you're home safe." Elle blew a kiss at Katherine and headed to her room. As she slipped out of her robe and her hand touched on her stars, she remembered the car full of blonds she'd nearly run into earlier in the day. She had a feeling she hadn't seen the last of the blonds, or the intriguing dark-haired man.

"You seriously kicked this bastard's ass." Traylon looked down at the bloody body of the Enforcer and felt a little chill. Locan had brought him back to the ship rather than leave him for discovery on the planet, Traylon couldn't wait to do a little questioning of the prisoner, if he ever woke up.

"Yeah well, he started it," Locan said quietly and walked away.

Traylon shut and locked the cell door then hurried after Locan.

"It will be a day or two before we can get any information out of him though," Traylon pointed out, not letting Locan get away with not explaining himself.

Locan and Traylon were both trained in many forms of combat; killing or maiming to the degree that Locan had done tonight was not often used. Locan could have incapacitated the Enforcer in a way that would result in his awakening within the hour with nothing more than a bad headache. Locan had lost control down there, and Traylon knew it. This was what he worried about, knowing that Locan refused to accept the Warrior inside him. If it ever took over, it might not let Locan come back.

"Hey man, I am not going to say anything to anyone. You are, after all, my boss here. I just want to know what's going on."

Traylon was loyal to Locan, but he also felt responsible for making sure everyone stayed safe.

Locan swung around and stalked back the two steps it took to close the distance between them. Traylon kept his no care expression plastered to his face, he refused to show Locan how much his deadly glare intimidated him.

"We are not dealing with a normal Prian rescue here. I can't just grab her and force her to join us. That means she is going to be down there, in danger, for a lot longer than I care to think about. The Enforcers have seen her, two got away. I will not explain my actions to a *boy* who thinks he is playing games." Locan spun on his heel and stalked off.

"I know who she is," Traylon said quietly, having followed right behind Locan.

"Then I expect you will understand that all normal procedures have just been put on hold until she is safely on Prias." The wall opened and Locan stepped through, not waiting for Traylon's agreement.

Traylon stared at the wall for a moment, stunned by Locan's reaction.

"That was interesting," Leda said behind Traylon.

"What are you doing out here, Leda?" Traylon turned to face her.

She was a pretty thing, spiky, white-blonde hair framed a round face and deep blue eyes. She was quite short; at only five foot she came up to Traylon's chest. He knew she was deceptively innocent-looking. She wasn't a trained Warrior, but she was nearly as deadly. Locan had made sure she was able to take care of herself. She was curved in a very womanly fashion and dressed as she was in a gauzy, floor length sleeveless gown, she was a sight that set most men's blood to boiling. Men who didn't know what a bitch she was, anyway.

"I was coming to inquire after our new prisoner and the

next steps to getting the Princess on the ship so we can get back already."

"So anxious to get back to Prias, Leda? I doubt it, be careful about showing that jealousy around Locan. He seems quite ready to treat L with all that she deserves. L is a royal, Leda, something you can't understand because you were born of a breeder." Traylon smiled sweetly, flicked a strand of her hair, and walked away, leaving her fuming.

Traylon almost felt bad for the girl, she tried so hard, but she just didn't fit in anywhere. That's the only reason she was on this ship with him and Locan, Locan had felt sorry for the girl all those years ago.

SEVEN

Locan hesitated outside the door that separated him from L, his hands pressed against the wood as he listened to the noises within for a sense of who and what he was dealing with. His Warrior senses were still on edge after the activities earlier, more specifically the danger she had been in. After cleaning up and changing into clothes of his own, he felt only mildly better than he had when he arrived on the ship with his prisoner.

Locan knew he would not feel at ease until she was safely on his ship, but assuring himself that she was safe for tonight would help. He focused his Warrior mind and pushed his senses beyond the door and into the rooms within. He could feel her presence on the other side as surely as if he could see through the wood and metal; she wasn't alone. He could hear three people, two of whom were making love from the sounds of it. He knew a moment of feral rage before he realized it wasn't L making those animalistic sounds of rapture.

Locan could feel her sleeping. Her calm, even breathing and steady heartbeat was as tangible to him as if it were his own. She was in there, she was safe, and she was asleep. He hated to disturb her.

Just one peek, just to be certain she's all right. He reasoned as he let himself in, easily disabling the locks. The room was dark, but his eyes adjusted quickly, and he could see that he stood in a large living area. To his left was a kitchen and a door that led to the couple. To his right was a hallway that led to the sleeping L, her pull even stronger now that he was this much closer.

Locan's feet moved him silently to her room and soon he was standing over her bed, gazing down at her beautiful sleeping form. His fingers itched to caress the silky strands of hair spread across the white pillow, his hand burned to touch her soft skin, his eyes focused on her soft lips, and he swallowed.

A growl tore through Locan's chest and out his throat. He forced himself away from her before he did something stupid. She was not for him; he was nothing more than a Guard member and she was a princess. Someone he was born to protect, not bed. Nothing but torment could come from desiring one as unattainable as her.

Once he was sure his lust was under control, he turned back to her and knelt beside the bed. He knew he was torturing himself, but he was helpless to make his feet carry him out of the room.

Exquisite, whispered in his mind.

Locan agreed and ignored the fact that it wasn't his own thoughts that had spoken of her.

She sighed in her sleep and his body tightened. Her arm was uncovered and Locan couldn't resist the urge to touch her Goddess marks. The two blue stars were so beautiful on her skin, and they symbolized so much for the future of Prias and its people. Just two more reasons for him to protect her, and not lust for her.

Locan's finger touched her lightly, but that simple gesture sent a shock of pleasure through him. He did it again and watched in wonder as the two blue marks shimmered as if they approved of him, or were they warning her of the danger of him?

Even more puzzling, another mark appeared before his eyes. "Goddess Cerulean, what does this mean? What is your plan for this princess who you are watching so carefully?" Locan whispered.

Locan knew what his plan for her was, and he had a very good idea about what his leader's plan for her was, as well as Temis', but if the Goddess was watching her, he had to wonder what her plans were and if they benefited the Prian people.

Traditionally the Goddesses and Gods, under the eye of the Mother Goddess, Achromic, and the Father God, Coal, protected and guided the Prian people who worshiped them in return. Years before Locan was born, the Goddesses and Gods would often appear to the people, guiding and being worshipped. Their disappearance had left the people of Prias confused and hurt, then the birthrate had dropped dramatically, then the Doctors had arrived.

Locan sat back on his heels and mulled over the possible desires of the Goddess Cerulean. Besides an overwhelming desire to be worshipped, the deities really didn't care about much, he'd been told. So, what did she have to gain from L, why now? Locan feared for L and the meaning of those marks.

Locan, you don't look happy about my gift.

The words slid through Locan's mind like an electric pulse, it was unlike anything he'd ever experienced, and he knew immediately what this was. A Goddess was speaking directly to him and there was no chance of ignoring it.

Goddess Cerulean. The thought floated from his mind as a gruff voice from somewhere hidden, some part of him that he tried hard to ignore.

Warrior, I see you. The Goddess responded.

Locan bit back a curse as he looked up into the face of the

Goddess Cerulean. Her blue body floated in the air, her blue hair swimming around her naked body, offering a minimal cover of modesty for her curves. Her black, soulless eyes narrowed on him in annoyance.

Locan quickly bowed his head. *I apologize, Goddess, but I am not certain which gift you are speaking of. I have so many given from one as powerful as you.* Locan spoke with his thoughts, not wanting to risk waking the sleeping Princess. He was hoping to soothe the Goddess with flattery. Daring a glance up, he noticed that she did indeed look mildly appeased.

The Princess L, of course. Her very conception was a gift from me. She was born safely by my good graces, and I have gifted her with wisdom to know fear of the Enforcers and not of you. You have already experienced the pull of her loyalty. She will draw a like response from all Prians. Those are great gifts Warrior. I expect to be repaid for my kindnesses.

Anything, once the thoughts that sprang from his mind were not his own, but the Goddess responded, smiling in satisfaction.

Locan clenched his fists, fighting the urge to scream that it was not he who had offered those words, but he knew better. *Of course, Goddess, I appreciate all you have done for the people of Prias. Surely L will be the one to free us and we can once again offer you great worship.*

The Goddess smiled. *Her destiny marks will guide her, and you will protect her. She is the Princess who has been awaited. We all watch to see how things play out. I will send my daughter to you, Violaceous will give you her mark and you will receive from her, gifts of power and magic, which I am sure you will need, even though the Warrior inside you is great.*

She was gone. She was there, and then she wasn't, and Locan was left with a feeling of unease over the journey ahead. Being visited by one Goddess was bad enough, but to have another one coming. No matter that Violaceous was of the half-mortal variety, it was still an unsettling thought.

Locan looked back at L and gave a silent prayer up to the Mother Goddess Achromic, the White Sun, the Goddess of goodness and faith, that she would smile upon all and keep her daughters and granddaughters and grandsons in line; not to mention her husband. The Black Moon, the God Coal, the God of strength and death, was one who Locan feared above all other deities in his home sky. In a matriarchy he had never been worshipped as fully as his wife, Achromic, or his daughters, Carmine, Amber, and Cerulean, and if there was one thing that all Gods and Goddesses wanted, it was to be worshipped above all others. It was how they maintained their power, which they were supposed to use to aid the Prians who worshipped them.

Locan couldn't help being a bit cynical, with the way Prias was now, he felt they had been all but abandoned by the deities they once cared so much for. So why was Cerulean here now? What had changed?

Locan looked down at L, he knew what had changed. The Princess was going to arrive on Prias, which could change everything.

Locan returned to the ship after setting Traylon up outside the building to watch. He was exhausted and knew he would be returning after only a few short hours of rest. Time was even more a factor now that she had been spotted by Enforcers who were not dead and not safely held on his ship.

Jabon's face twisted into an ugly smile as he listened to the retelling of the night's events. The scar running through the left side of his mouth made the unfamiliar movement a bit difficult; painful even. His most hated adversary was on the planet below, and so was the Prian Princess who shouldn't exist.

"You are sure the Warrior Locan didn't take the girl?"

"No sir, she disappeared while Kytin fought the Warrior, then Kytin was taken; to the Warrior's ship we assume."

Jabon frowned, a much more comfortable set to his face. "Well, that won't do, now will it? Our dear friend Kytin can't be allowed to tell any of our secrets." Jabon motioned to a small girl hiding in the corner, trying to be invisible to the three large men in the chamber. "Tanea, bring me Kytin's life-orb."

Jabon's eyes stayed on the two Enforcers in front of him, watching for any sign of weak disapproval. Everyone knew the punishment for capture, and he wouldn't tolerate his men questioning him in this. The small girl slunk to his side, head bowed, and handed him a small black orb.

Jabon reached out a hand before the girl could rush away, he held tight to her arm. She knew better than to struggle, but the whimper of fear and revulsion was not withheld. Not that he minded, he gloried in the fear he could induce in others.

"Tanea, dear, I am sure you will be happy to hear that these men have not earned the right to your body this day. Go now to your chamber until your services are needed."

He let go and she stumbled as she tried to run quickly from the room. Neither man moved to help her up, they kept their gazes focused on their leader. Jabon watched with a sneer as Tanea scrambled to her feet, lifted her long skirt slightly, and hurried out. She was a weepy sort, but she'd survived longer than some others had after being captured by him, rather than being *rescued* by Locan.

Jabon waited until the door shut behind her before taking the small orb between his thumb and forefinger.

"God Coal, our Black Moon, I call upon you to deliver death to Enforcer Kytin who has betrayed us with his capture." The small orb flashed a swallowing darkness of black light then shattered. The death screams of Kytin reverberated through the room.

"Leave me now. You will not rest, return to find her, you will not come back without her again." The words were delivered with chilling calm and both men bowed tightly, then left the room. There was no sadness over the death of their comrade, only a chilling knowledge that they were close, always so close, to the same fate. Yet they would serve happily with that knowledge because that is what they were bred to do. The God Coal had originally gifted Temis with the Enforcers, had sealed their loyalty to him and they were bound to want nothing more than to follow his orders. Jabon had been gifted their loyalty after proving himself useful. Temis was aging and needed a replacement as he moved into a figurehead and mastermind position. Temis was still someone Jabon didn't want to mess with no matter his age, he was powerful.

When Jabon was alone, he hissed and raised his tunic, peering down at the new stinging black circle on his belly, one of many. A painful mark for every time he had used the power. The pain would soon ease, he knew, and it was well worth it. He could feel the power of the God of strength and death rushing through his veins. It was an intoxicating aphrodisiac. He smiled knowing the best way to ease the new ache and feel his power vibrate all the more.

Jabon pressed a small button on his chair.

"Tanea, you will meet me in my bed chamber." There was no reply, but he knew she would not think to deny him. She knew what he would do to her if she did, especially after he had just used the Black Moon's power.

Jabon strode out of the room, the power that rushed through his veins humming. Coal would be pleased with Jabon for taking the breeder-born girl for his pleasure.

Prias was birthplace to some of the most powerful men ever

created, the Warriors. They could quite possibly take over any planet they wished, enslave its people, and drain its resources, but centuries of matriarchal rule had reduced these great men to lap dog guard members. Enslaved by the power of the Goddess Achromic. *Not anymore.* Jabon thought as he entered his bed chamber to find Tanea curled up on his bed. The time of the Black Moon was on the horizon, and he'd just identified the last piece of the puzzle. Soon the Princess would be on his ship, soon he would have more power than any Prian had ever dreamed of.

EIGHT

Locan entered the control room of the ship, once again dressed in Earth-appropriate clothing. Tight pants that reached his knees and a tight shirt that proclaimed *Lucky*. He felt like an idiot and if anyone so much as smirked at his attire, he would gladly put a fist through their nose. He had rested only briefly, but he was prepared to return and talk with L, time was short. Their prisoner died unexpectedly only a few hours before and Locan was sure it was Jabon's doing. He didn't know how Jabon did it, but he was certain that the poor Enforcer was killed as a means of keeping him quiet.

Bad news for L; Jabon would probably be sending out twice as many Enforcers to find her. Locan couldn't help but hope Jabon would personally attend to her capture. Locan wanted to face him again, almost as much as he wanted to see L safely back to Prias. The last time they had faced off, Jabon had gotten the upper hand by using a helpless girl as a shield. Nothing could make Locan harm someone so defenseless, which Jabon had known and laughed about as he escaped, with the poor Prian girl in tow.

Locan could still see the look of terror in the girl's eyes as she was carried away, and Locan could do nothing but watch. Jabon had delivered a near deadly wound to Locan's neck, and his vision had been swimming as he stumbled to his knees. If he ever faced Jabon again, he would make him suffer for every hurt he had no doubt heaped upon the girl.

That was three years ago, and since then Jabon and Locan had been racing each other planet to planet, searching for the lost Prians. Locan knew he had found more than Jabon, but for every one that he lost to Jabon, he tortured himself, and tried all the harder next time.

"Good morning, Locan," Traylon called happily from his post in front of multiple screens and computer devices.

"It will be a good day when we are gone from this place. Why are you here and not Leda?" Locan grumbled and walked to the cabinet where their weapons were stored. He selected a few, concealing them conspicuously within his tight Earth clothing. How did the people down there protect themselves when it was so impossible to hide a simple weapon on their person? They didn't walk around armed obviously—Locan had noticed that right away—so how did they protect their women?

"Leda wanted to take a turn."

Locan grunted at that. No harm in having Leda watch the building he supposed. "With any luck, I will catch her before she even leaves her place this morning and we will be gone by midday."

"Afraid it's too late for that. She is gone from her place," Traylon said with undisguised humor.

"What? Why the hell wasn't I informed? Do you have any idea what kind of danger she is in down there?" Locan was inches from Traylon's smiling face, ready to grab him and shake him to get that look off his face. L was unprotected and Traylon knew and had done nothing, it was unacceptable. "Explain yourself before I see fit to throw you in a cell."

Kill him, ran through his mind and Locan thought it was such a great idea, he didn't care where the words had come from.

"She left her building before the sun came up. Leda was capable of trailing her. So far nothing interesting has happened. She just went to the hospital."

"Hospital? What's wrong?" Locan imagined all sorts of horrors having befallen her to warrant a trip to a hospital.

"Apparently she works there," Traylon said with a knowing smirk. "She delivers babies, Locan. Imagine that, huh. Our Prian Princess delivers babies for a living. Do you have any idea how fitting that is? The Goddesses have been guiding her all her life I bet, taking a special interest in the girl."

"At least one Goddess anyway," Locan said quietly, stepping back from Traylon and letting his rage simmer down. "You still should have told me; she shouldn't be unprotected no matter where she is."

"Maybe, but Leda gets on my nerves, and I saw this as a great opportunity to get rid of her for a while. Besides, she is under strict orders to call if there is even a hint of Enforcers about. Leda knows how important L is. She won't let anything happen to her, and I have been watching carefully as well."

Locan pressed a button on the console and barked, "Leda what the hell is going on, why did you let Traylon talk you into leaving the ship without informing me first?" Locan didn't care that he was being unfair. *Does no one understand the importance of this one little Prian,* he wondered agitatedly?

"Locan, Sir, I apologize but you have to rest some time, and honestly there has been nothing exciting happening down here. Unless you count the fact that she just delivered a set of triplets that are screaming and carrying on like nothing I have heard in my entire life. I swear I never want to have even one of those disgusting things."

"Yeah well, I am on my way."

"Leda, you are such a sentimental bitch," Traylon said happily.

"Screw you, Traylon."

The door shut before Locan could hear Traylon's reply to that, but he could imagine it went something along the lines of, *you wish.* He didn't blame Traylon for taking the opportunity to send Leda away. Not that Leda was all that bad. It was just that the two of them were constantly at each other's throats. Locan often wanted to send them both away when they were all in the same room.

It really was his own fault though. Locan had seen that they didn't get along from the beginning, but still he had agreed to keep the woman on his ship. He just couldn't make her leave and go live among the Prian rebels who would treat her like an outcast among outcasts simply because she was born of a breeder. It wasn't her fault that her mother was a prisoner at the Hospital, impregnated by the Doctors. Luckily, Leda had grown up on the planet Maybar, a fairly civilized planet close to Prias that her mother had escaped to when many of the pregnant mothers, led by Queen K, had fled the Hospital.

Leda had never fit in on Maybar where she was a giant at five feet, and her adopted family had not done a lot to make her feel like she belonged. When Locan showed up and told her where she was from, she had been overcome with happiness, thinking that she would finally belong somewhere. She was over twenty at the time and she had ridden along with him and Traylon, recovering other Prians for the next few years. When they had finally returned to Prias, expecting to leave behind *all* the recovered citizens, Leda had seen that she did not fit in there either. Not only was she short compared to the full Prians, but she was also blonde-haired and blue-eyed and no matter that her hair was as long as the other women wore it, she would never fit in.

Locan hadn't been able to turn her down when she had looked into his face with such sadness and begged to stay on the ship. At least here she wasn't ridiculed for what she was, except by Traylon, but that was mostly reciprocated teasing. So Locan had agreed, and he paid for it daily with their bickering. She had proven herself useful at times however, after they left Prias she had shorn off all her hair to show she didn't want to belong and had started training daily. Her small body was tough, Locan knew that first-hand from practice fights, and she was determined to rescue others like herself. She was actually rather good at helping them understand what they were, and that they didn't have to feel like less because of it. Locan knew she did feel like less, no matter what she told the others and he felt sorry for her, though he would never dare tell her. He saw it every time they returned to Prias, and she yearned to belong there, yet refused to do what some of the other breeder-born children had done and live as a separate and lesser caste.

Locan could understand the hesitancy of the pure Prian citizens. No one understood what the Doctors and Temis had done in the Hospital to create them, though they all had an idea, and it didn't involve the semen of Prian males. Not knowing created fear, but none were openly rude to the breeder-born and most of the breeder-born accepted their life and made the most of it. Many had been rescued from planets where they were treated as outcasts anyway, at least on Prias they were surrounded by others like themselves, they weren't completely alone anymore.

Locan knew he was doing what he could for them, the rest had to play itself out among the people themselves, and an important piece of that was L. Prias needed a queen to rule, she could integrate them all, she could make things better—if he could keep her safe from Temis, Jabon, the Enforcers, and the Doctors. His mission wasn't going to be easy.

"Achromic, you'll have a new queen soon, bless her and use her for the good of the Prian people," Locan prayed quietly.

Locan left the ship and followed Traylon's directions to L's office. It was a nice building right next to a big blue hospital. Locan shuddered a bit, looking up at the huge utilitarian building, too much like the metal monstrosity that loomed over Prias. He'd never seen it himself, but the stories that the elder rebels told of it, brought to mind something like this.

He didn't hesitate outside the door to L's office, silently thankful she was no longer inside the hospital, which would have been difficult for him to enter. Here he could just walk right in feeling confident and determined, like nothing was going to stand in his way of talking with L.

He got no farther than one step inside.

The waiting room was crowded by five very pregnant, very distressed, women yelling at the receptionist about their appointments that were late. They were all fanning themselves and sweating and groaning about the heat.

"I am sorry, but Dr. Monroe had a delivery this morning and so all her appointments have been pushed back. She will get to you. Just have a seat, please," the receptionist spoke firmly and leaned over her desk, trying to impose her will on the women who were glaring at her from the other side.

Locan lost most of his resolve as he watched the pregnant women sprawl in chairs and glare at the receptionist. Then one started talking about things so vile, Locan thought he was going to lose his breakfast. He didn't know what a mucus plug was, but he had to leave before they said any more about it.

He stood outside the door for five minutes, prepping himself to re-enter the office. He refused to be intimidated by pregnant women. He was a fearless Warrior. Nothing could stand in his way.

"There is nothing to be afraid of in there, pregnancy and birth are sacred, wonderful things," he told himself firmly.

With forced determination, Locan entered the office again. This time, the women were all seated, and the receptionist was on the phone. He waited patiently just inside the door, planning to ask the receptionist to get Dr. Monroe so he could speak with her as soon as possible.

While he waited, Leda was pushed out of a room in the back.

"I told you Miss Leda; you are *not* pregnant. Now, I have other patients to see, I have to ask you to leave, now." L followed Leda out of the room and spoke agitatedly to her.

"Listen, *L*, I want another test and I refuse to leave here until I get one. I slept with so many guys last month I *have* to be pregnant," she spoke with more than her usual flippancy and disregard for any type of authority. She looked up and met Locan's stunned gaze, her face turning bright red. "On second thought, you're probably right." She rushed out of the building without another word.

Locan was too stunned to say anything and missed his opportunity to speak with L, who hadn't walked far enough into the waiting room to spot him standing by the door. He was unsure of what to do next. He really didn't want to disturb her when she so obviously had much work to do, but he knew she was in danger. His Warrior instinct was to protect, and he couldn't do that if he left. His male instincts made him feel more uncomfortable here than anywhere he had ever been in his entire life.

"Can I help you with something, Sir?" The receptionist was off the phone and looking at him with open confusion.

"I am here to see Dr. Monroe." He tried for cool and

confident; but ended up with questioningly hopeful. The receptionist's eyes lit up and swept him head to toe in obvious approval. She smiled warmly at him.

"She is really busy this morning, but she has a break for lunch at about twelve-thirty. Maybe you should come back then."

Locan nodded quickly, thankful for the excuse to leave, and rushed back out. He would keep a watch from a distance and be there for her lunch break at twelve-thirty.

At least that was the plan until he saw the male from last night enter her office at about twelve o'clock. He walked with a confident swagger that made Locan want to throw a knife into his knee.

Take the bastard out, he is in our way.

His mind registered the gruff words and blocked the thoughts of who had spoken them. They were, after all, the same line of thinking he was already on, not such a huge stretch. But they weren't his own thoughts and pretty soon he was going to have to investigate this new development. But not now and not here, he had work to do, and the male was threatening that. Not to mention, annoying the hell out of Locan with the easy familiarity with L that Locan would never be able to assume.

"Your aura is totally jealous right now, Warrior."

Locan spun around to find what could only be the Goddess Violaceous standing behind him. She was only slightly less intimidating than her mother for being half mortal. She had deep purple hair, short and spiky around her face. Her skin was lavender, and she wore a short purple skirt, much like he had seen on the beach yesterday, and a top that circled her body but left her shoulders and middle bare. Her eyes were green, the only indication of her mortal father. She smiled at him as he perused her and her eyes glowed, reminding him that she was as deadly as a pure Goddess and to step lightly with her.

"Goddess Violaceous, you honor me with your presence."

"Yeah well, Mother said you would need my personal brand of assistance. She is betting on your little princess in there to do what needs to be done. So, I am to assist you in your little problem."

"My jealousy?"

She laughed and sparks of purple fluttered around her. They floated to the ground and disappeared around her tiny bare feet. "Oh, how precious. No, your jealousy is cute, but not enough of an issue for us to concern ourselves with. Your refusal to accept your power, your Warrior. *That* will stand in the way of your success, Locan, and by association, ours."

She smacked her hand to the inside of his right forearm and grinned playfully. "Your destiny is now my concern, Warrior Locan, don't make me regret it." She continued on with a bored tone, "I bless you." She narrowed her eyes at him, making his insides cringe at her obvious power hidden inside her small form. "Don't screw this up Locan, you have to embrace every part of yourself, that includes your Warrior, fast, or you won't succeed."

"How am I supposed to do that safely?"

She removed her hand and smiled like he was the most amusing thing she had ever encountered. "You just stop ignoring him, silly."

She disappeared; there one moment and then gone. Locan looked down at his arm and frowned at the small purple star left behind from her touch on the inside of his right forearm. It trembled and power pulsed from that spot, it thrummed through his body making him feel like he did when in the throes of a Warrior transformation. Locan flexed his muscles, trying to relax and relieve the tingling. His arms puffed, his legs extended, starting to turn Warrior. He didn't want to turn

Warrior, not now. If he did, he was likely to do something he would regret; like rip the male's head off in front of everyone.

Locan pulled strength from the power Violaceous had granted him, using it to stave off the Warrior and calm himself. As he did, he heard a growl of frustration in his mind. Normally he would ignore such a thing, but this time he followed it and found a spot in his mind where a caged Warrior pounded against his imprisoning walls.

"Calm yourself," Locan spoke to the caged Warrior, soothing it. He felt it respond, look at him in astonishment and step back.

Finally, you see me, Locan.

"Perhaps, or perhaps I am just going insane," he grumbled.

Let me help you. It is what I live for and have so long been denied; my abilities wasting away in this cage. You only let me out to fight briefly and until L's loyalty called me forward, you would never hear me speak no matter how loud I yelled.

"Shit, I hear you now, Warrior, so what does that mean, what do we do?"

For starters, kill the Enforcers who are coming near.

Locan spun around, probing the area but coming up empty. "Where? I don't see any Enforcers."

You will. They are getting closer. My senses are more acute than yours, but you will sense them soon too.

Locan bristled at the implication that his senses weren't good enough, especially when talking about the safety of L, but he wouldn't second guess the Warrior. Locan concentrated, branched out with all his senses and as he did so, felt his Warrior join him, extending his sense even farther. He wanted to deny the Warrior, push him away, lock him up and pretend that this insanity had never happened. Violaceous' words surrounded him, and he knew he couldn't, not this time. He would have to investigate this other part of himself or suffer the wrath of the Goddess. His arm tingled where Violaceous had left her mark and with it he felt his senses sharpen.

The Enforcers were indeed on their way, but they were still far off. They were approaching fast, in a vehicle no doubt. He could also sense L, she was moving about in the building, she was safe. He had to make a decision, and fast. Either he went out and met the Enforcers, tried to stop them before they got here, or he could go in and try to get L away before they arrived. Neither option gave him all he wanted. He wanted L away, and he wanted those Enforcers for questioning.

As he struggled with the decision, L left the office. She walked alongside the male and headed off; in the opposite direction the Enforcers were coming from. That made the decision for him.

"Traylon, get down here and follow L. I'm going to intercept some Enforcers." His Warrior growled approval at his decision and Locan felt his body begin to grow as his Warrior came forward, ready for a fight, craving violence and destruction, exactly what Locan had feared he would want. How could Locan possibly embrace and expect to control such a violent being?

Traylon appeared beside him and Locan pointed him in the direction L had taken, then he settled down to wait. He felt them coming closer. There were four, and he hoped one was Jabon.

Our enemy approaches. I am ready.

"As am I," Locan growled, his body was now almost completely in its Warrior form and Locan knew he was nearly invincible like this. A large, black vehicle pulled into the lot and idled in front of the building. No doubt they were sensing the presence of a Prian Warrior now that they were so close. Locan crouched in ready position and waited. If they could sense his presence they might be able to sense the missing presence of L. Would they turn and run, or stay and fight?

They'd better stay and fight, his Warrior growled excitedly.

The back doors opened, and two Enforcers stepped out of the vehicle. They were the two from the club last night. They had tried to harm L. His Warrior roared and Locan felt his body bulge out to full Warrior mode, ripping his clothing to shreds. The two Enforcers hesitated only slightly when they saw him unfold his giant body from the crouch he had been in. The Enforcers ran forward, full speed for attack and each drew a long, curved knife. They intended to kill.

Locan lost himself to his Warrior, letting him do what he was there for. It felt great, like stretching out completely after sleeping in a cramped position all night. He drew a knife of his own, a small, curved blade that extended from his fisted hand like a talon. It was his favorite for hand-to-hand combat, he could get up close and personal with anyone he killed.

Locan crashed with the Enforcers, his fist arcing and blade slicing deeply into flesh. Neither would walk away from this fight, and right then, he couldn't make himself care. There were two more in that vehicle who could be held for questioning. One Enforcer fell, a wound to the neck. The other looked unfazed by the death of his comrade; he came at Locan with feral animosity. Locan blocked the Enforcer's knife with his arm and responded with a slice of his own knife across the man's shoulder. The Enforcer stumbled back. As soon as he regained his footing, he came at Locan again; these men were trained to fight to the death. There was no mercy given to those who failed in Temis' army. Death on the field was at least honorable, possibly less painful.

They circled each other, assessing for weakness. The Enforcer lashed out but tripped over his comrade and fell short of his intended mark, Locan's neck. Locan sliced through the man's neck, a death blow.

Locan stood tall, dripping blood, his own and theirs. His Warrior growled in delight as he studied what he had done. Two bodies lay at his feet, very satisfying. The black vehicle was gone though, damn. The men had died for no better reason than to be a distraction so the others could move on to find L. "Shit," Locan cursed. Sirens and screams bombarded him as his Warrior began to fade even more and he took back control of his body.

"Leda, bring me in, now!" Locan called, not caring if he disappeared in front of these people, it wouldn't be the most horrifying thing they witnessed today.

Locan called to Traylon as soon as he was safely on his ship. "Traylon! Status? Two Enforcers got away back there. They are driving a black vehicle."

"L is having lunch with a guy named Ryan. They are sitting at a table by the street, not very safe, but I am close and haven't seen or sensed any Enforcers." Traylon spoke in his usual unhurried tone.

"I've been compromised, no doubt their law will be looking for me. Keep an eye on her and let me know if anything changes. I will have to wait until she is back at her home before I come back down."

"Will do, it's nice down here anyway. So much better than that crowded old ship."

"I mean it, Traylon, if anything happens to her while you are watching, I will cut off your dick and feed it to Leda."

"Damn man, you are harsh. I'm watching intently."

Locan was unconvinced but had no other choice but to trust Traylon. "Watch Traylon closely, Leda, I want to know any change."

"Yes sir, of course," Leda said with enough actual respect

that Locan felt safe in leaving the chamber to clean up. He wanted to keep his own eyes glued to that screen and watch L's every move, but he was bruised and bloody and he needed to figure out where he was bleeding from before it became an issue.

"I will be back shortly," he assured her and left.

As he stood under the hot spray of water in his shower, his attention floated to the space in his mind where his Warrior was once again caged securely.

You know you don't have to keep me locked away like this.

"Right, if you were free to roam at will, then I wouldn't be in control anymore, now, would I?"

It isn't like that, trust me. Otherwise, you would see out of control Warriors all over Prias.

Locan backed away and blocked the Warrior's thoughts. They were reasonable, but he still didn't trust him. The Warrior was dangerous and unpredictable. He thought of the stories he had heard snippets of as a child. Stories of Warriors like his father, one of the greatest Warriors of all time. Ram had embraced this Warrior part of himself. Supposedly he walked around half Warrior most of the time. His poor mother, Elise, was a small woman, beautiful and proud. His father had eventually lost all control, and his mother had suffered greatly before she was killed.

Locan pounded his fists against the wall. His father had been insane, had been driven to horrible violent acts. This Warrior that lived inside of him, it had the power to make him do things just as horrible. Locan would never let the Warrior have that kind of control. He would not risk the safety of anyone around him, especially never a woman that he loved.

A fierce growl of disapproval ripped through his mind as he cemented his resolve. His Warrior was not to be embraced, but to be reined in.

Locan's arm burned suddenly, he clasped a hand over the purple star that Violaceous had left on him. The Goddess disapproved.

"What would you have me do?" he whispered.

His arm went from burning pain to tingling and his Warrior's roars became louder and louder until Locan had no choice but to acknowledge that he was there. Once he did, the feelings went away, and the Warrior shut up.

I just want you to hear me. I want you to use me as you see fit. Soon you will understand what a benefit I can be to you. It is what she wants as well.

By *she,* his Warrior no doubt meant Violaceous. "I may not block you out completely, Warrior, but I won't be embracing your kind of power any time soon. I don't need your kind of help."

We will see about that. How do you expect to walk the path Violaceous has set out for us if you do not use me as she intended?

"I don't know what she wants or intends, Warrior, I know only what I have been commanded to do by my leader. That is the path I walk now, not that which a selfish Goddess has intended." Locan half expected to be struck down for his comment. When nothing happened after a moment, he relaxed. Perhaps she wasn't as powerful as she wanted to be, or perhaps his punishment waited around the next corner.

NINE

Elle fell onto her couch after work, completely exhausted and thankful Katherine wasn't home yet. The morning had been crazy; triplets, then that crazy woman with the spiky blonde hair. She'd almost been thankful when Ryan had shown up to take her to lunch, after her secretary told her a giant of a man with a body she described as absolutely lick-able, was going to be back to speak with her. Elle wasn't positive, but she was pretty sure that man had been the same one who'd been following her. She had been getting tingles before she'd been informed of the man, it had to be him. No one else could make her arm tingle with awareness like he did, and it was very disconcerting.

She'd been relieved to leave with Ryan for lunch. It hadn't been so bad a time with him either, a little awkward as she apologized profusely for running off the night before. Then she'd returned to find out that two men had been killed in her parking lot. Not just any men, but the very men who had come after her in the club, or so it seemed from the description.

She didn't know what was going on, she wasn't sure she wanted to, but it obviously involved her whether she liked it or not. Why now? What had changed, suddenly, to make all these men follow her around? None of whom she felt sure she wanted anything to do with. She just wanted her old boring life back, was that too much to ask? Maybe if she could figure out why they were suddenly here, then she would know how to get rid of them all.

Her mind filled with a vision of a strong tanned face, long chestnut brown hair, and a body that made her drool. He was the most disturbing of them all. She understood how to deal with a man trying to harm her, she had a gun in her nightstand, but the one with the green eyes and sensuous mouth, she didn't know what he was after, and that was more disturbing than anything.

Dammit, what the hell has changed? A tingle on her arm brought everything into the light. Her aunt had died, she had found that box with her name on it, and she had suddenly developed a triple birthmark. Elle sat up slowly, eyes wide with fear. "What the fuck is going on?" Her mind filled with images of men, big men with blond hair and one with dark. The weird feelings that had been coming over her and then today, the bodies outside her office, she hadn't been too late to see them getting pushed into ambulances.

She didn't want to know her history anymore, didn't want to know where her mother had come from and why she had been left with Aunt Sara like that. It was becoming an all-too-real possibility that the answer would be something beyond a fairy tale. Or was this the opportunity she had longed for all her life? Was she finally close to knowing—good or bad—where she had come from?

Her arm tingled and she knew the answer even as she tried to deny it. She needed to know, and she was going to do what she could, no matter how terrifying, to find out. Elle scrambled into her room and grabbed the small shoebox out of her closet.

She tore the paper out of the box and stared down at the innocent looking piece of jewelry and journal. Her hand shook and a shiver ran up her spine as she reached for the bracelet. A sense of destiny filled her soul, and a sharp pinprick of pain stabbed her arm, somehow, she knew without looking, that she now had four blue stars on her arm.

She lifted the cuff and cupped it in her palms. It warmed in her hands and the tiny markings began to glow eerily green again.

"What the hell are you trying to do?" roared through the room seconds before a large hand knocked the cuff away from her. It skittered across the floor and under the bed. Elle spun around and faced her intruder with shock. "Are you trying to get yourself captured?"

His green eyes blazed down at her with fury and, she thought, perhaps a bit of fear. As she skittered away as fast as possible from the giant of a man, his face tightened in what seemed to be barely restrained fury and his hands were fisted at his sides. Elle braced herself for the attack she knew would be coming; no man looked like that before anything other than an attack, and she was sure he was deadly. She hated that she was cowering under his scrutinizing gaze, but could hardly breathe, let alone stand and fight.

He stared at her for a moment as if he were waiting for her to do something. She stared back, waiting to deflect the blows. Then he stepped back, slowly, one, then two steps and turned from her. He went to the bed and bent over, reaching under for the small cuff. It was tiny in his large hand.

"This is a tracking device. I am sorry to have scared you like that; it wasn't my intention. If you hold it, they will find you all the quicker."

Elle stood, although speaking was still beyond her. She took stock of the man; he had, after all, apologized for scaring her.

Perhaps that meant his intentions were not to beat or kill her—at least not right off. He was dressed oddly, wearing some kind of sultan outfit; a grey tunic and pants, both loose and billowing a bit as he walked. A wide leather belt circled his waist and from it hung what looked to be a very long, very dangerous blade. Her eyes stayed locked on that blade as she moved along the wall, inching closer to the door out of her room.

"L, please do not fear me. I am here only to protect and serve you in the best interest of all Prias." His words made no sense to her, but they were said with such conviction, they made her relax a little more.

He was obviously insane, but if he thought of himself as a protector of some kind, well then, she could certainly use that to her advantage here. "So, Mr. uh, sorry I didn't catch your name."

"Locan, Prian Warrior and Royal Guard member."

"O-kay. So, Locan, I need to make a quick phone call, if you could just excuse me for a minute." Elle hurried her steps; she was so close to the door now and he still stood over by her bed. Her hands gripped the open door, one foot was on the other side, she didn't want to turn her back on him until she was making a run for it. She counted down in her head, Three... two...

"Your mother would be very impressed with your choice of work here on Earth."

All thoughts of escape left her mind at the mention of her mother. This man, crazy or not, just might hold the key to her past. Her arm tingled as she contemplated staying and finding out for sure. She hesitated in the doorway.

"How do you know my mother?" She hated that she was so easily brought into his delusion, but there was just a pinprick of doubt in her certainty that this man was insane, and that was enough for her to want to hear him out. At least as long as she felt fairly safe in the situation.

"We don't have much time to discuss this here. I need you to come with me, I will explain everything once we are safely aboard my ship."

Crazy, screamed in her mind and she took a step back. This guy was certifiable, and she was alone in the house with him. She suddenly felt like every big-breasted blonde cheerleader in a scary movie. She was standing in front of the monster, perfect chance to escape at her back, but she just might choose to run up the stairs instead.

"Why shouldn't I think you're insane?" she asked quietly.

"Because you have marks from our Goddess Cerulean on your arm, because you have seen the cuff light up and because if you allow yourself to, you will realize that you feel a connection to me that goes beyond anything you have ever felt with a human, and you don't even know who I am."

"Damn," she whispered, she couldn't argue with any of those points. Elle looked into Locan's green eyes and felt a part of her warm, a part of her stretched as if wakening from a long sleep, it looked at Locan and saw a protector, not the crazed psychopath that her mind still wanted to call him.

"You feel it, don't you? You feel the pull of another of your kind. We are Prians, we will always know another one."

"I—I don't know," she said with a sigh, accepting that she was going to believe his insanity whether she wanted to or not. There was a part of her that was not going to let her brush his words off, and that part seemed to be growing, crowding out everything else. As that part of her grew, her arm tingled, exploded in tingles.

"Oh, dear Goddess," Locan choked out, his eyes locked onto her arm. Elle looked down and her eyes blurred when she saw that her arm was now covered in blue stars, from the back of her hand all the way up to her shoulder, hundreds of blue stars, all tingling and vibrating slightly as she stared at them in shock.

"Do you see, L; do you see that you are something more than an Earthling?"

Elle could do no more than look at him and nod, mouth agape and eyes slightly dazed.

"So, you see that you must come with me. You cannot stay here, you are in danger, and you will never know your destiny if you don't."

"The blond men," she said as clarity began to come back to her.

"Yes, they are—for lack of a better term—the bad guys here. I need to get you safely onto my ship before they find you and try to take you by force to theirs."

"I can't just leave," she said, incredulous. How could he even suggest that?

"But you must, it is imperative that you come with me." His eyes darkened intensely, and he took a slight step forward.

Elle stepped back, she didn't know this man, had no reason to trust him. "I will need time to think."

"There is no time L, I need to take you now."

"Elle, I'm home!" Katherine's voice called out, followed by a greeting from James.

Elle's eyes went wide with worry and fastened on Locan who was glaring out the open door. He had a long blade in his hand now and looked more than capable of using it without mercy or guilt. He hurried to the door and closed it with a thud.

"Elle?" Katherine called again.

"Y—yeah, I'm in my room! I'll be out in a minute!" she called in a high, strained voice. "Please, they are no danger to anyone," she assured Locan who was now standing beside her, as if to prevent her from leaving. He didn't touch her, but he didn't need to. The closeness of his body was all that was necessary for her body to heat with anxiety and what she could only imagine was fear. He looked down at her, his face held tight and strained. His eyes bore into her with an intense possessiveness and driven determination, she didn't think anything would convince him to leave her here.

"Leave with me, now."

"Ok," she croaked. Her mouth was suddenly dry. She was probably making the biggest mistake of her life, but she felt sure that it was the one she was destined to make anyway. "But the journal."

"What journal?"

"In the box, my mother's journal. Can you read it?"

"Grab it," he said gruffly.

She hurried to do as he commanded, then Locan grasped her arm firmly, pressed on his ear, and spoke to the air. Then the world disappeared around her and her mind blacked out.

TEN

Jabon roared and threw the first thing his hand landed on, which happened to be a bowl of fruit. He wanted to destroy something, and since he couldn't destroy what he really wanted, anything would do. Even the destruction of the two idiots that had returned with the worthless humans wasn't going to be enough to appease him now. So, he would allow them to live, in fear. That was more satisfying at times anyway. To watch them slink and cower, waiting for their worthless lives to end between his powerful thumb and forefinger.

Locan had the girl. He was no doubt already heading back to Prias with the Goddesses-be-damned Princess on his ship. Jabon was going to have to report this to Temis and the Doctors. There would be hell to pay for the failure. Another reason to keep the two Enforcers around, an offering to ease the way when they returned to the Hospital nearly empty handed.

The only thing that could possibly redeem him now would be if the Earthlings provided information on L, information that would make her capture possible. Thoughts of torture and pain filled him with joy, and as his mood brightened. The call in to

Temis didn't seem quite so bad. Perhaps he would spend a little time with Tanea first however, she always relaxed him like nothing else could. Jabon put his finger on the call button that connected him directly to Tanea's chamber.

"Jabon, you had better have good news for me." Temis' dark voice filled the room, stopping Jabon's finger halfway down on the call button.

"Temis, Sir, I was just about to call you. We have apprehended some Earthlings. They are friends of the girl." Silence met his enthusiastic reply. Sweat beaded his forehead as he waited for Temis' reaction to the weakly disguised bad news.

"And the girl? What about that whore's daughter?" The words were strained, obviously angry.

Jabon worked hard to keep his voice even as fear crept through him, and he spoke. "Well, she was taken, by Locan, before we could get to her. That is why we took these other humans. They will serve us in some measure of getting the girl. No doubt she will do anything to save her friends."

"She might want to, but do you think Locan is stupid enough to let her?"

"I will be happy to take care of Locan," Jabon said, absently touching the scar on his cheek.

"She must not arrive on Prias with the rebels. You have three weeks." Jabon knew the moment that Temis was no longer listening. It was like a choke hold being loosened; he wasn't sure how Temis did it, but he managed to be a physical presence even over a great distance, as if his voice held more than just the sound of his passionate words. The God Coal still had a hold on Temis, giving him power. If Jabon was a little more confident, he'd approach Coal about completely abandoning the aging figurehead and devoting his full power to him, but he wasn't sure the God would go for it, might smite him for asking.

Perhaps in time, once he had proven himself a bit more. Once he had the girl in his possession, *then* he would have a bargaining chip worth the God's time.

Jabon collapsed in his chair, finger still poised over Tanea's call button. "Damn." He cursed and moved his finger to another button. "Find Locan's ship, follow it and don't let them see us!" he shouted.

"Yes, Sir," was the quick answer.

Jabon sat, brooding, his thoughts turning dark and self-preserving. Their ship was bigger than Locan's, which also made it a little slower and less maneuverable. If Locan was determined to get to Prias as quick as possible, then they had no chance of intercepting them. It would be a three-week chase of futility. Their only chance would be to get them to stop along the way.

A crooked smile pulled on his face. He knew just what to do.

Elle gained consciousness slowly, thoughts floating around her head but refusing to solidify. She remembered the big beautiful dark-haired man, she remembered a net of blue stars, and she remembered fear. But mostly she remembered her mother, or rather the man having knowledge of her mother and claiming, in a roundabout way, that she was other than human.

That was the thought that brought her eyes wide with awareness. She immediately lifted her right arm and saw it was indeed covered in blue stars. She dropped it and squeezed her eyes shut again. It hadn't been a dream, that man, Locan, had indeed come into her room and told her those confusing things. He had insinuated some crazy things. He had wanted to take her to his ship and to her mother's home planet. It was crazy, but then he had grabbed her arm, told someone to bring them up and the world had disappeared around her. She didn't remember anything after that.

Elle opened her eyes again, unable to deny the truth of what she remembered. She looked around her. She was alone in a small chamber, lying atop a small bed. The room was completely white, walls, floor, and bedding. There was a chair and small desk, both white also. The only thing of color in the entire room was the door, which was grey.

She sat up slowly, assessing her head, it was aching from the shock of everything, and her stomach protested a bit at the movement. She ignored it and planted her feet on the ground, sitting on the edge of the bed.

Her mind vacillated between complete rejection of everything and an unexplainable acceptance of it all. She wasn't sure which she wanted to stick with and decided investigation into her surroundings might be necessary for acceptance of either theory. She knew she had, at the last minute, decided to go with him, so this was her own fault. Unfortunately, she couldn't blame Locan for taking her against her will.

Elle was about to stand and try to get out the door that seemed to have no handle, when it whooshed open and in walked a semi-familiar face. Elle recognized the cute face framed by pixie cut blonde hair and big blue eyes. It was that insane woman from her office! Only now she was dressed in an outfit almost exactly like the one that Locan had been wearing in her apartment, though hers had a feminine flair to it. It was in a peach hue and the sleeves were slit to reveal creamy skin. It had a V-neck which showed just the beginning of her curves beneath. The tunic was belted with a white belt and attached to it were multiple pouches, but no weapons.

"You are awake. Locan will be pleased. He almost lost it

when you fainted dead away upon arrival. I swear I have never seen him freak like that, of course you *are* important to the mission." The girl rolled her eyes, obviously not as impressed as Locan apparently was.

"Leda," she said, remembering the woman's name. "What were you doing in my office, really?"

She smiled. "I was making sure you weren't captured or harmed while Locan was getting some much-needed rest. I wasn't allowed to actually tell you anything, but I couldn't leave as long as Locan wasn't there to watch over you."

"And what can you tell me now?" Elle asked, more than a little annoyed that everyone knew so much more about her life than she did. The thought of being watched and followed by these people was a little disturbing. "How long have you guys been watching me?"

"Not long and I can't tell you much, honestly, Locan would have my ass if I did. I'm just here to check on you. Since you're awake I can get you food or Locan, that's about it."

Elle thought about that, she was hungry, and dirty. She was still in her work clothes, which were now sleep wrinkled. "How long have I been here, sleeping?" she wondered.

"About eleven hours. Locan kept waiting for you to wake up but finally gave up after the eighth hour and went to get some rest himself."

She had slept all through the evening and night, no wonder she was hungry, had to pee like crazy and, neither was the most pressing matter on her mind at the moment though. "I want to know exactly what is going on."

"I will get Locan for you then. He said to wake him as soon as you awoke anyway." Leda turned away but Elle stopped her.

"That is really not necessary. I don't want to disturb him. I will take food and a shower, maybe some clean clothes. If he has only been sleeping for a couple hours, I don't want to disturb him."

"As you wish," Leda said with what Elle could only think of as resentful sarcasm.

Why on Earth... er... on whatever planet, would Leda dislike her? It's not as if she hadn't offered to get Elle whatever she needed, short of information anyway.

"Bathroom?" she asked with a half smile.

Leda walked over to the wall opposite the bed and laid a hand on what looked like blank space. A door whooshed open revealing a bathroom, then she turned and left the room.

Elle hurried to use the facilities then went back to sit and wait on the bed. After a moment Elle couldn't resist finding out about the main door. If she were locked in, there was going to be an issue when the next person came through. She would not stand for that kind of treatment. As Elle approached, the door slid easily open. "Huh, guess I'm not a prisoner." She said to herself as she stepped out into a narrow hallway.

"Of course, you're not a prisoner, what would give you such an impression? If it was Leda, I will have to speak with her about treating our most honored guest in such a way."

Elle was startled by the voice. She whirled around to the right and stepped back. A man stood close. He was a large man, almost as large as Locan. He had black hair that hung around his shoulders and silver eyes. He was smiling and leaning against the wall, looking innocent and amused.

"I—I guess I just wasn't sure what the deal was."

"The deal, my dear, is that you are an honored guest aboard Locan's ship, and I am Traylon, here to fulfill your *every* desire." He bowed slightly and put enough innuendo into the smooth words that Elle instantly put up a wall. This was the kind of man she stayed clear of. "Is there anything you require? I would be happy to give you a tour of the ship or assist you in whatever manner necessary."

"Back off Traylon," said Leda, returning, "if Locan heard you, he'd throw you in a cell. On second thought, keep it up, I will go wake him now. It's where you deserve to be anyway."

"Oh Leda, you are just jealous because you are yet again only a pale comparison to another female aboard this ship."

"Screw you, Traylon, you are nothing but a nasty horn-dog and if you think the Princess will have anything to do with you then you are more delusional than I thought."

"Princess?" Elle whispered with awe, both Leda and Traylon stopped talking and looked guiltily at her.

"Great job, Leda, you know you weren't supposed to say anything to her. Locan is going to have your hide for this. Oh, I can't wait to tell him how you not only offended the Princess with your rough language, but you actually told her something it was his right to tell her."

Leda threw the tray she had been holding, hitting Traylon squarely in the face, then stomped off the way she had come.

Elle watched the whole thing with detachment, her mind reeling around the single word, *princess*. It was like a Disney movie dream; the orphan finds out she is really the princess of a faraway land. She had played and dreamed it many times as a child. The idea that it could even possibly be a truth, it was incomprehensible to her. She backed into her room and watched the door slide shut, blocking out the sight of Traylon cleaning up the mess of food on his body and around his feet. She sat on the bed, then laid down. She didn't think she could take much more surprising news right now.

After an hour of failed attempts at reasoning out the situation in her own mind, she gave up and decided she wanted answers, now, and she didn't care who gave them to her. If she had to search out Locan, then she would. Elle stood and walked to the door. The whoosh of it opening automatically was enough of an oddity to almost make her change her mind about leaving the semi normalcy of the bed, but she couldn't avoid it forever. Out there were answers she had longed for all her life, who her mother was and the reasons why she always felt so different.

With determination, Elle stepped into the hall. She paused, she had no idea where to go; to the right and left the hallway continued with doors just like the one she had come out of lining the way. To the right there was a set of glass doors at the end of the hallway, to the left the hallway curved around and, she assumed, continued on. Leda had gone around that corner after hitting Traylon with the tray of food, so she assumed that way led to a kitchen. She decided to investigate to the right first. Glass doors like that had to lead somewhere important, and if it was important, then there would hopefully be people there. A thought crossed her mind and made her halt all movement. People, these weren't people, *she* wasn't people, if she were to believe them.

"Oh my God, I am an alien."

"Actually, you're a Prian." Elle swung around to find Locan's large form behind her. He had come upon her silently and stood so close she could smell the freshly showered scent of his skin, which made her think of how awful she must smell after her long day at work then sleeping so long in the same clothes. "A Prian Princess, but I hear you already know that."

As Elle's mind became less distracted with thoughts of being an alien, she became aware of a tingling all up and down her arm. As if each of her stars was vibrating with happiness because of Locan's presence. Elle tried to ignore the odd sensation as best she could. "I hope you weren't angry with Leda for revealing that bit of information. It really wasn't her fault; Traylon had made her angry and—"

"Don't worry, I know quite well how those two react to each other. I'm glad you are up, have you eaten?"

"No, I'm hungry, and I would like a shower, but mostly I want answers."

"I think I can help you with all those." He turned and began walking down the hall. Elle couldn't help her mind wandering to him helping her with all the mentioned tasks. Her eyes roamed over his broad shoulders and slim waist. He was wearing the same tunic and pants style outfit as before; Traylon had been wearing it also. Not that he had looked nearly as good as Locan in it. The tunic split at waist level and revealed glimpses of a silk draped ass that made her face heat with a desire she rarely felt. She wondered what kind of undergarments Prian men wore.

Elle snapped back to reality when Locan peeked back at her, obviously having asked a question she had totally missed while checking out his ass. "Umm, I'm sorry, what?" she managed with only the smallest hint of embarrassment in her voice.

"I asked if you found your room satisfying, I realize it is quite small, but all of the sleeping rooms are small on this ship. My ship is built for speed, not comfort."

"Oh, its fine, but how long will I have to be using it? Are we already heading away from Earth? Fuck, that sounds just too weird." Elle shook her head and tried to comprehend the fact that she was on a spaceship.

Locan ignored her questions as he walked down the hall and around the corner. He led her through a double door that whooshed open and brought them into a large room with a kitchen on one wall and a large cafeteria style table along the other. "Have a seat and I will make us something to eat. Is there anything in particular you would like?"

"Umm, is it Earth food?" she asked, worried about food from another planet agreeing with her Earth food stomach.

"It is mostly, yes, we restocked while there so you should be quite comfortable eating what we have." His voice showed amusement and as a small smile lifted his lips, she was entranced by the effect it had on his usually intense face.

Elle sat down as he turned to prepare them a meal. It was easy to sit there and watch him. He handed her a plate with a sandwich and some tomatoes on it. Then went back for a couple glasses of water and sat across from her with his own meal. They ate in silence, Elle's ravenous stomach making it impossible to want to stop long enough to chat. Locan seemed fine with the silence. He merely sat there eating his own food with a deep look of concentration on his face.

When they had both completely cleaned their plates, he took the dishes to the sink and rinsed them.

"Is there nobody else on this ship?" Elle couldn't help but imagining the Starship Enterprise with millions of people and maids and cooks and all that.

"Just the four of us right now. So, we all have to take care of our own messes, not that you should, I am happy to serve you, after all you are the Princess."

She felt guilty watching him do everything, but honestly it took him all of three minutes to clean the mess anyway. She waited and sipped her water. When he returned, she was anxious and ready to demand answers if he didn't start offering them up.

"So, what do you want to know?"

Elle barely held back her scoffed *duh*. "Everything," she said simply. Let him tell it as he would, she wanted to know it all.

"That is a long conversation, why don't you get cleaned up. I will make sure Leda and Traylon aren't killing each other, and then we can talk all about Prias."

Elle wanted to argue, but she really did need a shower, and he was being reasonable. If telling her *everything* as she was demanding was going to take a while and he needed to get something done first, then she couldn't really argue.

"That sounds good, except, I don't suppose you packed me any clothing, did you?"

Locan frowned, looking quite bothered by the question. "I didn't think to pack any of your comforts from home. I am so sorry to have neglected so obvious a thing. I hope you can learn to make do with what Prian women do. I am sure Leda will be thrilled to share her things with you until we arrive."

"Yeah, I am sure she will," Elle said doubtfully, "but it's not really necessary. I'm sure I can just wear this until then. How long will it be?"

"Three weeks, roughly."

"Dang. Well maybe just a few things then, if she doesn't mind. I don't want her to think she has to."

"But she does."

"Not because I am some kind of princess on an alien planet."

"No, because I am her captain and I say so, and you are Princess L, of Prias, and she will serve you, as will we all." Locan strode from the room before she could argue, leaving her to sit and await his return.

As she waited, she leaned her head back against the wall and closed her eyes. There was just no more denying it, she was on a spaceship heading to a distant planet where her mother was from, where she was a fucking princess! It was insane, it was also every dream of a little girl come true. She groaned and pinched her nose to fight the stress headache that wanted to overtake her.

"Are you alright?"

Elle sat up and smiled politely at Leda. "Oh yeah, just

trying to come to terms with everything. It's all very overwhelming, if you can imagine."

"Sure, it's got to suck to find out you're a princess. Follow me, I will give you some of my clothes." She turned and walked out of the room, obviously assuming Elle would follow.

Elle did follow, although she wasn't sure she wanted to, the hostility was palpable, and she had no idea why. "I really appreciate your letting me borrow something to wear, just until I can wash this stuff at least."

"Don't worry about it. As I am sure Locan told you, we are here to serve you." Leda walked on in silence, her feet pounding the floor with unnecessary force and her hips swaying angrily. She walked to a nondescript door in the hallway, and it swished open for her. Elle didn't follow her in, but from what she could see, it was much like her own room, only this one was covered in rich fabrics, wall hangings, rugs, blankets, and pillows. Leda obviously liked more color than Locan permitted on the rest of the ship.

"Wow, I really like your room."

Leda looked up from the closet, which was a wall panel that was completely invisible until Leda had touched it and it'd popped open to reveal a good-sized armoire. "Oh, thanks. I suppose yours is pretty bare, no one stays in the rooms, other than our three, permanently. The others are just for transportation purposes, not very homey. Here," she handed Elle a pile of cloth and practically pushed her from the room.

"Thanks, now where is the shower?" Elle was embarrassed to have to ask, especially since Leda obviously did not want to be accommodating in any way but she'd been in her bathroom already it didn't have more than a sink and toilet.

"Follow me." Leda walked down the hall and to a door that, Elle assumed, was the room she had been in earlier, but she had no real way of knowing, all the doors looked the same and it was just as nondescript inside.

Leda walked to the wall opposite the bed and touched her hand to it, the wall opened and revealed the small bathroom. Leda walked to the wall opposite the toilet and touched her hand. A shower opened. Then she left.

"Thank you," Elle called after her, "bitch," Elle added under her breath.

ELEVEN

"I hope you didn't offend her with your sour face, Leda. Goddesses, you'd think even *you* could be happy about the acquisition of the Princess. She is going to change everything." Traylon huffed as Leda entered the control room.

"I don't doubt that," Leda said and sulked to her station where she was monitoring the surrounding areas for activity.

"Tell her, Locan. She should be stoked, not acting like someone just shot her pet. L is going to change everything for us, Prias will be a place of peace and tranquility like nothing we have known in our lifetime. No more Doctors and their freaky Hospital-inseminated—"

"Traylon!" Locan shouted, cutting off the typically thoughtless remark. It really was no wonder that Leda hated him, and most of the outcasts celebrated his departure. "Leda is free to feel as she wishes, as long as she doesn't take her anger out on L or annoy me with it overly much." Locan turned away, cutting off any further remarks from either of them. They were hell to work with most of the time.

He was sure Leda wouldn't do anything overtly mean to L

or offend her with intent. She was just naturally unhappy most of the time, and more so since L was found. Most likely just because she knew this mission was cut short and they would be heading straight back to Prias even though their ship wasn't full. Getting L to Prias was top priority. Leda hated being on Prias, no doubt she was cranky about it. Locan didn't totally get it, but he got it enough to let her have her anger.

Locan went back to pretending to monitor the ship's status. It was hopeless, however. All he could think of was L. His instincts were on overdrive right now. He was a descendent of the Royal Guard and she was a Prian princess; everything in him shouted to protect her. Leaving her unguarded, even on his own ship, felt wrong. He kept finding his mind drifting to the other two members of the crew and how they could possibly pose a threat to her. It was insanity and yet he was helpless to do anything to stop the thoughts.

He was a liability staring at screens with such distraction. "I am going for a walk," he announced with a growl to the two as he pushed out from his console. Neither spoke as he left quickly, no doubt they sensed his unease.

Unfortunately, there wasn't far he could go on the small cruiser and after only ten minutes he was feeling more restless than a caged beast.

Now you know how I feel. his Warrior growled.

"Oh, shut up."

"Excuse me?"

Locan turned around to find L standing in her doorway. He hadn't even realized that he had gravitated to her room, but he wasn't at all surprised that he had. He felt helpless to fight his instincts to protect her, which only made him want to try harder to deny them. He would not be ruled by that other part of himself. He would not let it destroy what and who he was.

"I was talking to myself. I see you have cleaned up, are you ready to talk about Prias?" She was wearing Prian clothing, tunic, and pants in a silvery grey color. Her hair was braided to the side, the white streak that spoke of her royal blood weaving in and out of the braid elegantly, and her purple eyes stood out of her fresh scrubbed face even more than they had when she wore her Earth makeup.

Beautiful, his Warrior proclaimed, and he had to agree.

"I do believe now is as good a time as any. Unless there is something you need to be doing. I don't want to take you away from your duties. We do have a few weeks before we arrive."

"Not at all, follow me. I am sure you are quite curious about everything; I know I would be. We will start with a tour of the ship."

"I have one question first," she said quickly, biting her lip nervously.

His eyes were drawn to her lips, and he frowned at the sidetracking of his mind. "What is it?" He asked, a little too gruffly.

"I—I was just wondering, how is it possible that you speak English?"

Locan looked up to her eyes with surprise and gave a little laugh. "I downloaded the language of the area when we first had the heading, a quick step into the ship's medical chamber."

"Convenient, so, I could do the same, and learn the Prian language before we arrive? Then I could read my mother's journal?"

"Of course. I would be happy to assist you in that whenever you'd like."

She smiled brightly and he took that as a sign that he should continue with the tour.

The ship consisted of two slightly curving hallways and a

large room at either end of the ship. At the front, through the glass panel doors, was the control room. At the back was a medical room and in between were sleeping chambers and the kitchen along one hallway and a couple larger rooms along the other hallway. One of these larger rooms was Locan's personal office, and this is where their tour ended. Locan deliberately choosing this room over the more sociable living area room so that he could emphasize his position of power and control as captain of this ship.

Locan offered her a drink, which she declined. He poured himself some of the liquor and sat behind his desk. "I am not sure where to begin," he said as he sipped. There was so much to tell her. "Perhaps with a bit about the planet and Prian history?" L didn't say anything, just sat there patiently waiting, and damn if she didn't look like a royal as she did it. It would be no stretch for her to become Queen of Prias. She had that look and energy about her that made people, well Prians anyway, stop and listen to her. His eyes strayed to the net of stars covering her arm. It was, no doubt, loyalty from the Goddess that was drawing on his Prian blood so strongly. He couldn't help but smile at the thought, she would call to them all, and she would unite them all. He just hoped she would want to.

"Prias is a very small planet, about a sixth the size of Earth. It has only one large landmass, about half the size of the Earth's United States. Not all of that is inhabitable land however, and so the population long ago settled into a fairly condensed area with rich farmlands near large streams of fresh water. A shallow sea covers the rest of the planet."

L's eyes were wide with curiosity, and she seemed to hang on his every word. He wished it were all beauty that he had to speak to her about.

"As you can imagine, it can be difficult for a group of people to live so closely, but we have always been a people devoted to peace, and through the rule of our Queens and the worship of our Goddesses and Gods, we have long been at peace. We were quite happy with our simple existence. We are technologically advanced compared to Earth; however, we have always chosen to live simpler than that. You will see what I mean when we arrive."

"It is hard to imagine, I guess a lot of things will just have to wait until I experience them firsthand," L agreed. "I am still trying to wrap my head around the fact that other worlds and aliens exist. It just isn't what most people on Earth believe, certainly not the mainstream accepted belief. Are there a lot of other *things* like us, like Prians and humans?"

Locan nodded. "There are many planets with varying degrees of civilization and many different forms of life. Not all are what you would call humanoid, and not all are what anyone would call friendly. Many planets are barely out of the stone age and some even farther behind than that. You should count yourself lucky that you landed on such a nice planet as Earth."

"I know that I am very lucky, I was raised by a wonderful woman." L's voice cracked a little as she said this.

"Where we are going is outside the main city, in the near-uninhabitable part of Prias. We were chased there by Temis, who I suppose is your great uncle."

"I have an uncle? Wow. But I take it he is not one of the good guys?" she asked, a hint of disappointment in her voice.

Locan wasn't sure how to proceed from here. Judging her reaction was hard, and he couldn't be sure she believed everything he said. The last thing he wanted to do was make her feel like he was pressuring her to do as he wished.

"That is for you to decide, I will tell you he is definitely not on the same side as me."

"Fair enough, please continue, sorry I interrupted."

"Temis was your grandmother's brother. He was an

unimportant extra relation to the royal family, it being a matriarchy. It is my belief that—well never mind, the facts are that he brought the Doctors to our planet, supposedly to help with our low birth rate problem that had been becoming increasingly evident. The Goddess Achromic, the Mother Goddess has always been worshipped and has ensured that the planet was fertile in its people and crops. Then one day, it seemed as if she just left us, no one knows why, but things got bad fast. Temis offered a solution with the Doctors. That was before my time, I was born a rebel, so I don't have firsthand knowledge of the time before, but what I do know, is that among the rebels there has always been a problem conceiving, though not as bad as in the city perhaps. In the city there still is much fear, and so it is believed among those who have stayed, that the only way to get a child is through the Doctors. They hand out children to those who support Temis and— Wait, sorry I want to only give you the facts as I know them. I want you to decide how you feel about them. Years ago, when your mother was just a young lady and—"

"What was my mother's name? What was she like?" Elle leaned forward, her face intense, so hungry for knowledge of her mother.

"K was her name. You are L and your grandmother was J. You are a letter, and you are named in order. That is the tradition of Prian Queens."

"Wait," L gave him an incredulous look. "How the hell do you have the same alphabet as the English language?"

"You don't believe that *Earthlings* came up with something as wonderful and complex as the alphabet, do you?" He couldn't help but scoffing. "I told you, we are far more advanced than humans on Earth and we have known about the planet for an awfully long time. It was a planet that our ancestors visited when we were first beginning to explore space travel. They found the planet lacked many things, and taught them a system of written language, I think you will be surprised to learn that our spoken languages are not so dissimilar either."

"I'm not sure I can wrap my brain around all of this."

"Don't worry about what isn't important, concentrate on what is now and important."

"Which is my mother's history," she said with a determined nod.

"Yes, I think so. K looked much like you; I have been told. Red hair, purple eyes and of course the streak of white at your temple that marks you as royalty. She was beautiful, as are you." Locan spoke the words and instantly regretted them as he watched a shadow cross L's face and she sat back in the chair.

"By the time your mother came to rule over Prias, Temis was already deeply involved with the Doctors and had built a monstrous building, the Hospital, where they were keeping women and breeding them. Your mother had no idea, she was young, innocent, and only following the example of her mother before her, who had been so grief-stricken when her soul-husband died that she had not cared what was going on around her. Your mother fell in love with a member of her guard, and you resulted, but when Temis discovered her pregnancy, begotten without the aid of the Hospital, he took her into it under the guise of keeping her safe. She managed to escape, along with many other pregnant women. She ended up on Earth and had you. Myself, and a few others from the rebel colony, have been searching for the missing Prians for years, and so have Temis' Enforcers. It has been a race to find *you* in particular. The legend of Queen K having a daughter off planet has been something that has kept the rebels' spirits up for years. Predictions of a return of you, L, has kept the Prian rebels alive with hope. You will lead us all to victory over the evil that has taken Prias for its own."

L's face was indecipherable as she listened silently to his story. "How do you know so much about my mother's story?"

"It is legend among the people. There are those among the rebels who were in the city when your mother was there. Our leader talks of his firsthand experiences in the royal home. L, you have to unite us, prove to the non-believers that there is a royal still here and willing to rule rightfully and fairly." Locan couldn't stop himself from emphasizing each and every word with a rise and lean forward. By the end he was standing and leaning so far over his desk he could smell her soap, the same soap everyone on the ship used, but somehow it smelled better on her.

"I—I—I don't—"

"Locan, we need you in here, now!" Traylon's voice called frantically over the ship's intercom.

L didn't move after Locan hurried from the room; she sat in shock. The things he had said were incomprehensible, and he expected her to not only believe them, but to embody them. Her name was a letter, not a word, she was a princess who was predicted to help save their planet from her evil uncle. It was all too much. He saw her as some kind of predestined savior of a people she didn't even know for certain existed. She saw herself as a damn good ob-gyn. Her thoughts for the first time returned to her life on Earth; her job, all her clients and her roommate. What were people going to think? That she'd just ran away, or maybe that she was murdered, and her body never found? They'll probably question Ryan about her disappearance, she hoped he didn't get in trouble.

As she contemplated all that Locan had said, her arm began to tingle. The stars seeming to vibrate with energy in response to her intense emotional reaction to everything. She stared down at the net of stars covering her arm and admitted that there was something going on here that was beyond her. Did that mean that there were Goddesses up above who had already decided she was going to do something great whether she liked it or not? She wasn't sure about that, but somehow these marks had magically appeared; she couldn't deny that there was something beyond what she thought she knew about normal going on here.

"I am willing to keep an open mind, but I won't make a decision about anything I don't see firsthand," she said to whatever entity might be listening. Her stars shimmered visibly for a second then stopped tingling and silence sat heavily around her.

She took a deep breath and stood, when she turned around, she screamed.

"Here I am, see me firsthand, and get your shit together, girl, you are supposed to be on my side."

A woman floated there, her bare toes pointed and held just barely above the floor. The woman was completely blue, except for her entirely black, soulless eyes. Her blue hair was long and flowing around her naked blue body and as she spoke, her words seemed to be emphasized by blue sparkles of irritation popping around her. Elle felt her blue stars pulse in tandem with each sparkling pop.

"I don't know what you expect me to do. I have nothing invested in the Prian world," Elle said, bravery she hadn't known she had, coming forward in the face of this terrifying entity.

"You will, I believe that and so do the others, but that doesn't mean they all want you to succeed. I am betting on you. I have invested time and energy to see that you succeed. I even sent my daughter to Locan, although he has yet to do as he must. Don't *you*, let me down."

With that command, she was gone, simply disappeared, no

puff of dramatic smoke or anything. Just there one moment and gone the next. Not even a second later, Locan was barreling into the room. At least it appeared to be Locan, sort of. He was twice the size of Locan, and his eyes were glowing blue intensely. Elle backed away, frightened of this creature.

He looked around the room, assessing her and the rest of the room with swift efficiency then advanced on her with long strides.

"What was it, why did you scream?" His voice was full of concern, and it was at such odds with his intensely dangerous look that Elle wasn't sure which to go by. She was against the wall, and he was so close that she couldn't move away from him. She closed her eyes so she wouldn't have to see his intimidating form and instead concentrated on the sound of concern in his voice. "Are you alright?" he asked quietly.

"Umm, I think so. A woman? A blue woman was here."

"Cerulean," he said without hesitation or surprise.

Elle opened her eyes and almost wanted to close them again as she watched his body shrink down to his normal, still intimidating, size right before her eyes. His intense blue eyes went back to their brilliant green, still full of concern for her.

"What the fuck are you?" she asked before thinking. He backed away, giving her room to breathe. His gaze became guarded, and she felt guilty for asking such an openly rude question like that. Especially when she was starting to realize she didn't even know what *she* was. Judge not and all that crap.

"I am a member of the Royal Guard, or at least I would be if one still existed. Royal Guard members are a breed all their own on Prias. We have the ability to invoke the power of a Warrior, to make our bodies grow and strengthen in the face of danger to the member of the royal family we are set to guard."

"Like a magical power, or more like Dr. Jekyll and Mr.

Hyde? The Hulk? Are you The Hulk?" she said with more doubt than she had intended, clear in her voice.

"It is what it is. There is nothing one can do to either prevent or induce it. This is just what I am because of who my father was. There is no Earth comparison, and it is no work of fiction, I assure you," his voice was reluctant, almost regretful as he spoke.

"So, I shouldn't be frightened of you then, is that what you're saying?"

His green eyes narrowed, and his jaw tightened, his gaze pierced hers and she felt like he was holding her physically with the force in his eyes. "I am a danger to everyone, doubt that not. I am driven to protect you, yes, I do not wish you harm, no. The Warrior on the other hand, he can make me do things unintentionally. It is why I lock him away more fiercely than any other of Royal Guard blood. I will not accept him, and I will not embrace him, and no Goddess is going to convince me to do otherwise."

"Dammit Locan, what the hell are you doing, I need you in here!" Came Traylon's voice over the intercom again.

"Shit!" Locan cursed and turned from her. "We are being followed by Enforcers. I need to get in there and help guide us through some tricky spots to lose them. Be aware that the Goddesses and Gods are always working on their own agendas. They are not to be fully trusted; they are to be feared and appeased. Especially when they are watching you as closely as Cerulean obviously is. But I will die to protect you, doubt that not, either."

With those words, he strode from the room and Elle slumped to the floor where she stood, shaken to her core and mind trying to shut down from the overload.

Some while later, she found the presence of mind to pick herself up off the floor of Locan's office and drag herself to her room, which she only found after first opening five doors that were not hers. She collapsed onto her cot and tried not to think of anything that had happened in the last two days.

She concentrated on breathing in and out until she drifted to sleep.

TWELVE

After the successful eluding of Temis' ship, which Locan had been sorely tempted to turn around and face instead of run from, Locan stalked back down the hallway to search out L. He found her asleep in her bed, safe. He allowed himself a moment to watch her and wonder what she would think if he told her what he had just discovered. That Jabon had kidnapped her roommate and her roommate's boyfriend. Even now he had them on his ship, threatening their lives if Locan didn't stop at the nearest planet.

Locan had a feeling he knew exactly what L would say, which was exactly why he couldn't tell her. If they stopped and risked L's life before getting to Prias, a lot more people would die, it just wasn't worth the lives of two Earthlings.

Locan walked out of her room feeling like an ass, but she was safe, and that was the most important thing.

"That was fast," Leda said as he emerged from L's room. She was leaning against the hall near her own door, looking at him with a raised eyebrow.

"Whatever you're thinking, don't. I am sworn to protect and that is above all else."

"Even lust?"

"Yes, Leda, even lust. A member of the Royal Guard would have to go against every instinct to cross that line with a royal. It's just never done."

"Except that *her* mother was supposedly impregnated by a member of her Royal Guard, a Warrior in his own right."

"I know the story," Locan growled.

"Which not only means it's possible, but it also makes her half Warrior. She's not the product of two of the upper class. I wonder what the citizens of Prias will make of that?" Leda walked into her room, leaving Locan with troubling thoughts.

He knew that L had another half, she wasn't purely the daughter of K, but would that matter in the eyes of Prians? Usually, a princess would marry a man of the upper class, never a Guard or simple citizen. He could maybe work this to his advantage though, if she were half Warrior then she had some fight in her, and she was going to need that.

Elle couldn't believe how good she felt when she woke up from her nap, it felt like it must be late afternoon now. She was in a strange room on a freaking *spaceship,* with people she didn't really know; yet she'd slept better than she could ever remember sleeping. She usually woke up and tossed and turned, she was fairly certain that she'd woken up in the exact position she'd fallen asleep in, and she must have been out for a while because she woke up feeling rested.

The lights in the room came on when she sat up, and her head whipped around, looking for intruders, but she was alone. She made her way to the bathroom where she splashed water on her face and tried to smooth out some wrinkles on her borrowed clothes, she was going to have to beg another set from Leda or at least wash her clothes she'd been in when Locan had brought her on the ship. The slacks and button up blouse weren't exactly casual comfortable, but at least they were hers.

When she emerged from the bathroom, she had one thing in mind; her mother's journal. If she was going to understand what she was getting into, that journal was the best resource. She just needed the language *downloaded* into her brain apparently.

"I wish there was a window," she sighed as she looked around the empty room. A circular space on the outside wall started to spin and unwind and a window the size of a dinner plate revealed itself. She rushed to it, entranced by what she saw outside.

A sea of deep, inky blackness was dotted with shining points of light, like looking up at the stars from the top of a mountain where no city lights were in the way to compete with the light from the stars. It was beautiful, but what really made her gasp, was the enormous pink planet that they were passing at a close distance.

"Palpatar."

Elle spun around at the voice and found Locan standing close behind her. She should have known he was there; her arm was tingling in a familiar manner. "I can't even comprehend what I'm seeing, not truly."

"I imagine it's all still a bit shocking."

She huffed, "A bit! I'm half sure I am about to wake up from a dream or a forced vacation in the looney bin."

"What if you just keep waking up here on my spaceship?" he said with a laugh.

"Then I guess I'd better learn the language."

"Food first?"

"I would love a cup of coffee, actually."

Locan made a disgusted face but nodded.

"You're not a coffee drinker?"

"The bitter black liquid is not to my liking, no."

"What does a Warrior take in the morning to wake up, then?"

"Tea."

"Tea?" She couldn't hold back her surprise, such a delicate answer from such a big man.

"It's not Earth tea, it can only be found on Prias."

Elle cocked her head to the side and thought about that, how different her eating and drinking habits were about to become. "I guess I'd like to try it."

Locan smiled, "Follow me then, I'll make us both a cup. Afternoon tea is nearly as good as morning tea."

She followed him to the lounge area and took the seat he indicated as he moved about making tea in a very Earthly fashion. Maybe some things were the same all over the universe.

"Do you want sweetener?"

"Does it need it?"

"It's not traditional, no," he said as he handed her a hot cup.

She took it with a smile, "Then I am sure this will be just fine." She could feel his eyes on her as she sniffed the hot liquid, it was a spicy sort of strange smell, not unpleasant but definitely not recognizable either. She ventured a sip and regretted her adventurousness, it tasted like dirt mixed with cayenne pepper and mint. She set it down and forced herself to swallow.

"That bad?" he said with a laugh.

"I'll stick with coffee."

"Me too, that shit is something else!" Traylon said, walking into the room with a bright smile. "I think I drank four cups a day when we were on your planet. Locan only tried it once," Traylon said with a dramatic eye roll. "I can make you some though."

"You'll have to say goodbye to Earthly delights, my dear, we didn't stock a lifetime supply," Leda said, joining them.

Elle refused to admit how much that statement made her

throat tighten and her eyes burn. She had left behind everything she'd ever known, for what? "I suppose I'll live."

"Of course, you will, you will want for nothing, Princess," Traylon said with a dramatic bow.

Locan snorted. "You'll want for plenty I think, but nothing that you can't live without, that's for certain."

Elle appreciated his honesty, and she gave him a weak smile and even sipped a little more of the tea, just to prove a point to Leda who was watching her with a bit of a disgusted look. "It's really not that bad after the first initial shock, it's unlike anything I've ever tasted before."

"It's shit compared to this black delight," Traylon said as he started the coffee grinder.

Leda huffed and got herself a cup of tea, then sat as far from Elle as she could in the small room. Locan looked thoughtful and Elle set her cup down but held onto it as if she would venture another sip soon; she wouldn't.

"So how long does the language download take?"

"It's a simple language with few differences in sound structure, though perhaps a little softer than your particular dialect. I think the computer will be able to implant the necessary knowledge in a minute or two."

"You getting your native tongue downloaded?" Traylon asked.

"Yeah, I think it would be ridiculous not to, seeing as we *are* heading to that planet, and besides, I want to be able to read my mother's journal."

Leda gasped, "You have her journal? Does it speak of the others?"

"I have no idea what it speaks of, I can't read it." Elle shrugged.

"Probably selfish drivel," Leda said under her breath, but nowhere near quiet enough to avoid everyone overhearing.

"Leda! You will not speak of the Queen that way," Locan growled.

"The woman who abandoned her people to atrocities? Who stood by while *my* mother was bred who knows how many times before she was forced to escape and kill herself to ensure my survival on a planet where I was hated?" Leda stood as she spat her angry remarks, laid her hands on the table, and glared at Locan.

To his credit, Locan didn't react at all. Elle was shocked, expecting that he would have reached across the distance and shut her up violently as she yelled at him. When he spoke, his voice was soft and calm, but she could see that his body was bulging, and she remembered how large he had been when he'd rushed to her rescue before. He was holding back his anger; did that mean Leda's accusations were accurate?

"Leda, you will keep your opinions to yourself. You will not speak of L's mother in such a manner, and to assume you have any idea what was going on in her mind when she was in rule is ridiculous."

Leda huffed and left the room. No one said anything else for a while, Traylon finished making coffee and handed her a cup, taking the still full cup of tea away. Locan was back to his normal hulking size by then.

"Thank you, Traylon, cream and sugar?"

"Yeah, I grabbed some of this stuff." Traylon handed her some flavored powdered creamer and a bag of sugar.

"Perfect," she said, even though she preferred her coffee with real milk and agave syrup, this was better than the tea by far.

"When you're done, we'll head to the medical unit," Locan said.

"Do you think my mother was the cause of all that?" she

asked carefully, staring into the dark liquid as she stirred in creamer.

"I think she came to power when the kingdom was in trouble and she thought she was doing the right thing, following in her mother's footsteps, and trusting her uncle. She did what she had to do."

"But she could have done something sooner?"

"Perhaps." Locan shrugged. "Maybe the journal will answer that for all of us."

"Perhaps," Elle said and drank the coffee.

She wasn't able to wait long; she made it through half the cup then took it to the sink and washed it out. "I'm ready," she said with as much confidence as she could. A nervous knot sat in her stomach. She wasn't sure which was causing it, getting the language put into her brain, or being able to sit down and read her mother's words. What if Leda was right, what if her mother had been a selfish, stupid woman?

"Good luck!" Traylon called as she followed Locan out of the room.

They took a right and headed away from the control room of the ship. The hallway curved as they walked.

"Is this a flying saucer?" she asked with a giggle, sure he wouldn't get her joke.

"This is a spaceship," he said with no emotion.

"Yes, but what shape is it outside, I guess is my question."

"Shape, well I guess it is shaped like a drop."

"A drop? That doesn't make any sense."

He stopped with a frustrated huff and turned, grabbing her hand roughly, he drew a shape on her palm. She almost missed the shape, so distracted by his touch. "A drop," he said again.

"Oh! A teardrop shape, I get it. Which is the front?" She looked up into his green eyes, the back of her hand warm and tingly where it rested in his palm.

"Here," he said softly, tracing the rounded part of the drop shape near her wrist.

She felt a shiver run through her, and when he dropped her hand and turned away stiffly, she felt an uncomfortable loss.

Locan stopped then and touched a panel on the wall which whooshed open to reveal the medical room.

Elle stepped in; it didn't look like any kind of medical room she'd ever been in. There was what appeared to be a tanning bed, a cot, and a wall of cabinets. Nothing that looked like medical equipment. When Locan had showed her earlier he hadn't really explained anything she was seeing.

"Does this do everything you need it to do while traveling?"

"Trust me, it is well equipped to take care of most ailments and injuries." Locan walked over to the tanning bed and started touching buttons. "This is our healing pod; you'll lay in it, and it will gently input the language."

The lid of the healing pod opened to reveal a cushioned bed on bottom and a top covered in blinking lights and what appeared to be small doors. She assumed they might open and reveal various medical tools depending on the needs of the patient.

A female voice spoke in a language she didn't understand and Locan responded similarly. Then the female voice said, "Earth English. How may I be of service today?"

"L would like the Prian language input," Locan responded. "Go ahead and lay down, L. I will close the lid and the computer will talk you through it, I'll be right here if you need anything."

Elle was unsure, but after all the amazing things she'd witnessed recently, she didn't doubt for a second that this tanning bed could input a language into her brain. "You'll stay here?" she asked quickly as the lid descended.

Locan smiled sweetly, and she liked the way it softened his features. "Of course, just relax."

She didn't relax, but she didn't jump out of the bed either.

"Welcome, L," the computer spoke softly, and the bed started a slow hum underneath her body. "Do you prefer to sleep or be alert throughout the procedure?"

"Asleep," she answered without giving it much thought. If she could avoid any pain or discomfort, she was all for that.

"Very well, breathe deeply."

She did as instructed, and before she knew it, she was waking up to Locan gently shaking her shoulder. "L, wake up."

"I'm awake."

He smiled broadly. "You can understand me!"

She realized he wasn't speaking English and bolted upright with excitement. "I understand you!" she shouted in a language she couldn't believe she knew.

Locan helped her stand, and she shivered a little with excitement. "I must go read my mother's journal."

Locan laughed, "Go, let me know if there's anything world-shattering in there that might help our cause."

"I will," she assured him, then hurried from the room. She only opened one wrong door before she found her room this time, she was going to have to mark the damn thing with a sticker or something. Luckily, the room she'd accidently opened first was just a storage closet. She'd hate to accidentally walk in on Traylon changing or something.

She grabbed the journal and flung herself on her bed, ready to soak up her mother's words. A tear slid down her cheek as she ran a finger over the cover. "Tell me your story," she whispered.

I don't know what to say, how to make it better, I know it's too late. But I hope that someday my daughter finds this, I hope she survives, and I hope she can forgive me.

My dearest daughter,

L, if you're reading this, know that I love you more than life and I would have given anything to spend a lifetime with you, but it wasn't in the stars. Our lives were not meant to be lived together, I was meant to deliver you into the world so that you could fix the things that your ancestors did wrong, what I did wrong.

I'm so ashamed.

L put the journal down and took a deep breath, it wasn't a journal, it was a letter to her and seeing her name written there in her mother's handwriting changed everything for her. Tears stung her eyes and she had to steady herself before opening it back up.

THIRTEEN

I can't take full responsibility for all our people's troubles of course; they started long before I had ever come to rule. It had started even before the death of my father, your grandfather, Mitt, when I was five, and before Temis brought the Doctors, Dr. Saval and Dr. Raval, when I was four. They started with the disappearance of the Goddess Achromic when I was born, she blessed me as her last act, I'm told. She appeared at my mother's bedside after I was born and left her mark on my leg, she was never seen again.

Temis brought the Doctors because they supposedly held the cure to the world's recent reproductive problems. They were going to fix everything. Why wouldn't your grandmother have trusted her dear brother? Family was supposed to watch out for each other.

The people of Prias had been mostly barren for four years by then. Your grandmother, affected to a degree, was only able to bear one child, me. Thank the Goddesses I had been a girl, there always must be a princess to be the Queen one day. Never had Prias been without a queen to rule our utopian society and a princess to inherit that throne. Without this, our people would have lost the faith much sooner. It would have proven that the Goddesses had abandoned us, maybe they have. I wonder sometimes if you aren't better off on another planet.

The Doctors that Uncle Temis brought, had come from a neighboring solar system, one that they said was advanced. The simple people of Prias had taken them at their word, thankful for their knowledge and help. The Queen trusted them, so everyone should. I did too, I never questioned the Doctors or Temis, and now I fear it may be too late to save Prias. Please realize that years passed and no one, including Queen J, questioned them so I grew up thinking everything was fine, no need to question or look closely. The Prian people happily built a metal monstrosity of a Hospital that the Doctors said was necessary for the cure. From there the Doctors and Temis slowly began to take control.

My mother, forever mourning the death of my father, completely ignored what was happening around her. I didn't realize she was oblivious; I thought she was privy to all that happened on the planet. I grew up thinking everything was as it should be. In our society there is no history of discord, no instance of a queen not making the absolute best decisions for her people, and never has another tried to usurp control that was given by the Goddess to the next queen in line. Each queen is not only blessed by Achromic, as I was at birth, but she inherits the power of the Goddess when she takes on the crown, this power allows her to control the Royal Guard who some say are descendants of the Goddess' race, not the Prian race at all. This power and control is absolute, they will do anything they are told, follow any command, and lay their lives down to protect the Queen and her royal family. I never got that far, I was officially crowned, but something was wrong, I never got the power. Perhaps Achromic really has abandoned us.

When the Hospital was built, the Doctors requested all women of breeding age enter and undergo fertility testing. It was supposed to be voluntary, but I found out later that the Enforcers worked in the dead of night, collecting innocents whose families had declined turning them over, and who had not had the sense to run. Any who were fool enough to cry out in public against the Doctors or Temis were stricken down before they could be heard by my mother or me. The common people lived in fear. The wealthy were reaping the benefits and turned their backs to what was happening. It sickens me to think that we let this happen, that we stood by while our society was destroyed.

Inside the Hospital the young women who were fertile were impregnated repeatedly, their babies passed out to appropriate families. Families Temis decided should be rewarded for their loyalty and wealth. Our once utopian society full of farmers, ranchers and craftsmen was suddenly a nightmare full of wickedness and subterfuge.

No babies were born in the city outside of the Hospital, I think this is what allowed Temis and his Doctors to maintain their power. The people were terrified that our people would be extinct if it weren't for the help of the Doctors. Quickly the gap between the commoners and the wealthy widened. The commoners, even if they wanted to revolt, were helpless, they could leave the city and take their chances in the wild or stay and hope that they may eventually find themselves in a position to take on a child that was born at the Hospital. While fearing that any child they already had would be taken from them and put in the Hospital to be used for breeding.

I have heard rumors that deep in the treacherous wilderness, far beyond the reach of the governing men of Prias, there grows a city of rebels. People who fled the terror of the city instead of cowering in the shadow of the Hospital. Their rumored existence threatens all that Temis has managed to achieve. Anyone who is heard whispering about it suddenly disappears, no one dares ask about them for fear they too will be among the missing. I like to think that if I had known of these things earlier, I would have done something about it, but I'm not sure, not sure I would have believed enough to care. Besides, what power do I have? Achromic is silent to my pleading even now and I cannot command the Guard as I should. If I had known, I might have made different choices after my mother died.

For three years after the death of your grandmother, J, I ruled our people under the close guidance of Temis. I was too busy vying for the attentions of your father, Carini, to care about anything else. He had the good sense to remember his place. He was a Royal Guard member, born to protect the royal family above all else, even his own desires. We were never meant to know each other the way I wanted, but I couldn't accept that. He was so beautiful, so strong and clever. I hope he was clever enough to escape, that he made it out of the city.

So young and dumb, so in love with the idea of love, I had blocked out everything else. I was a stupid selfish child. I pursued him, not caring what it would mean if we were ever found out.

He refused to make love to me because he was sworn to protect me. I was meant to wed someone of the highest class of the Prian people, not a commoner like himself, he would say. Carini believed this with all his being and would not give in to our desires. This strength and determination is what had made him a candidate for such a prized position in the Royal Guard, it was also what made me want his love all the more. I felt certain he was meant to keep a part of my soul, if only he'd accept it.

As our people suffered ever increasing oppression, I hatched elaborate plans to make Carini fall in love with me; finally, I succeeded. He came rushing to my aid in the middle of the night. I had stood in front of the mirror for an hour practicing the look I would give him. I knew it would win his heart.

Carini could no longer deny what he felt for me, and we quickly fell deeply in love. It was everything I had ever imagined love could be. Each night we stayed in each other's arms until the sun came up. During the day it killed me to be apart from him and we found every dark corner we could to grab a quick embrace. I had no idea what kind of fire I was playing with, and if Carini did, he never let it stop him. I gave him a piece of my soul and he gave me a piece of his, we were soul-wed, and in my mind, that was enough.

My uncle became suspicious when Carini dared show jealousy towards a suitor that had been recommended to me. That night Carini didn't come to see me as usual, I waited until the sun appeared before letting the tears fall. Did he abandon me? Or had he finally been punished for our love? In the morning he was gone from my Guard with no explanation, just replaced by another. I cried for days and refused to see my uncle. I knew he lived, I could feel his soul alive in my body though it brought minimal comfort. The only thing that moved me out of my suffering was the discovery that I was carrying our child. You were a reminder of the love we'd shared for so short a time. It seemed like such an impossible event, and I thought perhaps my uncle would then have to bring him back, he was the father after all, we could be married, and he would be king. It was unprecedented, but I was Queen! I got to make the rules, right?

These thoughts kept me happy company for a month while I waited to find the perfect words to tell him. Then Temis came to visit, and I finally was willing to see him. I was going to proclaim my happy news and make my joyful demands. He took one look at me and instantly knew I was carrying you. He convinced me that you and I were in great danger, and I must go to the Hospital immediately, promising to send for Carini at once.

I believed him, why would he lie to me?

Once at the Hospital, I was faced with the horror of what my mother and I had allowed to happen to our once beautiful and proud people. Temis slapped a cuff around my wrist and informed me that I was to marry him and tell everyone that the child I carried was his. If not, he would destroy me and you. I refused him, but he only laughed and threw me in with the other women to 'think it over.'

I soon discovered that the women whom I had thought to be there of their own free will, were prisoners. It was there that I finally heard the rumors of the people who disappeared and those who ran away to join the city of outcasts. I finally knew how stupid and selfish I had been.

I was enraged by everything I saw and heard. I had been played for a fool, my mother had been deceived by her own brother, and our people were suffering. Our wonderful people who worked hard and enjoyed a simple existence were now reduced to beggars and breeders. The people who were considered near equals to me and our royal family were happily contributing to the dismantling of society. Using everyone around them and following out orders given by Temis, as if he were ruler there instead of me.

How could this have happened?

I could not let it continue, and I refused to let you die, but marrying Temis was a horrifying possibility. I didn't know what, if any, options I had, and the bracelet ensured I couldn't stay hidden for long even if I did manage to escape. It's a tracking device with only two ways to remove it, death or taking off the hand, which would likely result in my death.

I thought for days, and finally a plan formed. I told Temis that I would marry him, but not until after the baby was born safely. He agreed.

I bided my time while I grew large, gaining strength I knew you would need to survive. When I knew the time was nearing for your birth, I enacted my plan. Along with many of the other *girls, pregnant and suffering, we made our way to the flight pods and escaped.*

It's been weeks and I am not sure when I will land, but I know you are about ready to come out whether or not I'm still stuck in this pod. I hope you wait; I hope we land somewhere safe and friendly; but most of all I hope that you can hide and forgive me for what I must do to keep you safe. If you ever find this, if you are ever able to read it, I want you to know that I don't expect you to leave whatever life you have to save the Prian people, but if you do, know that I believe you can do great things for the Prian people.

I love you; I will never know you and I am sorry for that. Whatever life you choose to pursue, do it with honor and do it with whatever joy you can find. If you ever find yourself on Prias, know that I heard rumors of the soul of the city lying beneath it. If there'd been time, if there'd been anyone safe to tell before I escaped, I would have. Perhaps someday you will deliver the message for both of us.

Love,
Your Mother, Queen K

Reading her mother's letter was emotionally exhausting and L fell asleep when she finished, her mind spinning with all the information. Her mother had been young and dumb, there was no denying that. But none of the things that happened were her fault; she was dealing with the result of what had come before her and as soon as she'd been faced with the truth, it was too late, and she'd done the only thing she could. L could forgive her. She wished she had something more convincing to tell Leda though.

FOURTEEN

Locan snuck into L's chamber with a tray of food when she didn't emerge for too many hours. He wasn't sure what she was going to find in that journal, but he was hanging his hopes on it convincing her that helping him was the right thing to do.

She was curled up on her bed, the book closed and clutched to her chest. She was truly beautiful. He dared a step closer and wondered if he could take the journal without her knowing. She sighed in her sleep, and he stepped back, if she woke, she probably wouldn't be too happy to find him lurking even if he was carrying a tray as an excuse.

So soft. A voice slid through his head as his eyes caressed her smooth cheek.

Locan growled and set the tray down, then left the room before his Warrior could convince him to do something he'd regret.

Locan joined Leda and Traylon in the control room of the ship. He monitored the screens and tried to think of anything but L. Just when he thought he was forgetting to think about her, she walked in with a grin.

"Hey," she called out.

"Did you finish the journal?" Traylon asked excitedly.

Leda hunched her shoulders and a crease set between her eyes. She refused to acknowledge L's presence and Locan raised his eyebrow at her. The disrespect was noted, he was going to have to talk to Leda and he really didn't want to.

"It wasn't actually a journal, it was more of a letter, to me, she wrote it while she was in the escape pod."

"Did it solve any great mysteries?" Traylon prodded and Leda perked up, obviously listening.

Locan knew Leda wanted to know about her own mother, desperately wanted a connection to anyone. He doubted she was going to find that, ever, and he felt sorry for her, though he'd never tell her that.

"It was a history lesson, and I know who my father is, or was, that's probably a more accurate statement."

"A mother *and* a father, how lucky for you," Leda grumbled.

Locan gave her a sharp look. Luckily L didn't seem bothered by Leda's attitude, it might be the only thing that saved Leda from real consequences.

"Temis got rid of him when it became obvious that my mother and he were in love, he was a member of her Guard," she said the last part to Locan.

Locan's eyes widened, and his body puffed slightly as his Warrior awoke. "The rumors are true?"

Yes, his Warrior purred in his mind, filling his head with forbidden images of naked flesh and scorching kisses.

"That's what the letter says," L continued on as if Locan wasn't in that moment fighting with himself to not walk across the room and enact his Warrior's fantasies. "He was a member of her Royal Guard, she seduced him, and they fell in love, then he was taken away."

"He was a failure," Locan spat.

L looked at him with shock.

He was in charge of his own life, his own desires, his Warrior argued.

"A Royal Guard member is meant to guard and protect at all costs." Locan said as much to her as to his Warrior. "He should never have been able to ask her to debase herself to the point of giving herself to him. It would go against his every instinct."

L rolled her eyes and stuck a hand on her hip. "Oh really, are you a love expert, Locan? You think you know what controls the heart so thoroughly?"

"Ha! Locan has never felt a twinge of love his entire life," Leda hissed.

"Love doesn't know social class, that's not just an Earth construct, that's biology," L argued.

"You obviously need to learn something about Prian biology," Locan accused. "A Royal Guard member is something Earth can't explain except with their mythology."

Now I'm a myth? Let me out and I'll show her what's incredibly real about me.

"We are not even Prian, but we are bound to serve Achromic's chosen rulers," Locan continued. "A gift from the Goddess herself to protect her chosen people."

"Regardless of your personal experiences with it all, the letter says what it says," L said with a shrug. "Besides, it said something about that, Achromic blessed her at birth but then disappeared and when she became Queen, she didn't inherit Achromic's powers, maybe that made the difference with the whole Royal Guard rules?"

Locan mulled over that possibility.

"And it doesn't say how to defeat the damn Doctors or Temis, I assume? Or you would have mentioned the important information by now," Leda said, thankfully changing the subject.

L smiled at her. "No, it didn't. It did say something about the soul of Prias being under the city, whatever that means."

Locan frowned. "The soul of the city?"

L shrugged. "I think I need to learn to fight," she stated firmly.

"Leda will teach you," Locan said in a tone that should have left no room for argument.

"Sure thing, *boss*," Leda grumbled.

The pleased look on L's face made Locan happy.

"I'm going to go shower and sleep, thanks for the food, whoever left it in my room. Something about space travel and learning you're an alien is exhausting."

"Sweet dreams, Princess, let me know if you need a bedtime story," Traylon teased.

Kill him.

Locan didn't disagree. L rolled her eyes and left.

"What am I going to do with you two?" Locan snarled when the door closed behind her.

"He should be neutered," Leda suggested.

"And you need a year in charm school," Traylon shot back.

"You both need to realize she's the Princess and that means we all are shit in comparison, we all live to serve her, and we all put our lives at her feet. If she doesn't get to Prias and take our army to the city, we won't ever have what we once did."

"*We* never had it, neither did our parents for that matter, what exactly do you think we are fighting for? What if it isn't what you think it is, what anyone says it is?" Leda questioned.

Locan didn't have an answer, so he walked out of the room. All he knew was the rumors of the utopia that once was and his inner drive telling him to fight to get it back. It was all he'd known his entire life, which didn't change now that they actually might have the key to success.

·   ·   ·

Locan sat in his office later that night staring down at maps without really seeing them, a cup of some Earth alcohol in his hand. What if the rumors were true, what if Queen K had been in love with a Royal Guard member and even had a relationship to the point of having a child? If it wasn't true that a Royal Guard member would be physically and mentally unable to do such a thing, what else might not be true? How much of what he believed could be long held myths about his planet and his people?

Give me a chance and I'll show you exactly how that's possible.

Locan gritted his teeth at the voice. "Shut up," he said aloud. Did it all have to do with Achromic, and her absence from Queen K?

Are we on speaking terms now?

"No." What would have happened if Achromic had shown up later on, blessed and inhabited the Queen as she was supposed to? Would their relationship have been ripped apart? The male punished for insolence?

Well then, don't listen to this. L is in desperate need of more than our protection, can you not feel her loneliness, her fear and heartache. Think of all the ways we might bring her comfort and joy. Think of how we could—

"Shut it!" Locan yelled, throwing the cup at the wall, and watching it shatter, amber liquid dripping to the ground.

"Whoa, dude, you need to learn to chill."

Locan wished he had another cup to throw at the violet Goddess who was now floating in the room with him. "What do you want?"

"Are you going to keep things from the Princess in order to get her to Prias sooner rather than later?"

"I am going to do everything I can to keep her safe and get her to Prias, yes."

"She's going to be mad when she finds out you let her friends suffer at the hands of Jabon and the Enforcers."

"So be it, I am not trying to win her affections, that's not my mission." His Warrior growled in disagreement.

Violaceous crossed her arms and lifted one bright pink eyebrow. "Your Warrior wants her; you plan to keep denying that?"

"Even if it kills me."

"It might," she warned.

"What do you know of your grandfather's involvement with Temis?" Locan needed all the information and if Cerulean and Violaceous were visiting him, he was willing to bet Coal was visiting the other side.

Her smile was wicked and showed surprisingly sharp teeth. "Granddaddy has his fingers in this pot deep. I would watch out for that." With those words, she disappeared.

"Well fuck you, too," Locan grumbled.

"Talking to yourself?" Traylon asked as the door whooshed open.

"Better than talking to you."

"Ouch, that hurts, boss."

"What do you want, Traylon?"

"I want to know if you plan to stop on Esbee for fuel."

Locan had forgotten about needing fuel, they should have stopped before they hit Earth, but they were in too big a hurry. "We don't really have a choice, do we?"

"Nope, just asking mostly so I know if we should try to get in and out before the Princess wakes up or if you want to take her on a little sightseeing trip."

"On a radioactive trash heap planet like Esbee? You just want enough time to visit Thlara."

Traylon shrugged.

"We can't risk Jabon catching up to us."

"We won't make it all the way back without fuel."

"No sightseeing, no Thlara. We stop now and we are back on our way in as little time as possible."

Traylon's face showed a flash of disappointment. "I figured that's what you'd say. I'll set the track; we'll dock in thirty." Traylon's eyes darted to the mess Locan had made. "You sure you're okay?"

"Yep." Locan pushed a button on his desk and a tiny cleaning robot zipped out to clean up the broken glass and spilled liquid.

Traylon's face grew serious. "You know you can talk to me."

"I can also talk to Leda, but you don't see me doing that either, do you?"

FIFTEEN

L's eyes shot open; someone was in her room. It was dark and she couldn't see anyone, but she felt a presence. "Hello?" she said cautiously. "Lights on," she commanded the computer.

The lights came up and revealed a floating green light. It grew bigger and brighter, then formed into the shape of a young girl. A young, green girl with blue eyes, delicate features and short black hair. She was dressed in a white toga style dress and gold sandals.

"Let me guess, you're here to tell me what I should be doing?"

"I'm here to tell you to get your ass out of bed and go save my sister!"

L wasn't sure she'd heard the girl right. "Excuse me?"

"Can you feel it? The ship has landed."

L rushed to the little window and stared out, it was very dark, but the girl was right, the usual hum of movement was gone, and she could see solid land out there. Possibly the outlines of buildings. "Did we arrive on Prias?" Maybe Locan had misspoken when he'd said it would take weeks.

"No, we are on Esbee, a terrible filthy planet."

L turned from the window confused. "And your sister is here? Aren't you guys like, Goddesses?"

"I'm half mortal and my full mortal sister is out there."

"What do you expect me to do? Go tell Locan, he's the Warrior who loves to save helpless women."

"Locan's only mission now is to keep you safe, he won't defer from that path, *you* have to go."

"What the hell am I supposed to do?" L was feeling a little frantic, she was no fighter, and she was certainly no secret spy. How was she supposed to *save* anyone? Especially an alien on an alien planet!

"Here," the green girl said, holding out what looked like a clear blade with a gold handle.

"I can't kill someone," L said with conviction.

"You don't have to, just threaten to, the man who is holding her is a coward, he'll back down immediately."

"Then why can't you go in and get her?"

"I can't, I'm forbidden from interfering with her."

None of this was making sense to L, she crossed her arms and gave the girl a sardonic look. "I'm not doing you any favors without a better explanation than that."

The girl's entire body flashed with an eerie green light. "I was born of a mortal here on Esbee, my father is a criminal who found a way to capture my mother and keep her until she bore me. For years he held me captive after I was born, and my mother was set free. He thought he could turn me into a weapon. Unfortunately, my powers are fertility and growth, everyone around me gets pregnant and I can help your crops take off, but that's it. When he realized I was worthless in his plans to dominate the city, he cast me out, but my full mortal sister is still there. She suffers under his care and is almost of an age where he will doubtless find her useful as a bargaining tool in business." A silver tear streaked down the girl's face. "I have no hope to save her unless you go in, he cannot capture you."

"Why not?"

"He is a coward underneath his bluff, if he can't use his sorcery to hold you, which only works on the Goddesses, he will give up easily when faced with a possibility of his own death." The girl took a quivering breath. "Please, her name is Sansorin and she's only twelve. I would owe you a favor, a favor from a Goddess, even a half mortal one, is a great thing. I am Verduous and I pledge myself to you."

Verduous flew forward before L could react and touched her neck, a sharp pain sliced through her. "What the hell?"

"A mark of my favor, it connects us, and I will answer your call whenever you need me. Please, save Sansorin, she's too young for the horrors that await her at his hands."

Verduous started to fade, and panic welled up inside L. She took the knife from the fading form. "I don't even know where to look."

"Go to the fueling station guard, ask for directions to the house of Parslin, let no one see you, stay to the shadows and wear this."

As Verduous completely disappeared, a brown hooded cloak dropped to the floor.

"There isn't much time, Locan plans to be fueled and gone within the hour." Her voice floated through the room, seeming to come from everywhere.

"Shit," L hissed as she picked up the cloak. She knew she was going to go, there was no way in hell she was going to let a twelve-year-old girl be used as a bargaining chip for some kind of alien would-be mobster, but she wasn't dumb, and she wasn't going alone. "Computer, where is everyone else?"

"Locan is outside of the ship. Traylon is in the engine room and Leda is in the control room. There are no other life forms on the ship."

"Perfect." L threw on her borrowed clothes, then she strode from the room carrying the knife and cloak. She went straight to the control room.

Leda was there and she was alone.

"Come with me," L said quickly. "We need to leave the ship, there's someone who needs help."

"Umm, fuck you and your demands, *Princess*. I don't have to do what you say and Locan would kill me if we left the ship."

"I'm going, with or without you, do you think Locan would be angrier if you came with, or if you just let me walk off onto an alien planet alone?"

Leda narrowed her eyes and grumbled under her breath. "What's going on?" she finally said aloud.

"There's a twelve-year-old girl down there who needs our help."

"And how do you know this?"

L lifted her hair in the hopes there was a visible mark left by Verduous.

"Verduous?"

"Yeah, apparently her full mortal sister is down there and in trouble." L held up the knife. "She gave me this."

"A Sorian crystal knife, it will cut through any armor," Leda said with awe.

"I don't plan to kill anyone, just threaten them," L assured Leda.

"We better hurry, Locan is going to be pissed but if we've already saved the girl by the time he figures it out, he might be less inclined to kill me."

"I'll tell him it wasn't your fault."

"Good luck with that," Leda grumbled. "Follow me, we'll have to sneak through the emergency hatch."

"Thank you, Leda."

"Don't thank me, just don't get hurt and maybe Locan will be reasonable."

L followed Leda down the hall and through a small door into a storage closet. She opened a hatch in the floor and stairs shot out to the ground. The air that filtered up through the opening was cold and wet; it reminded L of being on the coast in fall, it was fresh, but it was a bit jarring. There was a scent to it that wasn't familiar. It was almost smoky but not any kind of smoke she'd ever come into contact with. When her feet hit the ground, she was surprised by the almost buoyant feel of the turf. It looked solid and grey, but it had a soft feel under her shoes. Leda looked back at her and made a motion to be silent. Then she pointed toward the back of the ship. L looked where she pointed and could see dark figures moving about, refueling the ship she assumed. L threw the cloak on and pulled the hood up to cover her face then crouched and followed Leda's quick escape.

"We are supposed to ask the station guard to direct us to the house of Parslin."

"No need, I know exactly where to go."

"You do?"

"I've been traveling with Locan and Traylon for a while, I know this planet and all its horrors. Parslin is a piece of shit and he's been trying to own this town for years. There were rumors that he once managed to hold a Goddess prisoner, Cerulean I assume, Verduous is her daughter."

"That's the story she told me, and the girl, Sansorin is her full mortal half-sister."

"Did she offer you anything in exchange for this dangerous endeavor?"

"A favor."

Leda paused for a moment and looked back with surprise. "That's quite something."

"I would save a child for far less," L replied.

Leda just snorted and turned, then continued hurrying away from the ship. L wasn't prepared for what they encountered when they got to a gate leading out of what must be the refueling area.

A small figure turned to face them. He was only about four feet tall and just as wide. His skin the color of rust and deeply creased with wrinkled skin that seemed to be stacked on itself in such a way she thought she could possibly lift a flap and find a whole other face underneath. He had tentacles extending down from his chin, they twitched and moved as his small blue eyes looked them up and down. His nose was a vacant space on his face and his mouth was large, bulging lips surrounded huge teeth that looked like they were likely quite sharp.

"What can I help you lovely ladies with? Looking to make a quick buck?" His eyes moved over them as he spoke and his hand wandered to his crotch, giving it a deep scratch.

L gripped her knife, but Leda spoke up, asking for directions to a bar they were not heading for. L realized the alien had spoken the Prian language, he must have assumed they'd come off Locan's ship, which also meant he would be telling Locan where they went when Locan freaked about them being off the ship. It was smart of Leda to throw him off course with the bar question.

L followed Leda through the streets that looked uncannily like those of a rundown city on Earth, except for the feel of the planet under her feet and strange smell in the air. They made their way to a relatively nicer-looking brick building with a large black front door. They passed a couple of people along the way but mostly it seemed the town was asleep. They looked like the man from the gate, all very hard to look at if L was being honest.

Leda stopped in the shadows of the building across the street from their destination.

"So, what's the plan? We can't just knock on the door and say, hey give us your daughter," Leda said.

"I was hoping we could, actually," L admitted.

"That's a terrible idea."

"Do you have a better one?"

"No," Leda grumbled.

"Follow my lead, will he speak Prian?"

"Yeah, it's a common second language in this part of space."

L hurried up the steps, knife ready. She wasn't sure where her confidence was coming from, but her arm was tingling, and her neck was warm. She lifted a hand and knocked.

The door was opened by a woman with a broom in one hand and a scowl on her face. She spoke in a strange language, but the tone was annoyed, and L was guessing it was something like, *who the hell are you knocking on my door in the middle of the night.*

"We are here for Sansorin," L said in the Prian language.

"Prians, I should have known, uppity and demanding, don't give a damn that you're interrupting a family asleep at night."

"I apologize for the late hour. Sansorin, now," L demanded, not sure where this forcefulness was coming from, but the tingle on her arm and neck gave her a clue.

"Sansorin is a child, she doesn't take strange visitors in the middle of the night." The woman moved to close the door. L put her body in the way, Leda right behind her, hand holding the door open.

"It's not really a request," Leda hissed.

The woman turned and ran.

"Well, that wasn't too hard, but where is the girl do you think?" Leda asked with a smirk.

"Do you think the maid is going to run for help, or just save herself?"

"Maybe we don't have to find out," Leda pointed to the top of a staircase.

A young girl stood there. She had all the same features as the other aliens but on her they were smaller, more delicate and the color of her skin leaned more toward salmon than orange. L wouldn't call the girl pretty, but she wasn't quite so frightful.

"Sansorin?" L asked carefully, making sure her blade was hidden beneath her cloak.

"My sister told me to expect a savior tonight." She held up a bag. "My father is out of the house; we should go quickly."

The girl came down the steps and L was certain they were going to succeed with an almost disappointingly easy rescue mission. Footsteps on the street outside promised more excitement.

A drunk voice slurred behind them in a strange language.

L and Leda turned to face the man coming up the stairs, Parslin, she was sure. He had a smile on his face, and he was wobbling slightly.

"Well, hello there, big boy," Leda drawled quietly, luring him in and keeping his attention off Sansorin, who was creeping forward behind L.

"Aren't you a pretty little thing," Parslin responded in Prian. He was soon close enough to recognize his daughter behind them and he straightened, glaring. "What the hell is going on?"

"We are rescuing Sansorin, you *don't* want to try and stop us," L hissed and held the knife in view, threatening.

"Like hell you are, bitch." He pulled a blade of his own and snarled.

L had no idea how to fight and she was immediately regretting her choice to be the one holding a weapon.

Leda jumped into action, tackling the man. They tumbled

together down the steps and when they hit the bottom, L was there ready to do anything she had to in order to protect Leda.

Leda was on the bottom and when Parslin sat up, raising the blade above his head in two hands as if he were about to plunge it into Leda's chest, L reacted without thought. She lashed out with her own blade. It slid through Parslin's neck like it was nothing, blood erupted from the wound, covering L and Leda, then he slumped, now a headless corpse.

Leda pushed him off with a disgusted yell, Sansorin screamed behind them, and a growl from down the dark street broke out above all the other noise. L dropped the blade as she looked down at what she'd done, unable to comprehend the taking of a life, it was the opposite of everything she'd ever wanted to do. Blood was pounding through her body, she could hear nothing more than a rumble and when she was swept up into the arms of an enormous and semi-familiar man, she let herself weep, and shiver, and be comforted.

Slowly she came to herself, the pounding in her head slowed, and voices surrounded her. She was still being held tight and she realized Locan was growling and yelling at Leda.

"It wasn't her fault, I made her come with me," L whispered.

Locan looked down at her with such ferocity, she had to bite her lip to keep from screeching. "She never should have listened to such idiocy."

"Idiocy? I had to save the child!" L snapped, now fully aware and ready to defend Leda and their actions.

"The child?"

"Sansorin," L explained looking around, but saw no one.

"I think she ran away when you came barreling down the street like a fucking maniac," Leda growled.

"We have to find her!" L was frantic, the child would never survive here alone.

"I'll find her, I think she went inside," Traylon said.

L turned as best she could, still being held in Locan's arms, to see Traylon head up the stairs and into the house. L turned back to see Leda standing now, but a bit awkwardly, one hand pressed to her side. "You're hurt," L said and wiggled to try and get out of Locan's grasp. He only tightened his grip. "Calm your shit down and let me go," she demanded.

"No," he growled.

"Locan, Leda is hurt. You can punish her later." L tried to keep her voice calm, she put a soft hand on Locan's chest and looked up into his angry eyes.

He growled but let L down, she rushed to Leda's side and inspected her wound. "He stabbed you while you fell?"

"Yeah, I think so. Nothing that can't be fixed on the ship, if Locan lets me back on."

"As if he could keep you off, you kept me safe and you are loyal to him," L shot a look at Locan daring him to argue.

Locan narrowed his eyes and grunted.

"Found the little sprite," Traylon said, coming out of the house, Sansorin trailing behind with wide eyes.

"You're safe, you'll come with us," L said with a smile and wished someone would have thought to at least cover her father's body before bringing her back outside.

"He—he's a *Warrior!* My sister said they are like, totally scary," she whispered, eyeing Locan from under her lashes. He was nearly back to normal size now, but his glare was intimidating at any size.

"Yes, but he's promised to take care of me and do what I ask, and I ask that he take care of you. You have nothing to fear, I promise," L explained.

Sansorin nodded and gripped her bag tight.

"Traylon, why don't you help her to the ship, I think Locan is going to need to assist Leda." L felt good being in charge of the situation, it reminded her of the delivery room, she knew what needed to be done and she could set everyone to their task. She could make sure everyone got out alive.

"I'm fine," Leda gritted out.

Traylon nodded, gently guiding the girl down the street. When they were a few steps away, Locan raised his eyebrow at L. "I never promised to do what you say."

"I thought it was implied with the whole Royal Guard thing," she said, waving her hand in the air vaguely.

He laughed and it made L's spine tingle in a delightful way. Then he picked Leda up, despite her protests. "Let's get off this shithole planet."

"What about that?" L motioned to the body.

"The locals will deal with it in the morning I suppose. No one will miss him," Locan said with a shrug.

They got back to the ship without incident, Traylon settled Sansorin into a room and Leda went into the medical pod. L went straight for the shower and when she was out, they were already flying again. She figured she was still going to have some questions to answer about her little side trip, but they were going to have to wait. She slipped into bed and was asleep almost instantly.

SIXTEEN

A week later, L was feeling only slightly better about the situation she was in. She was starting to think of herself as a Prian, though she ignored the princess part. She was the daughter of a beautiful woman, K, who was neither a junkie, nor a criminal. She was L, and she had been loved and saved by her mother who had been forced into a horrible situation. It wasn't exactly what her fantasies had been growing up, but they weren't too far off either.

She hadn't spoken alone with Locan since the night they'd brought Sansorin aboard the ship. Sansorin had settled well on the ship and was very curious about everything. She drove Leda nuts with her questions, but L appreciated hearing the conversation, and the answers Leda reluctantly gave her about life on Prias.

Locan seemed perfectly happy to practically ignore L, and she became friendly with Traylon, after telling him for the last time that she had absolutely no desire to sleep with him. Leda seemed to hate her less after their adventure and Leda had taken on the task of teaching L and Sansorin some basic self-defense moves. The exercise kept her tired enough to sleep at night, but she did miss her daily run by the lake.

She was trying to enjoy a meal in the dining area across from a stone-faced Locan and a chattering Traylon when an alarm went off. Not a run for the nearest fire exit kind of alarm, more of an incoming message kind of alarm. She looked around, not sure what to think. Locan and Traylon both rushed to the control room and L followed, curious. Leda was there, already looking at different screens and pushing buttons. Sansorin was there as well, watching everything eagerly.

"Where is it coming from?" Locan asked as he took a seat in front of a panel of buttons.

"I am trying to figure that out. The only thing close to us is Septar, and I don't think they would know how to contact us, they aren't that advanced."

"No, but a stranded ship might be able to get a message out. It was definitely a distress signal," Locan said with annoyance.

The sound came again, and Leda frantically pushed buttons. "It is definitely coming from Septar," she said with surprise.

"What do you want to do?" Traylon asked.

"We can't risk stopping, not with L on board," Locan said.

Traylon nodded and stepped away from his post. Then a voice came through, it sounded like a child begging for help, but L couldn't understand the language.

"What is she saying?" L demanded.

Traylon looked at Locan who gave a slight nod, then Traylon pushed a button and suddenly the sounds formed into coherent language.

"Help, someone, please, is anyone out there? We crashed on Septar, and my mother is pregnant and injured, we need help. Is anyone out there?"

"Oh my God! Locan, we have to help them!" L shouted,

rushing forward as if she could comfort the child if she could only figure out which button would send a responding message.

"We can't, it's too risky," he said, simply.

"Too risky? There is a child with an injured, pregnant mother, *that* is risky. We have to stop!"

"Did you forget that we are trying to stay ahead of Jabon? We're faster, but not that fast. If we stop again, they *will* catch up."

"We can't just leave them there," L whispered, her voice thick with emotion.

"We can't save everyone between Earth and Prias," Locan said, motioning to Sansorin.

"Why not?" L demanded.

Locan narrowed his eyes at her. "Fine, but you do not leave the ship. Septarians are savage."

L couldn't help herself; she rushed forward and gave Locan a hug. He stiffened and didn't return the embrace, she pulled away, embarrassed.

L pretended to straighten her clothes. "How long until we arrive? Can we tell them we're coming?"

"Sending messages from this far away is too risky, anyone could be listening. It will take most of the day to get there, we can respond when we get close," Locan said stiffly.

L watched happily as Traylon changed the ship's course and Locan looked worried.

"Oh goody, an adventure!" Sansorin said, clapping her hands.

L retreated to her room and stood looking out the little window. She'd spent a lot of time staring out that window, mesmerized by the passing stars and planets, wondering at the inhabitants of each. How many were like her? It seemed unlikely that she'd have the same basic form as Earth inhabitants. Was it the perfect form? Was that why it developed on so many planets? Would the inhabitants of Septar be strange and hideous?

"Pretty, isn't it." Leda said, coming in unnoticed.

"Yeah, it is. I was just thinking about how different, or rather not different, inhabitants of these planets might be. Are Septar's inhabitants like us? Or more like Sansorin?"

"They are very tall and skinny and because their sun star is so close, they have developed black and red eyes and very dark skin. They are cave-dwelling tribes, very underdeveloped socially, patriarchal. It's usually a sign of a lesser society if they continue to recognize brawn over reproduction. Earth is considered undeveloped by most of the universe which is why it remains uncontacted for the most part."

"Reproduction, is that all Prian women are good for?"

"You tell me, *Princess*. What will you tell your people?"

L turned away; she didn't like thinking about that sort of thing. It wasn't anything she had ever wanted, not really. To be in charge of an entire planet, no thank you. "I am going to Prias to learn about who I am and what I come from. If that results in people coming out of oppression, well then good, but I am not interested in leading or commanding anyone."

"You know that's not a choice, right? Locan didn't risk his life to find you so that you can just walk away from your birthright. If I—"

L turned back to Leda in a huff, tired of being treated like an idiot by this little angry girl. "If you what?"

Leda matched her glare for glare, hands on hips. "If I were Princess, I sure as hell wouldn't be planning to take a back seat to people's suffering. I wouldn't let the children of breeders live like animals among animals, as if they had anything to do with the way they were conceived. I would—I would—" Leda paused and took a shaky breath. "I would care enough to find out all I could about the God damn place before we got there."

"Why do you think you have any idea what I want?"

Leda lifted her chin slightly, defiant. "I have been gifted by the Goddess Amber, Goddess of energy and honor. I can feel where your loyalties lie, and they aren't where they should be. I can read your energy and feel how you long for your simple Earth life."

"Can you blame me? This is some crazy shit!"

"Yeah, finding out you're a princess from another planet is rough. I found out that I was destined to be treated as something less among rebels or sit in the Hospital and pop out babies. My mother was just a breeder, who knows who my father was, maybe not even Prian, but it doesn't matter because on this ship, I am Leda and I have been doing everything I can to find you so that you can help everyone."

L threw herself onto the bed and put an arm over her face. "What if I can't? I've never been good with people."

"Ugh, don't you know anything! That's because you aren't an Earth being. Of course, you aren't good with those idiots. It's different with Locan, isn't it? Even with Traylon and me? Prians are drawn to other Prians, it's the work of the Mother Goddess, Achromic. She wants all of her children to know each other, she's the Goddess of goodness and faith, so have some! Her husband, the God Coal, he's the God of strength and death, sows seeds of discontent among her people." Leda whispered the last as if she were afraid of who might be listening.

L felt a shiver run up her spine and the hair on the back of her neck stood. Her right arm tingled, a sign she was beginning to associate with the path that was chosen for her.

"I believe you, Leda, and I am sorry I haven't taken things more seriously. I guess I have kind of felt like I was walking through a dream, but if this shit is real, I don't even know how to handle that."

Leda smiled. "Now I can relate to that! I was freaked out

when I first met Locan and Traylon. It was a good thing they'd picked up another girl before me or I don't think they would have gotten me onto the ship in the first place; and believe me, I always knew I didn't belong on Maybar. I was half convinced they were going to sell me as a sex slave on Esbee, but I got on anyway."

"I didn't feel like I belonged most of the time either, I guess we just needed our own kind."

"Speak for yourself. Those bastards on Prias don't accept me any more than my forced foster parents on Maybar did."

"That can't be true."

"Why? Because it isn't pretty?"

"It's just not right."

"No, it isn't, Princess." Leda left the room and L wasn't sure why she had come in at all. Just to guilt her into making a statement she supposed.

Leda walked to her own room and was soon joined by the Goddess Amber. She floated naked a few inches above the ground, her entire aura glowing yellow, her flame-orange hair reached her ankles and moved like a river of lava. Her deep, black, soulless eyes shone out of her perfect face and bore into Leda.

"Did you do it? Did you ascertain the Princess' loyalties?"

"I think so, she seems to understand how important her position is. I just hope she can handle it once we get to Prias."

Amber looked out the window and frowned, "You have taken a turn, why are you heading off course?"

"There was an emergency call from Septar, we are on our way to check it out. The Princess insisted."

Amber looked thoughtful. "So that's what you want to play," she said mostly to herself, then looked back at Leda, looking almost surprised to find herself still in the presence of her. "Watch your backs," she said, then disappeared.

Leda wasn't sure if she should tell Locan about the encounter. She hadn't told him when the Goddess had first started visiting her, shortly after L had tried to get them both killed rescuing Sansorin. She sort of enjoyed the little secret she had, and the yellow star high on her right arm was a badge of honor as far as she was concerned. She would just have to make sure she was on high alert on Maybar, nothing would get past her. She had sworn to the Goddess Amber that she would protect the Princess, that she would get the Princess to Prias and that she would do everything in her power to get the Princess to take the position that was needed to save the Prian people.

She would do all she could to succeed. Leda tied an extra knife to her belt then went back to the control room.

SEVENTEEN

L made her way to the control room; sure they were near the planet by now.

"I say we just tell the Princess that they told us they don't need our help, we keep on our way no harm done," Leda grumbled.

"Except to the helpless woman on the planet and her children," L said sharply, walking in at just the right moment apparently.

"Of course, we weren't considering that," Locan reassured L.

"Wouldn't want to keep you safe or anything," Leda huffed and left the room.

"What's her problem? It's not like she likes you or anything," Traylon said with a laugh.

"Traylon, you should watch your words in front of the Princess," Locan warned.

"I don't offend that easily," L reassured Traylon. "But seriously, Leda is an angry thing."

"Yeah, well she had it rough, growing up on Maybar. She

was about to be placed in a home where women are trained in the art of pleasure before we found her. When she found out that she was going to her home planet she was so excited, but when we got there, it didn't take long to realize that none of the Prians take too kindly to those born of breeders. I think they're scared. No one knows for sure how they are created in the Hospital. None of the mothers ever escaped, except those who left the planet," Locan explained.

"What do they think they are?"

"I don't know, just something else, can you feel it when you are with her? There is a draw, she is definitely Prian, it isn't like when you are next to a person on Earth or Esbee, but it isn't the same as being next to Traylon, or me?"

L looked thoughtful about this. "I feel a different draw between you two though as well, it's like you two are not the same either," she said thoughtfully, never having really thought about it before. When she was near Traylon it was like being home, with a brother perhaps or father. When she stood next to Locan it was more raw, like being at home with a lover or husband. Next to Leda, well that was like being next to the kid in class who not so secretly hates your guts but you both belong there because that's the only class available and you're stuck whether you like it or not. L decided to keep most of that to herself. She cleared her throat. "Did the Doctors inseminate the women themselves? They are from another planet, right?"

"That is one theory, yes. Another is that it is some kind of science experiment that involves only the mothers, without the aid of an actual father. Like I said, no one knows."

"What about the Enforcers? They didn't have the same Prian draw when they were near me."

"Oh no, they are from somewhere else entirely. Hired hands is all, with no loyalty to Prias," Traylon explained.

L looked at the door Leda had left through. She felt sorry for the girl, and guilty for even considering a wish that she could go back to Earth and forget this ever happened. There were a lot of people depending on her and she could only hope she was able to help.

"We are approaching Septar," Traylon said, interrupting L's thoughts.

L looked at the screen that showed where they were heading. A huge red planet was racing toward them. It looked like what she'd always imagined Mars to look like; dry, and hot, a desert as far as the eye could see.

Traylon was making quick maneuvers, pushing buttons and steering. The planet was soon filling the screen and L could see that it wasn't a desert at all; but was covered in a forest of orange and red trees. Traylon landed them smoothly in a clearing, L was impressed and felt a little safer being in this flying space craft, he obviously knew what he was doing. She could now see that the grass was a vibrant shade of red and L couldn't wait to go out and touch it.

"Can I breathe out there, just like Earth?" L asked, not caring that all her excitement was audible in her voice. She knew she probably sounded like a kid on Christmas morning.

"Yes, and no you will not be leaving the ship. Leda and I will check out where the call was coming from. You will stay here with Traylon and Sansorin."

"Hell no, I need to check out the pregnant mother right away, what if it isn't safe to move her? I need to be there to assess." L put her hands on her hips and met Locan's glare. "I'm the professional in that department, Locan."

He looked like he wanted to argue but finally gritted out, "Fine, but if there is even a hint of something not right; your little ass is coming straight back here. Traylon you will come along; we need everyone guarding the Princess."

"That means me, too!" Sansorin said excitedly. L wasn't

sure when she'd entered the room, she had been so absorbed in the landing. The girl was stealthy, moved like water and had startled L more than once in the last few days

"I guess so!" L could barely contain her excitement; she was about to set foot on another planet for the second time, and in some other solar system! She suddenly felt like she needed to go to elementary school again and learn what her universe was all about.

"You're going to need this," Leda said, attaching the crystal knife to L's belt.

"I am not a violent person," L said, touching the knife delicately with her fingertip and shivering at the memory of the last time she'd used it. She had immediately handed it over to Locan when they had gotten back to the ship, not wanting to be in charge of such a weapon.

"I expect you to defend yourself if necessary, Princess, we all know you can." Leda hissed.

"Of course, I would defend myself and you guys too, but I wouldn't want to hurt anyone."

Leda rolled her eyes and walked away mumbling, "Sweet Goddess Amber, I don't know if you're betting on the right one here." Leda grabbed her arm and hissed, then turned at the door, "I will be by your side, Princess, no harm will come to you. I will see you guys outside." Then she walked away.

"If she could just decide whether or not she likes me, yeah that would be great," L said sarcastically. She hadn't missed the way Leda had rubbed at her arm before deciding to be nice again. L would bet there was a Goddess mark there. L looked over at Locan, but he didn't seem to have noticed anything and she wondered if Leda had told him a Goddess had presented herself to her. She wondered if she should mention it or keep Leda's secret.

"She doesn't have to like you, she just has to keep you alive," Locan said.

"*I* like you," Traylon said with a wink.

"You know what, Traylon, I think I might like you better than Leda."

Traylon laughed and Locan scoffed.

"You will need this," Locan said, handing her a tiny earpiece. "Just press it and we will all hear you, it's just a precaution, don't think it makes it safe for you to go off on your own out there."

"Yes, Sir," L said mockingly as she stuck the tiny clear device in her ear, it fit comfortably.

The air was hot but perfectly breathable and although the colors were different than on Earth, the foliage didn't seem all that alien. L reached down and touched a blade of grass, it felt waxy and thick, probably better held in moisture in this hot environment.

L turned and looked back at the ship they'd been living in for the past weeks. She hadn't gotten a good look at it on Esbee, it had been so dark. It was a blackish silver color that seemed to change as she looked at it; it certainly wasn't a type of metal that could be found on Earth. It was sleek and smaller overall than she would have expected, but still big.

"Impressive, isn't she?" Locan said with pride.

"I can honestly say I've never seen anything like it."

Leda came running up to them huffing, "All clear, no Septarians in sight."

"Did you get eyes on the downed ship?"

"No, we must be too far off. I only did a quick sweep, should I circle out farther?"

L was impressed with the seriousness that Leda seemed to be taking Locan's orders, her *I don't care* attitude seemed to be mostly reserved for L. "Let's go then, if they are in trouble, we are wasting time," L said.

They wove through trees that were covered in thorns, deterring any who might think to use it as a source of nutrition or housing. L spied some kind of animal making its way through tops of trees, but she wasn't sure if it was a bird type creature or perhaps a small monkey like thing. It was fast, she just saw a flash of black and a rustle of red leaves.

"Stop," Locan whispered. They were coming to another clearing like the one they had landed on. Locan and Leda crept forward while Traylon and L watched from a distance.

"What kind of danger is Locan expecting?"

"All kinds, he is cautious by nature, but when there is a princess to protect, he won't leave anything to chance."

"Aren't I protected by the Goddess Cerulean? She's marked the hell out of my arm." L held up her arm to substantiate her point.

"The Goddesses and Gods don't interfere with mortals like that usually, they more push and guide. Present a situation perhaps that will get them what they want. It's like if they want you dead; they will put a vicious animal in your house, but they won't make your heart stop. Does that make sense?"

L looked at him like he was nuts. "Yeah, sure clears it all up. I will watch out for lions and tigers then."

"What?"

L smiled. "Animals on Earth, I guess you wouldn't know."

"Verduous isn't afraid to get involved," Sansorin said.

Traylon didn't have a response.

L touched the green star on her neck, Verduous had pushed, but she hadn't gone in and saved her sister, was it because that was too much of a direct interference? What would happen if she called in the supposed favor? Would there be a million stipulations and fine print rules? She had kind of been counting on it to be her Get Out Alive Free card, but maybe she needed to be more careful about its use.

They watched Leda and Locan crawl forward on their bellies and pause at the edge of the forest. After a few minutes, Locan stood and motioned them over. There was a ship in the clearing that looked a little smaller than the one they'd gotten out of. This ship looked more utilitarian than theirs too, it was a beige color and from what she could tell, had some sharp edges, Locan's ship was all smooth outside, the same as in.

"I don't see any movement, I want you two to wait here while we check it out," Locan said

"But—"

"No, just stay here, L, I am not going to let you flaunt yourself in front of every kind of danger between Earth and Prias. I will tell you when its safe and I will make sure you get to any pregnant women as soon as possible, but we still don't know this isn't some kind of trap to rob us." Locan's words were full of concern and his face was serious.

L knew he was right. "What do we have that anyone could possibly want?" L asked as Leda and Locan made their way toward the ship.

"Other than the Princess of a very rich planet?"

"No one knows anything about me being with you guys."

"Okay, so they would just be after our ship and supplies. The universe is full of scavengers and pirates. They would take you for ransom, Leda and Sansorin for pleasure and kill Locan and I, then take apart our ship and sell it for parts."

"They'd be sorely disappointed if they thought Leda was a pleasurable creature," L said with a laugh.

Traylon laughed, "Good one."

L almost felt bad, but figured it was fine to poke a little fun at the grumpy girl. They watched as Locan and Leda approached the ship slowly, stopped a few feet away and called out a greeting to whoever might be inside.

"It's an old ship, the kind used for transport of material mainly," Traylon said.

"From this planet?"

"Definitely not, they don't have even close to this kind of technology, I would guess it's from Nebulan. It's a planet about a month from here and also very utilitarian, not the kind of place you'd want to go on vacation."

"So why do you think it's here?"

"Probably was making trades in the area and ran into trouble. This is an unfortunate place to crash land though, they don't have resources to help, which is why they sent out the signal."

It seemed reasonable enough to L, and she watched and waited as Locan and Leda tried to gain the attention of anyone aboard. A rustling behind them drew their attention and Traylon went on alert, pulling out a large knife and shoving her and Sansorin roughly behind him.

"Ouch," she grumbled but he ignored her. Her eyes darted around the alien terrain, but she couldn't see anything moving, no indication of life. "Animal?" she asked quietly.

"Could be, but I'm not willing to risk it." He stood then and grabbed her arm; they took off in the direction of the stranded ship.

Locan and Leda had disappeared on the other side of the ship, but L could hear them shouting out again to whoever might be inside. There was no response and L was starting to worry that they were too late. She stumbled a little as they hurried toward the others, Traylon slowed slightly but didn't stop moving.

"Is this necessary?" she grumbled.

"The animals on this planet are less friendly than the people, so yeah," Traylon assured her.

"I thought you could protect us," she teased.

"I can, but I prefer not to die in the process."

They had reached the ship and he stopped, shoving her and Sansorin back against it and stood in front of them. There was still no visible threat, and she was fairly sure he was just overreacting.

"Locan," Traylon said, and L heard it clearly in her earpiece and from him, it was an odd effect.

"What is it?" came Locan's worried voice.

"We heard something so we are on the other side of the wrecked ship, just a heads up, there might be an animal near."

"Or a horde of cave dwellers," Leda grumbled. "And no pregnant mother desperate for your help by the way, L."

"Leda, shut it," Locan ordered. "I don't see an open entrance, and no one is answering our shouts, we should head back to our ship. Wait there for us."

"I guess that's that; no saving a life today," Traylon said, glancing back at her.

L wasn't convinced, she wanted to get on the ship. "Why can't we get in and look? That call for help didn't come from nowhere."

"Doors don't open for just anyone, babe."

An arrow slammed into the ship over her head, stopping all chances for arguing. Traylon spun back around, knife out, he shoved her, then Sansorin to the ground with his free hand. "Locan, we've got company," he growled into the earpiece.

L could see a line of figures clad in barely anything and painted with red markings. They looked savage, ready to fight, and quite possibly eat whatever they killed. *Shit!* Her arm started to burn, and she knew she was in trouble. She didn't want to die here, on a planet that was neither her heritage nor her known home. This couldn't be her destiny. She was about to call out to the Goddess Verduous and call in her favor when a door whooshed open beside them. A small girl poked her head out just far enough to see them. When she spoke, the language was indecipherable, but L didn't care, she rushed into the opening and the promise of safety. She could hear the ting of arrows hitting around them as they moved. Traylon followed, carrying Sansorin; Locan and Leda were only steps behind.

EIGHTEEN

Locan spoke in the child's language and the door shut them in. Arrows hit the door as it closed.

"Locan, you're bleeding!" Leda screeched.

"I'm fine," Locan growled, pulling an arrow from his thigh. "Just a scratch." He had felt it hit, but he was halfway to Warrior and his muscles were so enlarged that he hadn't felt it as any more than a slight irritation. He ignored L's look of horror as he threw the bloody thing on the ground and willed his Warrior back in his cage.

There is danger here, why is she here, why did you not complete our mission?

Locan ignored the Warrior and assessed the situation. No injuries aside from his own, the clan outside was small and would likely move on quickly. They were decorated like a hunting party, not a war party and likely had only stumbled upon them and this ship by accident. They would probably be heading back to the caves to gather others who would come and strip this ship. The relative safety here was short lived and if the scavengers found their ship in the meantime, they would be in real trouble.

"Where is your mother?" he growled at the young girl. She was Nebulanian and the language was thankfully known to him well. A planet of criminals mostly, poor traders at best.

"She is in the back; she says the baby needs to come now."

"Bring us to her," he said, then turned to L. "She will show us to her mother. We may have to move her, it isn't safe to stay here long. Leda, stay here and watch out for the clan, they will be returning with more to scavenge this ship no doubt. Traylon, take Sansorin back to our ship and keep it safe. Take it back up and we will contact you when we are ready to come aboard."

"Yes, Sir," Traylon said. Leda and Sansorin just nodded. In times like this, Locan knew he could trust his people, and it was why he put up with all their shit most of the time.

"It may not be safe to move her," L said as they followed the young girl down a narrow hallway.

"It is definitely not safe to stay here," Locan said simply.

L huffed but didn't argue.

As they moved farther into the ship, the darkness grew more complete. Aside from the luminescent floor, there were no lights on. The power supply must have broken, perhaps that was why the ship landed in the first place.

But where the hell is everyone else? His Warrior questioned, and Locan blocked him harder.

"Where are the others?" he questioned the girl.

"They left us, went for help and never returned."

"When was that?"

"Three days."

Locan was satisfied with that answer. Men on the ship would not have risked a woman and child on a trip to get help, they obviously didn't find any friendly locals.

"In there, she was sleeping when I left her." The girl pointed at a door that looked like it led to a sleeping chamber.

L didn't hesitate, she couldn't understand the girl's words, but the pointing was enough. She stepped forward as if she had no sense to watch for danger. Locan reached out and pulled her back, stepping into the dark room first. "We need light," he said.

"I will get lamps," the girl said and hurried away.

He could make out a cot and what looked like a lump in the middle, could be the mother. L was close behind him, peering into the darkness. "Ma'am?" she said quietly.

The door behind them slammed shut and a roar inside his head told him before he even checked. They'd been locked in.

"Fuck!" Locan growled, slamming his fist against the door. "You little shit! Let us out of here!"

"Leda, the little shit trapped us, it's a goddamn trap," he growled, pressing on the earpiece.

"Of course, it is! Why the hell did you listen to this bleeding heart idiot princess?"

Locan had to take a deep breath and clenched his fists to hold back the rage at Leda's disrespect. He knew it was coming from a place of fear though, so he could forgive her, this time. "Leda, I suggest you shut the hell up and watch your language or I am going to have to discipline you when we get back to the ship."

"Sorry," she grumbled unconvincingly.

"Find us and watch for the child. Traylon did you guys make it back to the ship?"

"Almost."

"As soon as you can, get in the air and beam us up."

"Yes, sir."

Locan turned to L, she was shivering slightly and rubbing her arm. "It will be fine; Traylon can get us out of here and directly back to the ship."

"Something's not right," she whispered, her eyes darting around the small room. "I can feel... something."

Locan crossed the distance and frowned. "What is it?" He

trusted instincts, and even more, he trusted the wisdom that came from Cerulean.

"I don't feel well," she said quietly then slumped.

No! His Warrior screamed and his body swelled as he pulled her limp body into his arms. Then he felt it too, a swimming in his head a sucking of his energy. *We are going to pass out, punch a hole in the wall, you know we can, we need air from the rest of the ship, inside walls are usually thinner. Let me take over, I can do this.*

Locan dropped her body as gently as he could, then threw himself against the wall beside the door and reared back, punching, over and over until his knuckles were bloody. He didn't stop until he felt a rush of cool fresh air.

I could have done it faster. His Warrior huffed as Locan finally let the blackness take him.

Ferlin had a job to do. If she succeeded, he would let her mother go. She hadn't lied to the innocents, her mother was in trouble, she just wasn't here on this ship, and she wasn't pregnant. When she heard the thunk of a body fall, she pushed the button to open the chamber door. She stepped over the man's hulking body; he'd actually managed to punch a hole through the wall! She didn't want him as an enemy, but she was left with little choice.

Ferlin hurried to the woman and grabbed her legs, dragging her from the room and down the hall, over the body of the other, smaller woman. She wasn't the one. He had said the one to take would be the one everyone protected. This was the one he wanted. It took a lot of huffing, but she managed to drag the woman's body to the door of the ship. When she pressed the button to open the door, he stood there.

"Ferlin, you did good."

"Now release my mother," she demanded.

He dropped a bundle of rags on the ground with a laugh, "She was good entertainment for my men, but I think she lives. Now I'll take that." His red eyes lit up and a disgusting smile broke across his face. "We won't be able to have as much fun, but the prize for her capture is going to be great."

Ferlin hurried to her mother's side as he walked forward to pick up the woman. She silently prayed to the Prian Goddesses that someone watch out for the woman. Ferlin didn't want to see her harmed, she just didn't know what else to do, her mother was all Ferlin had.

She huddled protectively over her mother until she was certain they were all gone. Septarians were not friendly and the fact that she was left alive, even though that was the agreed upon result, was a surprise. She wanted to take her mother into the safety of the wrecked ship but knew there was just as much danger there at the moment. When the others woke up, they were going to kill her. She was still doomed, "Mother please, wake up. I don't know what to do."

Tears streaked down her face.

"You little bitch!"

Ferlin turned to see the woman she'd hit on the back of the head stumble out of the ship.

"I had no choice! They had my mother—" she started to explain but the woman gave her a deadly glare and she shut up.

The woman pressed her ear and spoke. "Traylon, are you up there, we have trouble." The woman looked at Ferlin. "Bring me up, with two prisoners, can you get a lock on Locan and L?" The woman walked close to Ferlin. "You're coming with me." She knelt down and touched them both. Ferlin's world went fuzzy for a moment and then she was on a bright clean ship looking at the other two who had been with the rescue party.

"What the hell happened down there, Leda?" The man, Traylon she assumed, asked.

"It was a trap, no surprise there. Put them in a cell," Leda growled.

"My mother needs medical attention," Ferlin pleaded.

Leda looked like she was going to deny the request, but Traylon rushed forward and pulled back the mother's cloak and gasped. She was nude and bloody, barely breathing.

"Shit," Traylon whispered. "Leda, take her to the medical unit, watch them both. I will go back for Locan and L, neither are responding."

"The man is still on the ship," Ferlin said quickly, hoping to show that she was willing to help now that they were safe. "They took the woman, I had to, they had my mother!"

"Who?" Traylon demanded.

"The Septarians."

"They expected us?"

"Yes."

"Then they aren't working alone. I'll get her into the medical unit, start the computer searching the area for the Enforcer's ship, I'm betting Jabon is catching up quickly."

Traylon picked up Ferlin's mother.

"Her name is Baltina, we are from Nebulan."

"She's not Nebulanian," Leda snapped.

"No, she's Prian," the girl said quietly.

"Shit," Leda hissed as Traylon hurried out of the room.

Ferlin had to run to keep up.

NINETEEN

L woke up and immediately rolled over to puke, her head was pounding, and her eyes were a bit blurry. She laid back once her stomach was empty and tried to remember what had happened. She was lying on a very hard mattress, was she still on the wrecked ship?

"Locan?"

No answer, she dared move her head a bit, her eyes swam with darkness at the movement. When they finally refocused, she saw bars and stone walls. She was in a cell, in a cave?

"What the fuck," she grumbled.

She pressed a hand to her ear, but the communication device was missing. Panic threatened to overtake her. She'd been wrong to insist they stop, and now she was some alien's prisoner.

"Is the Princess awake?"

L turned to see a tall, skinny, dark-skinned alien, one of his eyes was completely black, the other a swirling of red and black. He wore white pants and shirt that looked like they were made of some sort of cotton-like material and a cloak of red was thrown over one shoulder. "You speak Prian?"

"I have found it necessary in my dealings to know all local languages."

"Locan said your planet is savage and undeveloped."

"It is, compared to others, but in the last few years, since I came into rule here, I have taken helpful assistance from others. We are developing quickly now. I am not sure I'd say we are any less savage though," his words were dark, and his smile revealed pointy black teeth.

L shuddered. "What do you want with me?"

"You are a valuable thing to a dear friend of mine."

"Temis?" she hissed, assuming the worst.

"Jabon actually, but I have dealt directly with Temis a time or two, your great uncle was once a powerful man."

"Was?"

"He's grown old, I'm told, and Jabon has risen to power at his heels. Soon Jabon will assume full power of Prias, or so he claims. For my assistance in his rise to the top, my planet's status in this part of space will also rise."

"You're planning to hand me over to Jabon?" L was trying extremely hard not to freak out. She figured the more she knew about his plan, the better she might be able to find a way out of it. Her fingers moved slightly, and she was surprised to find her crystal blade still attached to her belt. They must not have expected her to be armed, they didn't even check. She wondered if she could use it to cut the bars, it was supposedly immensely powerful, could cut through any armor. Maybe she could escape right now. Her hand gripped the handle debating her best move.

"He will be here shortly, yes, he has some of your friends aboard his ship."

L froze, her hand left the blade handle. "Friends?"

"Yes, two humans, they lived in your home with you apparently."

"Katherine and James," L whispered.

The alien's smile broadened, and his eyes lit up with an evil glow. "Yes, that sounds about right, if you try to escape, he will kill them." With that, he turned and walked away.

L felt tears sting her eyes, her dear friends were in danger because of her!

"Oh, and just so you know who is really on your side, Locan knew that your friends were on Jabon's ship, but he refused to negotiate for their safety. I guess he didn't tell you, didn't let you choose what happened to your friends."

Anger filled her, how could he? What horrors have they already endured because of Locan? She would do anything to help her friends, they were not a sacrifice for her own safety, and he knew she'd feel that way. That was why he hadn't told her.

"Damnit!" she hissed. She needed to do something sooner rather than later. If Locan managed to rescue her, she didn't think she'd ever convince him to help someone else again.

She suddenly knew what she had to do. She held a hand to her neck and spoke aloud. "Verduous, I'm calling in my favor."

Moments later a green light flashed and Verduous was standing in front of her, this time she was wearing a bright green tutu, a black halter top, and black combat boots. "Fuck yeah you need help, you're in a prison. Hold on." She held out a hand.

"No, I need more than a hand out of this place, I'm pretty sure Locan could get me out of here."

Verduous lifted one slim black eyebrow and pursed her lips. "And what exactly do you want?"

"I saved your sister; I want you to save my friends."

"Katherine and James," she said simply.

L's mouth dropped. "You knew! And you've done nothing to help, even after I risked my ass to save your sister?"

Verduous shrugged. "Our rules are complicated, we can't

intervene in an obvious manner, I couldn't walk in and take my sister, same as I can't walk in and take Katherine and James."

"But you could get me out of this prison?"

"I could open that door and let you know when the coast was clear."

L frowned at the less-than-helpful powerful being. "Could you get me on Jabon's ship? Trade one captivity for another? It's not saving me, not really."

Verduous looked thoughtful. "Doesn't seem like it would cross the line to outright help."

"Then I'm calling in my favor, take me to Jabon's ship. I'm assuming it's hovering in the atmosphere of this planet."

"It is, do you have a plan?"

"No, but feel free to let Locan know where I've gone and why."

Verduous laughed, "Will do. When you get on the ship, seek out Tanea, she'll help you."

L didn't have time to respond, they both heard the sound of fighting, the roar of outrage, and she knew immediately, Locan was on his way to save her. Verduous grabbed her arm and in a flash, she was standing in a small dark room.

"Where the hell are we?" L whispered.

Verduous motioned nonchalant and L realized they were in some kind of supply closet.

"You're going to want to be careful out there."

"Careful? I'm crashing the fucking ship! Tell Locan to find us when we hit the ground."

Verduous laughed. "I like you, Princess, I can see why Mom is betting on you to win. It's a good thing that I'm not invested in the outcome of Traylon's life." She snapped her fingers and suddenly Traylon was standing there, then Verduous disappeared.

Traylon looked at her with wide eyes. "What the hell just happened?"

"Hey, uh, we are on a rescue mission."

"Yeah, Locan and I were trying to rescue you."

"Too late, I rescued myself, sort of, now we are rescuing my friends."

"Okay... and where are we?"

"Jabon's ship, we need to find someone named Tanea, she's supposed to help."

"Are you fucking kidding me?" he whispered harshly.

"No, and if you aren't going to help me, then I'm going to do it myself and you *know* that's not going to go well and Locan would be so mad at you."

"You're insane."

"And we're stuck on this ship, so we may as well save them."

"And how do you plan to get them off of here once we do save them?"

"I'm not sure. Crash the ship?"

"That's a terrible idea, unless you're suicidal."

"Not particularly, no."

"This ship has escape pods no doubt, it's the only way off of here alive."

"Perfect! We make a great team," she said with a wink trying to not think about the danger they were in. "Do you have any idea where we are or how we might not get caught?" L said, biting her lip and trying awfully hard not to regret her rash decision.

"Looks like Verduous did a little more than just drop us on the ship," Traylon said gesturing around. He reached out and pulled a folded cloth from a shelf. When he held it up, L could see that it was a uniform of sorts. "I think these will get us past most of the crew."

"Works for me." L grabbed a uniform from the shelf and

quickly slipped the long brown robe over her clothes. Traylon reached over and shoved a beanie style hat low on her head then tucked her hair up underneath.

"Don't look at anyone, keep your eyes on the floor and follow me. If I had to guess, I'd say these are low class servant clothes, no color and coarse material. No one will look too closely at us."

"Okay, next problem, where the hell do we go?"

"We need access to the computer. Don't die, Princess," Traylon hissed, then opened the door.

The hallway they came out into was thankfully empty and looked much like the hallway on Locan's ship, only wider. L followed Traylon, not even missing a step when a group passed, speaking a language she didn't recognize. She dared a quick peek and saw that they were all a strange shade of green with white hair and long thin limbs.

"If you need to talk, do it in human English so no one else will understand."

L gave an affirmative grunt, not willing to risk words.

He kept going for a bit, then stopped at what appeared to L to be an empty space of wall, but when he gently touched it, a screen lit up. "Computer, show me where the Prian, Tanea is."

The screen lit up with a map and glowing arrows.

"How do you know she's Prian?"

"Because we went to save her, but Jabon beat us to her. Locan's never forgiven himself and I am certain the girl has suffered greatly at Jabon's hands. If she isn't completely broken, she'll help us."

L understood now why Verduous wanted them to find the girl; she needed rescue, too. She doubted the girl would be much help though, not if she were a prisoner as well.

Traylon was moving faster now, slowing only when someone passed so they wouldn't raise suspicion. L's arm started to burn with warning, and she knew they must be near the Enforcers, knew Cerulean was trying to warn her. But could she risk stopping?

"They're near," she hissed at Traylon's back.

"Who?"

"The Enforcers."

"How—never mind." He grabbed her arm and pulled her into a room that opened up when he touched the wall, luckily it was empty. Unfortunately, it was clearly a bedroom and their presence there would not be ignored if the owner walked in.

"Shit," she hissed.

"We have few options. We are close to the girl, I believe. Are the Enforcers coming closer or are they stationary?"

"I don't know," she said incredulously.

"Yes, you do, you just need to pay attention."

L was about to argue but then the pain in her arm intensified. "Definitely getting closer."

"Get in the bathroom." He indicated an open doorway, then he pulled out a small gun.

"No way, I can help," she said with a confidence she didn't really feel and pulled out the crystal knife.

"I don't have the same instincts as Locan to protect you at all costs, but I don't want him to murder me, so you can stay out here but don't throw yourself into a fight unless I'm dead."

"Deal." L groaned slightly as the burn in her arm hit a peak, but then it slowly dissipated. "I think they passed."

"Good," he said, putting the gun away just as the door opened and there stood a woman dressed in head-to-toe black, even a veil covered her face.

Traylon acted fast, grabbing her arm, and pulling her inside, whipping her around and shoving her toward a small couch.

L pulled out the crystal knife and held it out toward the woman. "Who are you?" she demanded in English.

The woman didn't respond, just looked from L to Traylon, visibly frightened and cowering.

"Who are you?" Traylon asked quietly in Prian.

"I am Tanea," she said softly.

"Oh, thank the Goddess," L said, putting the knife away. "We are here to rescue you and a couple of prisoners from Earth."

The woman shivered and shook her head. "There is no saving me or anyone else. Jabon is too powerful."

"We have some powerful backup," L said, pushing up her sleeve and revealing her star covered arm.

"Cerulean is no match for Coal," Tanea whispered unconvinced.

"Maybe not, but we are here to try, and we need your help."

"What can I possibly do?" she sobbed and lifted the veil to reveal a face covered in deep bruises and a few healing scratches.

L sucked in a breath, frozen, but Traylon reacted immediately, rushing forward, and kneeling in front of the woman. He touched her shoulder and when he spoke, his words were full of determination and emotion. "He will die for this, doubt me not. Let us save you, *help* us save you and L's friends."

"L?"

"Yes, we found the Princess of Prias."

Tanea sniffled, then gave a small nod. "I will do what I can. Jabon has left the ship, to collect you from the planet below, he will return angry." Her hands went around her body protectively as she spoke. "And he will call for me."

"Show us to the prisoners, then we need to all make it to an escape pod."

"The escape pods are all locked, I've tried."

"We'll worry about that after," Traylon said with a soft smile. "Show us to the prisoners."

Tanea nodded, placed her veil back over her face, then stood. "Keep your heads down and follow me."

Tanea walked swiftly down hallways, they followed, and no one bothered any of them. They were a part of the invisible class on this ship.

"There will be guards in there," Tanea whispered, pointing to a panel on the wall. "We are near the rear of the ship and there are two pods further that way, not too far. Locked, like I said."

"You have done a great thing," Traylon said softly. He pulled out his gun and L pulled out her knife. "Stay behind us and run if we don't succeed, no one needs to know you helped us if we fail."

Tanea moved to the side and L stepped forward, next to Traylon. "Ready, Princess?" Traylon asked.

"I would never leave my friends to suffer just to save my own ass," she said with confidence.

"That is your Warrior half talking."

Traylon touched the door and it opened to reveal a large room, several cages, and three guards. The tingle on L's arm told her she was destined to be here; it didn't tell her whether or not she succeeded or survived.

They didn't wait for the guards to process what they were seeing, Traylon leaped forward and started shooting a dark red laser out of the gun. The first guard went down before the others could even react. They didn't waste any time calling for help when their comrade was hitting the ground, and L was thankful for that. One guard went for Traylon, pulling a knife from his belt and throwing it right at his hand, knocking his gun to the ground. The other came after L.

He sneered at her and swiped with a knife. L's Instincts, and bits of Leda's teaching, kicked in. She swiped back, hitting only air. Next to her, Traylon and the other guard were grappling on the ground now. Whoever found the knife or gun first was going to win that fight.

"I don't like to fight women, at least not outside the bedroom," the guard spoke in Prian, but she was certain it wasn't his first language, she didn't feel a draw to him like she did Prians, even if he looked quite similar.

"Don't get your hopes up, I'm more than I appear," L said with as much ferocity as she could muster.

"I hope to find out," he said, swiping forward and managing to slice a deep gash across L's shoulder, a spot she knew very well, her original Cerulean birthmark. The pain was sharp but the reaction that rippled across her entire arm of marks was invigorating. She gave a feral yell and lashed out with the crystal knife. It was a powerful weapon and easily sliced through anything it touched. This time it came into contact with the guard's wrist, and she didn't stop there. She stepped forward and jammed the blade into the man's heart, relishing the feel of the warm blood that spurted onto her own hand. When she pulled the blade out, he slumped to the ground. She felt nothing but grateful to relieve the universe of one more violent, abusive, male.

"We must hurry," Tanea said quietly from behind her.

L stood, staring down at the body, her own blood pounding in her ears, her heart racing. It felt like every nerve in her body was on alert, ready for the next dangerous thing to cross her path. She felt like a Warrior!

She shook herself and tucked the knife away. "Y—yes," she stammered.

"L, are you alright?" Traylon asked carefully.

She lifted her gaze to meet his, he was looking at her strangely and he was covered in blood. "You are alive."

"Yes, and so are you, but are you *alright*?"

"Yes, why do you ask?"

"You're bleeding."

"Oh, yeah." L reached up and touched her shoulder. "I think it's just a scratch, most of this blood is his."

"Locan is going to kill me," Traylon mumbled and moved further into the room where a very stunned and silent Katherine and James were clinging to the bars of a cell. "You are the human friends?"

"What the *fuck* is going on here?" James croaked.

"Elle, is that really you?" Katherine gasped.

"I'll explain everything later, we have to get off this ship before anyone discovers the mess we made," L said, hurrying over to the bars. "Tanea, do you know how to open these?"

Tanea rushed to a panel on the wall and pressed a button. "I spent some time in here," she said quietly.

The cell opened and Katherine embraced L in a warm hug. James gave her a cautious slap on the back.

"Let's go," Tanea said, hurrying from the room.

"You have so much to explain," Katherine whispered as they followed. "Starting with what the hell kind of language are you all speaking?"

"Prian," L explained.

They followed Tanea down a short hallway and Traylon spoke to the computer in a language L didn't recognize. It worked! The wall opened and they piled into a small pod, he spoke to the computer again in the same strange language and before L knew what was happening, she felt a jolt and then she knew they were flying through the air, back to the dreadful red planet below.

"Dude, I can't ignore the fact that the side of your face is fucking covered in blue stars," James said, breaking the silence that had settled over the group.

"What?" L screeched.

"I was going to mention it earlier, but your eyes were

glowing blue, and I was pretty sure Cerulean was actually in control when you killed that guard," Traylon said.

L just shrugged and let out a huge sigh. "Well, I guess someday I'll just be a big blue blob, maybe that's considered sexy on Prias?"

"Prias?" Katherine asked carefully.

"It's the planet I'm from, well, my mom and dad were from apparently. It's where we were heading when we made this little detour."

"Fuck that! I want back on Earth!" James shouted and Katherine nodded furiously in agreement.

"I'm sure we can take you back," L said, eyeing Traylon who had a very guarded look on his face. "After all, you are only here because they wanted to get at me."

"Hold on, we're approaching the planet," Traylon said, changing the subject.

There weren't enough seatbelts for the five of them. Traylon pushed L down in a seat and buckled her in, James and Katherine buckled themselves and that left Tanea and Traylon holding on as best they could as the small pod bumped and jolted its way to the surface. Traylon grabbed Tanea against her protests and held her as they hit the ground and skidded to a stop. Not nearly as smooth as Locan's ship landing.

When the pod stopped and the door opened, L couldn't have been happier to see the thick red grass of Septar.

TWENTY

It was the Warrior's time, Locan was tucked away. The Warrior knew how to handle this situation, he'd rampaged through the small collection of caves that had made up the village, nothing was left standing and still, there was no L. He let out a howl of outrage as his enormous fist flew through a door. His usually loose clothing was tight under his enlarged muscles and tattered from fighting. Blood covered him and he relished it, knowing he had punished those who'd dared take what was theirs.

He'd sensed Jabon near as he was destroying the caves but hadn't been able to locate the bastard. Left with no options, he was about to go back to his ship and smash into Jabon's, which he knew had to be floating up there somewhere. But then he felt it, the unmistakable pull of the Princess.

He turned from the task of smashing every usable item in the area and started running. The world went black except for a bright blue light, calling to him in the distance. "I'm going to lock her away; she'll never leave our sight ever again!" the Warrior growled. *You know that's a bad idea, Warrior, you know you can't lock her away, she'll only resent us.* Locan said, trying to reason with the Warrior.

"But she'll be safe," The Warrior argued. *I won't let you ruin everything; I won't let you harm her.* Locan insisted.

"Too bad you're locked away, Locan," the Warrior growled and continued running full force toward the light in the distance. "Leda, get ready to beam me up with L," he yelled pressing the button in his ear.

"You found her?"

"Not yet, but I'm almost to her."

"Is Traylon with her?"

"I don't know yet."

The world around the blue light started to shift into focus. There were others around her, and he let out a deep rumbling growl, was she in danger? He drew in a deep breath, and he could smell that she was bleeding.

"Kill," he growled. *How the hell do you know it's her that's bleeding?* Locan tried to reason with the Warrior, knowing he was out of control and any added danger to L was going to make him slip even farther.

"It is part of our gift, something you would know if you'd have bothered to ever talk to me while I was locked away in your mind," the Warrior hissed back. "And she's not alone!" The Warrior's mind clouded with rage, who had harmed her? He would kill any who had dared touch her.

"Locan!" L's voice floated across to him. There was relief there and a bit of joy that made his heart skip a beat.

She needs me, you have to let me back in control. You'll harm her!

The Warrior grunted and rushed forward, more determined than ever to prove what he was, what he could do, and what he would never do. He ignored the shouts of the others, pulled L into his arms, and ordered Leda to bring them aboard.

"Locan, you can't just leave them!" L was shouting as they

disappeared and reappeared in the control room of his ship. "Get the others!" L shouted at Leda frantically.

"Shit, Locan what have you done?" Leda gasped, looking at him with wide and frightened eyes. "Are you even in there?"

"Locan has let go, he knew I was here to do what needed to be done," The Warrior sneered, still holding L tight.

"Let her go," Leda demanded.

"I'm fine, get the others before Jabon finds them!" L snapped back.

Leda turned to start pressing buttons and the Warrior carried L out of the room. "You are bleeding, I can smell it, but also someone else's blood is on you."

L shivered in his arms. "Yeah."

His arms tightened around her. *We should have been there to keep her safe,* Locan whispered to the Warrior. *If you are all you say you are, why is she hurt now? Maybe neither of us are good enough to care for her.* "I will kill him," the Warrior hissed.

"I already did," she said with a half laugh. "Or maybe it was Cerulean, I don't really know."

She relaxed into his arms, and he felt his body start to relax, his muscles begin to reform and shrink.

Let me take it from here. She needs gentleness now, care, you know you can't give her that. Locan said.

"You are not afraid of us," the Warrior stated to L simply as a way of arguing with Locan's statement in his own head.

"No, if you were going to hurt me, my Goddess marks would be burning, not tingling. I know I'm safe with you."

The Warrior smiled over her tiny head. *You see, Locan, she is not afraid,* The Warrior thought to Locan.

"Not being afraid isn't the same as not being in danger." Locan said with a frustrated sigh.

L's trust relaxed the Warrior more, however, and by the time he arrived with her at her room, he was no longer able to hold control over Locan. Locan's arms pulled her tighter and he breathed her scent in deeply before setting her gently on the bed.

L was tired, all the adrenaline she'd been running on was gone now and the instant Locan had embraced her she'd known it was over. She was safe and she'd succeeded in saving her friends. She couldn't even be mad at Locan, though she knew she would be later.

"You shrunk," she said with a laugh.

"I am me again."

"You were always you, Locan."

He just grunted. "You need to show me your wounds."

L indicated her shoulder and sat silently while he gently poked and prodded at it. "Ouch!" she snapped when he got too close.

"You need stitches."

"Great."

"I will take you to the medical pod."

"Can I shower first?" She felt disgusting and waiting to wash off the blood of others was not something she thought she could do.

Locan's frown told her he disagreed.

"Please, Locan, I can't sit here with other people's blood on me any longer."

"I will wrap the wound for now."

"Thank you," she sighed.

Locan retrieved a small cloth and bowl of water from the bathroom, then gently washed the wound. L watched his face as he worked, intrigued by the deep concentration she saw there and wondered at the movement of his lips, almost as if he was talking but no sound was coming out. Was he arguing with himself? Or grumbling silently at her for getting into such trouble? Locan pulled out a knife and cut a strip from the soft cloth of his tunic. He wrapped it tightly around her arm then stepped away.

"It will work until you are ready for stitches."

"Thank you." L jumped up and hurried to the bathroom. As soon as the door shut, she stripped out of the clothes that were going to have to be thrown away, then looked in the mirror.

The sight took her breath away. Delicate blue stars trailed from her hairline, across her cheek and to her chin all along the left side of her face. One large star near her left eye seemed to glow slightly. "Cerulean, what have you done?"

"I do what I must to keep you alive, it's not as easy as I had thought it would be, after growing up on a weak planet like Earth. You are surprisingly brave; I suppose it has to do with your father having been a Warrior."

L wasn't surprised by the voice or the appearance of the floating black-eyed figure behind her in the mirror. "I wouldn't go so far as to say I'm brave, but I can't stand by while others suffer wrongly either. Did you have to mark up my face?"

"It is an honor to bear my marks," Cerulean said indignantly. "Would you rather I had let that male kill you?"

"I would rather not look like I belong on death row," L muttered.

"You have to stop thinking like a human," Cerulean snapped and disappeared.

L showered and tried to ignore the discolored water that swirled down the drain. By the time she felt clean and dressed in more of Leda's borrowed clothing, she was remembering the next problem. James and Katherine needed to go home, and she needed to convince Locan of that.

L hurried from her room to search for her friends.

She started in the control room. Leda and Locan were there, neither looked like they were in a good mood.

"Where are my friends? We need to get them back to Earth as soon as possible."

"Told you," Leda hissed at Locan.

Locan glared at Leda then L. "We cannot risk it, we have to get you to Prias as soon as possible. The fact that Jabon managed to catch up to us is disconcerting enough, but the fact that you risked your life multiple times for others has made this journey a reckless endeavor."

"I will risk my life any damn way I please! And I will not doom my friends to a life on another planet when we are perfectly capable of taking them home."

Leda huffed agreement, earning another glare from Locan.

"I can return them after you are safely deposited on Prias."

"No way, their lives have already been turned upside down. The longer they are missing, the harder it will be for them when they return."

"I don't care about them," Locan yelled.

"I know, but I do!" L yelled back. "And I'm the fucking Princess here so don't you have to do what I say?" She stood with hands on hips, glaring at Locan.

The door whooshed open behind her and somehow, she knew that whoever walked in, wasn't Prian. "Katherine and James, you want to go home, right?" she asked, without even turning to confirm her suspicion.

"Definitely, and *Princess?*" Katherine asked loudly.

"It's a long story, and we will have plenty of time to tell it while we travel back to Earth."

"No," Locan said simply.

"Let me talk to the Warrior," L said, suddenly hit by an idea.

"Fuck no!" Locan's eyes went wide, and he took a step away from her.

L took two steps forward. "I know the Warrior has my best interest in mind and my best interest is getting my friends safely home."

"Fine," Locan growled. "Take the goddamn Earthlings home, Leda. L come with me, it's time for stitches."

"Stitches?" Katherine asked with a gasp, "are you badly harmed?"

"Just a scratch on my arm. Locan already cleaned and wrapped it, but it's bleeding through. I suppose stitches are necessary." L embraced her friend and smiled at James who stood with a shocked sort of expression behind her. "Did you guys get settled into a room?"

"Yeah, we are fine, thanks to you! Go get stitched, then we need to talk." Katherine's eyes flitted to Locan and back to L. "About everything."

"We will," she assured Katherine, then followed Locan out of the room.

"Hey," she called to his back when the door was shut behind them.

"What?" he answered harshly.

"Thank you," she said quietly.

"I hope your recklessness isn't the downfall of all Prias," he said stiffly

"It won't be," she said with confidence.

Locan stopped and turned to face her, confusion and frustration showing. "How do you know, why can't you just let me take you to safety as quickly as possible?"

"I don't think that's fair to them, and I don't think you believe it is either, otherwise you never would have agreed. You *are* stronger than me, Locan, stronger than all of us. You could bend all of us to your will if you wanted to."

"That's not what I want," he said, incredulous.

"I know. That's why I trust you. I think we have to work

together, you, me and the Warrior, otherwise we won't succeed."

"He's dangerous."

"He's never harmed me."

"I won't give him the chance," Locan said quietly, his eyes met hers and she saw pain there before he turned and continued down the hall.

L smiled at his back, remembering how gently the Warrior had cradled her, how soft his words had been when he'd addressed her. Locan fought the other side of himself, but she knew no fear of the Warrior. The tingle of her stars told her she was right in that trust.

"His eyes are blue," she said quietly.

Locan's back stiffened but he didn't turn. "What?"

"The Warrior's eyes are blue. It was odd to look into your face and see blue eyes. Your green ones are so pretty."

Locan huffed.

"His voice is deeper than yours, but his touch is still gentle and warm, reassuring."

"I suppose anyone can be gentle at times," Locan agreed.

L rolled her eyes at his back and gave up trying, for now. She felt connected to Locan—and his Warrior—and she had every intention of seeing what was behind it.

When they got to the medical room, Traylon was standing over the medical pod. "What's going on?" L asked quickly, worried that someone was hurt.

"Tanea is healing, her wounds are deep and many," Traylon said quietly, and L noticed his hands were fisted.

"She's safe now," Locan said quietly, regret clear in his voice. "We have not always been successful in retrieving the Prian children before they were found by the Enforcers. Tanea was one of the unlucky ones. Not only did Jabon find her, but being female, he kept her for himself instead of returning her to the city to work the fields."

L reached out and touched Locan's shoulder, hoping to offer comfort. "You do what you can, but you cannot possibly save them all. It is something doctors learn quickly. Sometimes the odds are stacked too far against you, and you lose. She is lucky to be here now, she is safe with us."

"I will take care of her," Traylon vowed, and L saw something fierce flash across his uncharacteristically serious face.

Traylon felt something for the small girl. "I'm sure that is fine, as long as she agrees to your company. She may not," L warned.

Hurt passed over Traylon's face before he had a chance to cover it with a wide playful grin. "Who wouldn't want my attention?"

Locan grunted, "You, my friend, have too much confidence."

"And *you* don't have enough," Traylon shot back.

"Okay boys, how about you both step out. I'm sure Tanea will appreciate a female in the room when she's done in there and you need to clean up, Traylon." L ushered the men out and sat, waiting for the pod to open up.

When it did, Tanea emerged looking beautiful and perfectly healed and healthy.

"Where is your Warrior?" she asked, her eyes darting around the room.

"Locan is off doing whatever a ship captain does, I suppose."

"And the other one?"

"Traylon is no Warrior, he is cleaning up, he was watching over you until just a few minutes ago. I had to practically push him out of the room."

Tanea smiled and dipped her head, but not before L saw a flare of red hit her cheeks. "He seems nice."

L was filled with happiness to see that Traylon's affection for the girl might be returned. "Yes, he is. I am sure he'll be happy to see you're feeling better."

"Yes, better."

L knew it would take more than a medical pod for Tanea to overcome the emotional scars and bruising, but hopefully Traylon could assist with that too, in time.

As if summoned by the thought, Traylon walked in, freshly showered, and dressed in clean clothes. He carried a bundle in his hands and his face lit up with a smile when he saw Tanea standing there. "I have clean clothes for you, I thought you might want to get out of that."

Tanea looked down at her black robes and nodded. "Yes, this is what Jabon ordered me to wear when I wasn't in his quarters," her voice shook at the last words and Traylon stepped forward.

"You are safe here," he said firmly, touching her chin and lifting her gaze to meet his.

L smiled as she watched the interaction, it filled her with a longing though too, that kind of romance had never happened to her, and she wondered if it ever would. A vision of Locan's Warrior embracing her on Septar filled her mind and she sighed. He was a complicated man, two men? Both strong, gentle, frustratingly fierce in their desire to protect her. Locan and his Warrior both made her body tingle with awareness, and she suddenly wanted to explore that.

The thought was overwhelming, she strode toward the now-empty pod. "My turn to get healed, I suppose, Traylon why don't you show Tanea to her room."

L laid in the pod as the others left. She spoke to the machine and closed her eyes as it closed and started to whirr to life, assessing her and stitching her up.

It didn't take long, and she was stitched good as new. Then she went to make sure everyone was settled.

She wasn't expecting to find the little twerp who'd tricked them into landing on Septar.

"What the hell?" L yelled as she walked into the kitchen.

"Oh hi, Ma'am," the girl said in perfect Prian.

"Now you speak my language," L said, hands on hips. "Why are you here?"

"I saved her and her mother," Leda said, coming in behind her. "I guess I figured it's what you would have done," Leda huffed.

"Her mother?"

"Yeah, she's sleeping now, came out of the medical pod and passed right back out." Leda leaned in and whispered in L's ear. "She was in real bad shape, looked like the whole tribe had taken a turn with her and they are not a gentle species. I'm surprised she's not dead, honestly."

L bit her lip and looked over at the young girl who was eating happily and drawing a picture of what might have been some kind of animal L had never seen.

"I suppose you were only trying to save your mother?" L asked the girl.

"I was, and we are very excited to be going to Prias, it's where she's from."

L looked at Leda with a raised eyebrow.

"Yeah, she's definitely Prian, breeder-born."

L nodded; Leda had certainly done the right thing. "What's your name?" she asked the girl.

"Ferlin, my mother is Rylin."

"Welcome aboard," L said and smiled at Leda. "I'm glad you were able to save them," she whispered.

Leda shrugged, obviously uncomfortable with L's praise.

"And you thought we were going to land on Prias without a full ship," L joked, then left to find Katherine.

TWENTY-ONE

Three weeks later they were nearing Earth. Katherine and James were well adjusted to life on the ship. The shock had come when Jabon had first taken them, since then they'd been rethinking their view of what reality was and now that they were safe, they thought it was pretty cool that L was an alien princess. Traylon hovered over Tanea, trying his hardest to anticipate and take care of her every need, she wasn't as convinced of their compatibility as he was, but didn't push him away either. She had taken to mothering Sansorin, which Leda appreciated. Leda was no less broody, but she was surprisingly protective of Rylin and her daughter, Ferlin, spending much of her free time with the two. Locan was acting weird, ignoring L and everyone else too. He had holed himself up in his office most of the time, only coming out to eat and check on the ship. L could admit she missed him when he wasn't around, but she wasn't sure he'd welcome her company.

"I can't wait to wear my own clothes!" L said excitedly to Katherine as they watched the big blue planet appear on the screen.

"And eat sushi!" Katherine squealed.

"Oh my god, a hamburger! I want a hamburger with french fries," James said, wiping imagined drool off his chin.

L bit her lip, unwilling to talk about the things they were all worried about. They'd been away from Earth for more than a month, their jobs would have replaced them, called the cops likely to report them missing. Their bills were unpaid, and their apartment may have already been cleared out, unless the cops were watching it for clues to who abducted and possibly murdered them. Would they even be able to access their bank accounts? L didn't have any family to worry about her, but Katherine and James did, how terrified were they for their loved ones?

"L, can you talk with me in my office?" Locan said, startling her out of her thoughts.

"Sure," she said, a little nervous.

Katherine gave her a wink and mouthed the word *hottie*.

L just rolled her eyes and followed Locan out.

He didn't say anything until the office door closed behind her. He was standing behind his desk, his hands clasped behind his back. His face was stoic and unreadable. L didn't know what to expect from this conversation.

"I don't think you should go to the surface."

"Why?" she snapped.

"It's dangerous."

"Dangerous how? There's been no indication of Jabon's ship or any other Enforcer ship anywhere since we left Septar."

"I'm not concerned about the Enforcers, I'm—I'm concerned that you will reevaluate your commitment to saving Prias."

"You're worried I'll want to stay on Earth?" She was surprised by that.

"I've heard you and Katherine speak of nothing but what

you both miss about the planet since we left Septar, L, what the hell do you expect me to think?"

"Heard me? When the hell have you heard me? I have hardly seen you for weeks and you certainly haven't bothered to talk to me and ask me what's going on in my head! Asshole," she yelled and stormed out of the office.

She nearly ran into Leda and Sansorin as she hurried out of Locan's office.

"L!" he yelled as the door closed, but she ignored him.

"Whoa, what's up his butt?" Sansorin asked with a laugh.

"Hasn't spoken to me in weeks and thinks he knows my mind."

"Sounds about right, he's a bit full of himself," Leda agreed. "I told Sansorin she can go down to Earth when it's dark, she can wear something with a hood, and I don't think anyone will notice."

"Are you kidding me, she looks like she's wearing a Halloween costume," L laughed, and they just looked at her, confused. "I mean, I think you're beautiful, Sansorin, you know that, but Earth doesn't know they aren't alone, and I don't think our trip will go well if they find out tonight."

"Ugh, I never get to do anything fun," Sansorin whined, "Please?"

"If L thinks it isn't a good idea, then it isn't a good idea," Locan said from behind L. "You can't pass for human."

"Are you going?" Sansorin asked him.

"Of course, I must keep the Princess safe."

"I don't need to be kept safe on Earth. If you want to be useful, take Sansorin down for sightseeing and make sure she isn't noticed."

"While you do what, exactly?"

"Tie up loose ends, gather some items I'd rather not go without for the rest of my life."

"And see nobody," he growled.

"And see nobody," she hissed.

"We already came up with a plan to tell everyone," Katherine said excitedly, joining them in the hall. "James and I took off to Europe and got married, L came with us and decided to stay, she may never come back."

"I just hope they give you guys back your jobs," L said with a frown.

Katherine shrugged. "An adventure was had. If I lose my job over it, so be it. At least we are all alive and hey, I guess this means James is going to have to marry me!"

L laughed, "Your bright attitude is why I love you." Tears burst from L's eyes as she realized she was hours away from saying goodbye to her best friend, forever. It had been easy when she thought she was saving Katherine from knowing too much and being in danger. This was different.

Locan growled behind her. "Leda can gather your things; you should stay on the ship if going will be too hard."

"Fuck you, Locan," L said and hugged her friend. "We are going to eat sushi and watch Dirty Dancing. We are going to braid each other's hair and fall asleep in the living room." L wanted one last girl's night before she left Earth forever. "Leda, Sansorin, Tanea, Rylin and Ferlin should come too."

"Oh! Girl's night! Wine and popcorn!" Katherine agreed.

"Of course, that's all dependent on us actually having a home to go back to," L pointed out, wiping away her tears. "So, let's go figure that out first."

"It's evening. Traylon and I can beam down to your neighborhood and check things out without being noticed. Traylon and I are going to go first, and alone," he said firmly. "I won't risk any of you to a place we haven't checked out first."

"That's fair," L said with a half smile. If Locan wasn't going to insist she stay on the ship, then she would be agreeable to a little safety precaution.

They all gathered in the control room and stared at the screen. It was zoomed in on the dark alley behind her apartment building. Traylon and Locan materialized there dressed in Earth clothes they'd had on hand from the last visit and wouldn't raise any suspicious eyebrows.

They watched as the two men strolled casually around to the front of the building. And disappeared inside.

"Damn, why doesn't this thing have x-ray vision?" James complained.

"We are outside the door," Locan's voice floated in. "Everything looks the same and quiet behind the door. Go ahead and beam us inside."

Leda pushed a couple buttons, and no one breathed while they waited for a response. Would the place be empty, would their stuff be there unchanged? Would a new family be living there?

"Looks good. Pull Traylon back and send everyone else down," Locan said, and everyone cheered quietly.

"We're going home!" Katherine squealed and clapped her hands.

Traylon appeared in the room, then the others disappeared. L looked at Traylon, confused when she wasn't sent along with the others.

"What the hell?"

"You have to reassure him."

L wished she could deny knowing what he was talking about. She gave a heavy sigh. "I told him that I wasn't trying to stay on Earth."

"He doesn't believe you; he is scared, and he is barely holding it together. I've known him for a long time, and I can see it in his eyes."

"Ugh, fine, I'll tell him again, but I don't see how it will make a difference, if he doesn't believe me, he doesn't believe me. There's nothing I can do about that."

"All I'm saying is, if you could try and reassure him, Leda and I would appreciate it, he's been hell to work with the last couple weeks."

L frowned, she hadn't really noticed, since he'd been avoiding her, she had no idea how he was interacting with the others. "Fine," she grunted. "Now beam me down Scotty," she said with a laugh.

Traylon didn't get her joke, but he hit a button and she felt herself disappear. It was unreal when she appeared in the middle of her condo. It looked exactly the same and she hadn't thought she'd ever see it again, had been resigned to that and actually okay with it too. Now that she was here, she felt a little teary eyed and just a hint regretful to leave it all.

Locan was standing near the door, watching her carefully. Katherine and James were both on their cell phones making frantic calls, Leda, Tanea, Sansorin, Rylin and Ferlin were oohing and aahing over the various things around the house.

"I guess I'll order some food! If my debit card still works, maybe I have some cash in my purse," L said as an excuse to leave the room. She closed her bedroom door behind her and fell onto her bed, rolled to her side, and let the tears fall. The last weeks had been unreal and now that she was back in her own bedroom, she wanted so badly to convince herself it had been a dream, a really weird dream. She looked down at her arm, covered in blue stars and she knew it had all been far too real.

"Back to this depressing planet?"

L turned to see Cerulean floating in the room with her. "Why are you here, am I in danger?"

"No more than usual, no."

"That's good, I suppose."

"I made sure things were taken care of while you were gone. Your bills were paid."

"What?" L sat up, surprised.

"This is all a part of the journey, you were never going to let your friends be stranded away from home, though my prediction was that you'd save them farther down the line," she grumbled.

"You knew! Of course you knew, why the hell does everyone know so much more than me?"

"Knowledge is not always a blessing, but you know enough to do what needs to be done. Enjoy your last night on Earth." She started to disappear, but her voice floated back in an eerily surround sound sort of way. "And do something about that damn Warrior, if he doesn't accept who he is we're all screwed."

"Why am I in charge of Mr. PMS out there?" L grumbled but got no response.

She rummaged through her drawers and pulled out clean clothes that she was never happier to see. Leggings and an oversize shirt, underwear, and cozy socks. This was her movie night with Katherine outfit. After she changed, she offered the other girls the chance to rummage for clothes in her room, which they squealed over, even Leda was happy about the opportunity.

Katherine and James hadn't emerged from their bedroom, which left her and Locan somewhat alone in the living room. She sat on the couch and pulled her legs up to her chest, then motioned to the other side. "Come sit, no one's coming through the door to attack. Cerulean said I'm as safe as usual and she paid all the bills, knowing I'd be returning, or at least that Katherine would be returning, eventually."

Locan huffed; but relaxed slightly and sat on the couch. "Did she say anything else useful?"

"No," L said quickly, then took a deep breath. "She did say that you're having some kind of a problem?"

Locan glared at L and she was tempted to leave it alone. He was quite intimidating when he wanted to be.

"She said that if you don't accept who you are, we're all screwed."

Locan pursed his lips and shook his head. "The Gods and Goddesses interfere when it suits them, they can push and prod, but they don't predict the future."

"Then how did she know that I was going to be coming back here?"

"A good guess."

"So, what if her next good guess is you being an asshole and me taking a dirt nap as a result?"

"I would never harm you. Damnit L, can't you see that's all I've been trying to do? Trying to keep you safe? Safe from the Enforcers, safe from Jabon and Temis," his eyes closed and his breath hissed out, "and safe from my Warrior," he whispered.

"Your Warrior is not something I need to be kept safe from, Locan. I know that with every ounce of my being. He would never harm me, could never. I saw it in his eyes when he found me on Septar." L's words were intense, and she wished she could force Locan to believe them.

"You don't understand what he wants," Locan growled. "It isn't just your safety he's after." Locan's eyes dipped down L's body and she felt a shiver run through her as she realized what he was talking about.

"Oh, yeah I guess that's different, but I still don't understand how it puts me in danger." L pulled her knees tighter and tried to ignore the sudden fire that was set in her belly at the knowledge that Locan's Warrior wanted her.

"You can't understand, you know nothing of what the Warrior truly is, only what he has presented to you, you know not what he is capable of." Determination and fear filled Locan's eyes, and he looked away from her.

L reached out and touched his shoulder, wanting to offer comforting words, but she wasn't sure what to say.

Katherine ruined the chance when she rushed into the room yelling about her bitch boss who wouldn't give her back her job.

After that, there was no more alone time for her and Locan. L ordered food and although it was supposed to be a girl's night, James and Locan were allowed to stay and be a part of it. James went out for beer and wine, and they spent the rest of the night watching movies, eating, and drinking. She went to sleep in her own bed in the early hours of the morning. Sansorin stayed with her, the others volunteered to go back to the ship for the night and Locan stretched out on the couch which was far too small for his body.

Locan didn't sleep, there was far too much danger with L off his ship, but laying on her couch and hearing her steady breathing in the other room was akin to torture.

You heard what she said, if you don't accept me then you are quite possibly dooming her and the entire planet of Prias, his Warrior snarled in his mind.

"Your opinion is neither wanted nor valid."

Just because I can admit that she belongs to our soul, you would deny my good sense?

"Because you are selfish and violent and care for nothing other than what satisfies your body. You would destroy her and call it love. I would watch her wilt and die under your fist."

We are not our father!

"And I'm going to keep it that way!" Locan growled.

TWENTY-TWO

L woke up disoriented for a moment, she couldn't understand where she was until she heard the familiar sound of Katherine making coffee in the kitchen.

"Coffee!" she hollered happily and rushed from the bedroom, not caring that she was in short shorts and a tank top, this was her house after all.

"Good morning, sunshine, you slept in," Traylon called from the couch where he sat with Tanea, already drinking coffee, and eating bagels.

"Who went to the store?" L asked, grabbing a bagel and a cup of coffee.

"I sent James this morning for essentials."

"We should definitely bring some of these on the ship with us," Traylon said around a mouthful.

"Add bagels to the shopping list," L laughed and looked around. "Where's Locan?"

"He went back to the ship to freshen up, he'll be back shortly, I'm supposed to let him know when you get out of bed," Traylon explained.

"How long has he been gone?"

"About ten minutes."

"Don't bother him, I'm sure he needs some alone time."

"Don't we all," Tanea said quietly.

L glared at Traylon who just shrugged. "I'll wait a few, but don't try to leave or anything."

"I wouldn't dare. I'm supposed to be in Europe, remember? I can't exactly be seen in town."

"So, what *is* the plan?" Katherine prodded. "When do you guys pull anchor and head out forever?"

"Not forever," L insisted. "I don't see why we can't come back to visit someday."

"After you take your rightful place on the throne of Prias?" Katherine laughed, but there were tears in her eyes.

"Yeah, who would dare deny the Queen of Prias a little vacation across the cosmos?"

"Besides your grumpy bodyguard?" Katherine said with a raised eyebrow.

"He might take a little convincing."

"Oh, I'm sure you can handle that!" Katherine wiggled her eyebrows. "He's a freaking hottie, even though he's an alien, but I guess you are too, so tell me, are you two going to hook up on the long drive home?"

L just rolled her eyes; Katherine was never not trying to get her laid. "I think that would be an unnecessary complication."

"Or it would settle his ass down. That man is wound tighter than anyone I've ever met."

L had no response. She took her breakfast to the small table and stared at what was on the television without really seeing it. Katherine's words stuck in her mind. Would sleeping with Locan solve the problem of his attitude, or would it just make it worse, give him some kind of possessive edge to his crazy ideas of protecting her. Cerulean had said that they were going to fail if Locan didn't accept both parts of himself. Locan refused to accept his Warrior because of the supposed danger he posed to her. If she could prove that she trusted his Warrior and that his Warrior meant her no harm, would he do what the Goddesses thought was necessary?

"L?" Tanea asked, waving a hand in front of her face. Snapping her out of her thoughts.

"Oh, sorry, I was just thinking. What's up?"

"I asked if I could borrow more clothes, I have nothing of my own and I saw some great stuff in your closet."

"Yeah, go for it, I'll pack it all to take with us. You, me, Rylin and Ferlin are at the mercy of Leda's closet no more!"

They packed everything she didn't want to leave behind forever, which amounted to five suitcases and one box. So many things she didn't want to take because she knew she would have to do without eventually; makeup, soap, and lotion, all the things that were different on another planet and she'd have to adjust to, she was ready for that. Her favorite books were coming along with all of her clothing and shoes, a few photographs, and Aunt Sara's afghan.

"Is that the last one?" Traylon asked, pointing to a small bag on the bed.

"Yeah, that's it, everything else, Katherine can sell or give away."

"Are you glad we came back? Giving you the chance to gather a few things?"

L stood up and dusted off her hands, "I think so."

"Are you ready to go?" he asked carefully.

"I said goodbye to Katherine and James, so I guess so; but could you send Locan down, I want to talk to him before I go."

Traylon gave her a half smile and a raised eyebrow. "Sure thing, Princess." He grabbed the bag. "Be gentle, he's not as tough as he looks," he said, then pressed his ear and told Leda to bring him up.

L waited longer than she'd expected to before Locan showed up. His face was guarded and his voice impatient. "What's the hold up?"

"I need something before I can really feel like we are making the right decisions."

"Of course we are making the right decisions, look at your marks, you don't get those when you make the wrong choice."

"The wrong choice for whom? How do we know that the Goddesses want what's right for the Prian people?"

Locan looked thoughtful. "They worked hard for our people until Achromic disappeared I'm told. I can only hope that they are now on our side for their own selfish reasons."

"So, you think we should follow everything they say?" L asked carefully.

Locan frowned. "Yes, I suppose that's accurate."

"Then you have to trust your Warrior, or we won't succeed."

"Not going to happen."

"I can't trust you if you aren't whole, Locan."

"I *am* whole, the Warrior lives in my head, and he will stay there, I swear I won't ever let him harm you."

"That's exactly the problem, Locan. I am not afraid that your Warrior will harm me, I am afraid that you keeping yourself torn in two is going to harm *you* and lose us everything."

"The Warrior is not me," he said firmly.

"Fine, then let me speak to him, let me be the judge of whether or not he is a danger to me. Let's prove it for the last time."

"No way. He's far too dangerous to be let loose."

"No, he's not. If he was, then my stars would burn when he was near, when *you* are near, but instead I only feel—I only feel that he and you are a part of something I am meant to be a part of. That you being whole is something that will make me whole too." L got quiet at the end and tears threatened to spill from her eyes. She wasn't sure where her certainty was coming from, but she knew the words she spoke were real. More than anything, she wanted to see this man united, and she wanted to stand beside him as they pursued the freedom of their people. She stepped forward and touched his shoulder. "Please, Locan, I'm asking you to trust me. Let your Warrior free and I'll show you that it's safe."

L wasn't sure what kind of torment or debate was going on inside Locan's head, but his face revealed nothing as he stared at her with pursed lips. Eventually he pulled a knife from his belt and handed it to her.

"If he tries to harm you, kill him."

"Locan I—"

"Promise me," he said, pressing the knife into her palm. "Promise me you will not let him harm you."

L swallowed a knot in her throat. "I understand, Locan."

"Step back."

L obeyed, stepping back until the back of her legs hit the bed. She wasn't afraid of Locan's Warrior side, she hadn't lied about that, but his seriousness set her nerves on edge. She took a deep breath and concentrated on feeling everywhere on her body where a star marked her, feeling for any indication that what she was about to do, was a bad idea.

Her stars were frustratingly quiet.

"I'm ready, Locan."

"I'm not," he grumbled, but closed his eyes. As she watched, his body grew, bulged, and stretched until it seemed like his once-loose tunic and pants were about to burst, and his head brushed the ceiling. When he opened his eyes, they were blue and emitted an eerie glow.

"Princess, I can't believe you convinced him to let go."

"Did he really and truly, or is he still holding on, just in case?"

"Against his better judgement, he let go completely."

L stepped forward, intrigued by this enormous man who was Locan, but not. "And he watches, from somewhere inside there?"

"He does."

"He'll know what we say and do?"

"He will."

"May I touch you?"

He simply nodded.

L stepped closer and reached out, running a finger over one muscled arm. "Will you tell me why he worries so much?"

"He wouldn't like it."

"He doesn't like any of this," L reasoned.

"True. Our father was broken. He was severely injured in a battle fought in order to leave the city. He was taking his young wife and running to join the rebels. Some Enforcers caught them and threatened to take her to the Hospital and turn her into a breeder as punishment for them trying to leave. He managed to fight them off, killed them both actually, but not without great injury to himself. He took an axe to the face. It severed something important."

"He was never able to change back?" L gasped, her mind running to the possibilities of his mother getting impregnated by his father in this enormous form.

"No, and it was as if he'd become a completely different person, quick to anger and fights, never happy with life."

"Why didn't she leave him?"

"She loved him, their souls were mated, and she thought if she stayed, she could change him back to the man he was."

"But she couldn't."

"No one could. His brain was broken, and he was angry.

She became a frail and scared woman, terrified of her own shadow and barely able to function. She took care of us; she was as good a mother as she could be. When we were ten, our father killed her. She was bringing him his dinner and tripped, spilled it and he exploded, hit her so hard she died instantly."

"Oh my god," L gasped.

"When his crime was discovered, there was no other choice, he had to be killed."

"I'm so sorry," L whispered and embraced the enormous Warrior. "I am so sorry that was your life."

"We were taken in by the leader of the rebels after that."

"Your father was broken in battle, how can Locan think that he will be broken too, it doesn't make any sense."

"Fear brought on from childhood trauma rarely does."

"I want to prove to him that you are not a danger."

"And how do you think to do that?"

"I don't think I can prove that you aren't dangerous, but I can prove that I'm not afraid of you."

The Warrior just raised an eyebrow and waited.

"Sit on the bed."

"Princess?" he drawled.

"You're tall and I have a kink in my neck from looking up at you."

The Warrior obeyed; the bed creaked under his incredible weight.

L walked over to him and stood between his knees, she grabbed his face and leaned in, planting a kiss on his surprisingly soft lips.

She was trying to prove that she wasn't scared, she wasn't expecting the fire that would ignite where they touched. She'd planned to plant a quick peck and step back triumphant, but now she couldn't pull away, she found herself leaning in, pressing harder and parting her own lips invitingly.

His hands stroked up her backside and pressed her forward against his hard body. He was warm and safe, and a sigh escaped her lips as their bodies pressed together. She gave herself completely to the kiss, opening her heart and mind to all the feelings, all the lust and more that was filling her. It was amazing and she didn't want it to end. Her hands were in his hair, and she felt his chest rumble with a moan as he accepted her. A prickle ran up her spine and it felt like an electric shock ran straight into his mouth from hers, it was almost shocking enough to make her pull back, but his hand was now cradling the back of her head and held her tight.

When he finally pulled away, her head was fuzzy, her body hot and her breath panting.

"See?" she stammered. "I trust you completely."

"Princess," he whispered. "I think we have a problem."

Her eyes opened and tried to focus. "Problem?"

"I own you now," he said with a grin. "I tasted your soul in that kiss."

"What?"

"It's a Prian thing, your soul reached out to mine."

L stepped back, her head clearing. "I mean the kiss was good, but what the hell are you talking about?"

"Two souls who are meant to be together, the kiss tells it all. Of course, I knew it the moment I saw you, Locan just wouldn't listen. He can't deny it now though. You are meant to be ours, the perfect mate for the man and the Warrior."

"Bullshit," she snapped.

"I thought you said you trusted me."

"To not kill me, not to always tell me the truth."

"Then ask him yourself." His body shrunk to a more manageable size and his eyes returned to their normal brilliant green.

"Locan?"

"What were you thinking?" he hissed. "You had no right!"

"I had to show you," she whispered.

"Well, I hope you're happy because now he thinks he owns you."

"I—I couldn't have known."

"No, but you could have trusted me. Damnit you could have *asked* me if you wanted to know about my past too."

L didn't know what to say, Locan was hurt, she was confused, and it was obviously past time to go.

Locan pressed his ear and told Leda to pull them up, she was leaving Earth, and she had a lot more important things to be concerned about.

Locan locked himself in his office and put a fist through a table.

"Easy there, boy."

Locan turned to see Violaceous lounging behind his desk. "I don't need your opinion right now."

"Yeah, looks like you're doing a great job with everything."

"What do you want?" Locan growled.

"I want to know why you aren't sealing the deal with the Princess."

"You're kidding, right? She has no idea what it means to have touched my soul with that kiss, she meant to only show she wasn't afraid, she didn't know enough to protect herself from giving too much."

"You mean she's pure and free and gave you her all just because it was what her body wanted her to do?"

"You don't know what you're talking about."

"You don't know what you're missing out on."

Locan's hands fisted, and he ignored the shouts of anger that rumbled through his mind. "I won't risk her, and I won't debase her by putting a claim on her, she is meant for more."

"More than the best Warrior on Prias, more than a man who's dedicated his life to saving others?"

"You know she's meant for more than me and this *thing* inside me."

"She would never accept one of those idiots who bow down to the Doctors. You know she wouldn't."

"There are a few who joined the rebels."

Violaceous made a gagging motion. "That is such bullshit, and you know it. When the soul chooses, nothing else matters. How do you think her mother ended up with a Warrior baby-daddy? The souls started to choose different, doing what was best for the continuation of the species, and the planet."

Locan wanted to argue, but he couldn't. "It's not safe for her."

"If you wait long enough and she takes someone else as a lover, that won't be safe for anyone."

Violaceous disappeared then, leaving Locan and his Warrior seething with rage. The mere thought of L with someone else made him murderous, and the Warrior screamed in his head, also outraged by the idea.

"She will be with no one else," Locan said firmly.

I'm glad we're on the same page, the Warrior growled.

TWENTY-THREE

The weeks passed slowly; L was worried about what was going to happen when they arrived on Prias. Locan refused to be in the same room as her and she was seriously concerned about the whole 'piece of her soul' thing he'd talked about after their kiss. She was far too embarrassed to ask any of the others about it though, so she worried alone. She worked out with Leda and the other girls, learning more self-defense and a little offense, that she hoped she wouldn't have to use.

As the time drew near for them to land on Prias, she couldn't hold back any longer, she couldn't move on to the next adventure until she knew everything about the one she was still stuck on.

"Locan, I need your assistance, immediately," she called over the ship's intercom system.

"Where are you, I'll send Leda," he responded.

"I need *you* and I'm in my room."

"He's on his way," Leda called over the intercom and giggled.

L rolled her eyes, she hadn't exactly been subtle, but with the way he'd been avoiding her, she practically needed to knock him on the back of the head and drag him into her room to get him to talk to her.

When he got there, he stood just inside the door and stared at her with his hands behind his back. "What do you need that no other can assist with?"

"Will you step inside so we have privacy?"

"No."

L glared but proceeded. "I need to know what you meant when you said that I had given you a piece of my soul."

Locan glared and stepped far enough into the room that the door closed behind him. "It doesn't matter."

"Like hell it doesn't! Every night I dream—well I dream about things that I never dreamt before and I can only assume they are coming as a result of what passed between us."

L saw a flare of blue pass over Locan's eyes and she wondered if the Warrior was near the surface, fighting for control.

"I can't say where your dreams come from," he said flatly.

"What *can* you say? Or do I need to talk to the Warrior to get any real answers?" L was done playing nice.

"No!" Locan growled. "You will never see him again if I can help it."

"Why? I think I've proven he isn't a danger to me."

"You've proven nothing other than the fact that you're willing to put your life at risk for others, I think I already knew that."

L glared back and put her hands on her hips. This was not going as planned. Luckily, she had a plan B. Her face heated as she realized she was actually going to go through with it. She pulled her shirt over her head. She wasn't wearing a bra and she knew she looked good. All the training with Leda had taken her already svelte body to another level of toned. She stood before Locan in a pair of short shorts and nothing else, her red hair loose around her shoulders and so many blue stars on her body, she felt like a work of art.

The groan he let out was satisfying, the way he dropped to his knees and hung his head in his hands was unexpected. "Princess, you have no idea what you are asking for."

"I think I have *some* idea," she whispered. "Locan, I dream of you every night and I feel you near me every day. Yet you avoid me like the plague. Are you not drawn to me as I am to you? Did whatever happened between us only affect me?" L held the shirt over her bare breasts, embarrassed by her assumptions.

"No, definitely not. I just can't, I'm not meant to be with you in that way, I am meant to protect you."

"Bullshit!" L shouted and crossed the distance between them, her shirt forgotten. She knelt before him and pulled his hands from his face, forcing him to look at her. "If I gave you something, it was because I felt safe, cared for and desired. I wanted to give you whatever it was and if you took it, that means you felt the same way."

"You didn't know what you were doing."

"Maybe not, but I would do it again. Locan, I trust you with my life. I have no doubt that you would die to protect me, and I know you are a good person, you care for others above yourself, and your goal has always been to save our people. Why would I not want to connect with you?"

"The Warrior is—"

"No! You cannot use him as an excuse. I have had a lot of time to think, and I even asked Cerulean for advice. She said that you and your Warrior are two halves of a whole and if you don't accept him then you will never be at your best. She said that he couldn't hurt me any more than you could, and your fears are based on a terrible occurrence, a truly horrible thing, but nothing that would ever happen again. Locan, you have to accept him, or we might all be screwed."

"And you're willing to offer your body in exchange for this, willing to be his property, his soul-tied female? That's forever!"

"I am willing to be in a relationship with you and the Warrior, I am willing to accept you as you are, both halves. I've never been so sure of wanting another in all my life."

Locan looked like he was at war with himself. She watched his face go through a hundred emotions before he spoke.

"Princess, I don't think you understand—"

"I am so sick of hearing that! I may not have been born on Prias, but maybe that's a good thing. I have no prejudice; I have no system of who's good enough for me, burned into my brain. I grew up in the United States where we got rid of the class system generations ago. Nothing internally is screaming at me that you are less than me, that I should marry some soft-bodied aristocrat who couldn't protect me from a fly. I need someone who's as fierce as I want to be, who knows what we are fighting for and can actually get the job done. I want to stand next to a man who will walk through a fucking wall to save me or destroy an entire village when he can't find me." L let a little laugh escape her, she knew she was sounding desperate, but this was her last chance, she knew she'd never convince him if they were on Prias with so many other distractions. She had to put it all out there right now. "Locan, I want *you*. Would you deny us both what we want?"

A growl ripped through him, and his body bulged, his eyes started to pale, turning blue, the Warrior was surfacing. Locan pulled her to him then. "You have given us a piece of your soul, now you will take a piece of ours."

Locan covered her mouth with his and she felt a warmth flow into her, it latched onto her heart and for a moment she was certain it stopped beating, she gasped, struggling to breathe against his lips, then it exploded, her heart leapt, her lungs filled, and she was consumed by a feeling of completeness.

Locan pulled away, his eyes back to their deep green were full of worry. "Are you alright?"

L blinked, not sure at first. She was vibrating and she swore she could feel his desire inside of her own body. Not just his, but the Warrior's as well. "What—what am I feeling?" she asked carefully.

"When a piece of the soul is given, the other person can tap into the feelings of the other. You will know what we are feeling, if we are hurt or well, happy or sad."

"Horny," she said with a laugh. "Wait, and you could feel mine? I mean, since we kissed on Earth?" Embarrassment flooded her cheeks at the thought of how she'd been lusting after him daily, and nightly. Had he known? She wanted to crawl into a hole and die of embarrassment.

Locan only smiled wickedly and nodded. "You were truly testing our restraint these weeks, L. I considered throwing myself into the darkness of space to keep you safe from us, but it's too late for that now," he frowned.

"Hey," she said sternly, taking his face into her hands. "None of that. This is supposed to be a happy thing. We want to be together; we *will* be together, and we will save Prias."

"We will protect you, above all else."

"I know you will." L pulled his face to hers and began a slow, deep assault of his mouth, wanting to savor the experience of feeling his reactions as part of her own.

He didn't hold back, he responded immediately and picked her up without breaking the kiss. He carried her to the bed and laid her gently down.

"Computer, lock the door," he called out, his voice rough.

"Hey, I didn't know I could do that."

Locan laughed, "I didn't want you to know you could keep me away."

L smiled up at his green eyes, they held a hint of blue, and she acknowledged the Warrior there as well. This complicated beast of a man was hers; body and soul, and she had no regrets. He was what she'd waited all her life to find, no wonder a human man could never hold her attention for long. She was meant for so much more. A tightness surrounded her heart, and she knew it was him, his feelings overwhelming him the same as hers. She couldn't put it into words, love just didn't cut it, so she set about showing him with her body just how much she wanted him, how much she needed him, and how much she rejoiced in their union of souls.

Locan worried as Prias came up on the screen. He'd spent one amazing week in the arms of L pretending that their story was over, that they'd reached their happy ending and that was it. Now reality was seeping in. They had a lot to take on, so much responsibility lay on both of their shoulders. Not only that, but he still hadn't told L who her father was, Carini was not going to be happy about their soul joining.

"Is that Prias?" L asked excitedly, unburdened by Locan's worries, though he knew she could clearly feel them.

"That is home," Locan said quietly. The familiar green planet was currently just a ball on the screen, they weren't that close yet, it would be a couple hours before they landed.

"Tell me what I'm looking at," she prodded.

"This area is all wild, full of dangerous beasts and, of course, us rebels." Locan waved his hand over a large part of what she was seeing. "Prias has a large ocean that covers most of what you can't see. Like Earth, the land is dotted with many lakes and rivers. The water supply that is subterranean covers nearly the entire small planet as well. As you can see, the foliage is a little lighter on this part and that is where the city of Prias lies, covering only a small portion of the total area."

"Wow, so few inhabitants on a planet, is that normal?"

"For a small planet, yes. You must remember it is much smaller than Earth."

L looked thoughtful. "How long to go from the rebel settlement to the city?"

"An hour by ship, a couple days of hard travel over land."

"On foot?"

"We are a little more advanced than that," Locan laughed. "We ride, animals similar to Earth horses, only sturdier and more dangerous if you aren't careful. They have very sharp teeth and eat meat."

L gave a little shudder.

"He's only teasing you," Traylon said. "The beasts are quite gentle and only eat grass."

Locan sighed. "There's plenty to be afraid of down there though, so don't get your hopes up. Most of the animals do want to have a bite of your soft flesh."

"Well, that's what I have you for, right? My personal weapon," L said with a smile, reaching up to lay a kiss on Locan's cheek.

Traylon turned away with a sorrowful look on his face. Locan knew he'd failed again and again to convince Tanea to give him a chance. Locan felt sorry for his friend but thought Tanea might be making the best choice to keep her distance from him; he wasn't known for successful relationships and whatever she'd gone through on Jabon's ship, it had left deep scars.

Both of the other women he was bringing to Prias were deeply wounded, and scared to death of him, it seemed. One quick movement around Rylin and she was yelling and running from the room. Leda hovered over that one like a mother bird and when no one was looking, she touched the woman gently and they'd shared more than one soft look that made Locan wonder if they weren't lovers. It wouldn't surprise Locan one bit to find Leda preferred the company of a woman, and after Rylin's experience on Septar, he would expect nothing less than a complete aversion to males. He just wished she'd stop running as if *he* had personally hurt her, he prided himself on never harming a female and she reminded him of the way his mother cowered from his father.

How he feared L may one day cower from him.

His thoughts turned dark then, and he went through every possible scenario that could end with him harming L the way his father had harmed his mother.

Let it go, his Warrior growled in his mind.

Locan couldn't, but he wanted to, more than anything. Looking down at L filled him with so much pleasure and yet he was terrified, she was so small, so delicate. He reached out and pushed a lock of red hair behind her ear.

"Yes, I will keep my soul-wife safe," he whispered in her ear, delighting in the growl of approval his Warrior sent through his mind. The last week had settled the Warrior in a way Locan had never imagined possible. It was as if the piece of himself he'd given to L had held much of his anxiety and now he could accept that the other part of him loved her as much as he did, and it wanted nothing more than to protect her. He would never harm her on purpose, could never.

Yet he felt he would always be watchful for that to change. What if he received a head injury in battle? What if he became very angry?

"Will they be expecting us?" L asked, dragging him out of his thoughts.

"We will signal them when we are close, this far out we

need to keep ourselves hidden, we don't want to alert anyone in the city."

L frowned, "Do you think Jabon returned to the city?"

"It's possible. I was surprised he didn't follow us from Septar." Locan's thoughts drifted to fearful territory, when it had become obvious that Jabon wasn't following them, he'd immediately started to worry that he'd returned to Prias and attacked the rebel camp. The Enforcers hadn't been able to locate the camp because it was well hidden and moved regularly, but that didn't mean it would be impossible to find with the right motivation.

L could feel his worry and she touched his shoulder gently. "Whatever it is, we'll do everything we can. Our goal is still to free *all* of Prias from Temis and the Doctors, right?"

"Right," Locan agreed. It just wasn't as simple as saying the words.

TWENTY-FOUR

L busied herself with cleaning her room. She'd been too anxious to stay in the control room and watch the slow approach of the planet. Locan said he would come find her when they were close, so she was doing all she could to distract herself from the reality of what was about to happen. She was going to meet her people! Her mother and father's people. Not only that, but she was also about to set foot on a third alien planet, she was so much cooler than Neil Armstrong.

Locan walked in while she was dusting under the bed, not that it needed it, a little robot kept the floors immaculate. She stood and hurried across the space.

"What's wrong?" she asked quickly.

"I have been trying to figure out how to tell you something."

She laughed nervously, "You don't have a wife or girlfriend down there, do you?" It was a fear she'd been holding back, knowing it was highly likely, he was a very attractive and virile male, no doubt he had many women strewn all across the cosmos. Anger and jealousy bubbled up inside of her and she felt like lashing out at him.

"No!" he said, incredulous.

Her nerves eased a bit. "Locan, you're making me nervous. Literally! I can feel your nerves invading me."

"I know, and I'm sorry. You need to know that your father, Carini, he's alive."

"Alive!" she gasped.

"Yes, he's the ruler of the rebels, the man who took me in after my father had to be killed."

L took a step back and cocked her head. "Why didn't you tell me?" she asked carefully.

Locan looked embarrassed. "He isn't going to be happy with our soul-giving."

L rolled her eyes, "You *can't* tell me he believes in that status shit too; he impregnated my mother, and she was a full-on queen!"

"I don't know how he will feel about it, and that's what worries me. As your father, he has the right to undo the giving."

"Undo the giving?" L asked, confused.

"There is a way to give back the piece of soul, it isn't easy but is the responsibility of the female's father, if he disapproves. If he thinks the male is not suitable for his daughter."

L was aghast, "How could he possibly not think you're good enough, Locan?"

"I just need you to know it's possible."

"I don't care what anyone else thinks," she said, coming forward and grabbing Locan's hands, holding them tightly to her breast. "My heart beats for you, Locan, he can't change that."

His relief flooded her as he relaxed and kissed her quickly. "I am about to make contact; would you like to be with me?"

"I would," she said brightly and held his hand as they walked back to the control room.

Everyone else was already there looking varying degrees of eager and nervous. Leda was telling the girls about the planet, leaving out anything about the people who had shunned her.

"Carini tried calling in, but I ignored it," Leda said when she saw them.

"Probably for the best," Locan said, then pushed a button. "Carini, come in, this is Locan."

"Locan! Good to hear from you man, it's been a long haul, I hope you have good news."

"Very good. I have collected three lost Prians."

"All that time and only three?"

"You need to know," Locan took a deep breath. "One is L."

Silence met his words. L gripped his arm so hard she knew her nails dug into his skin, she could feel his nervousness mix with her own and it was nearly overwhelming.

"K lived long enough to give birth to our daughter?" Carini said so quietly, it would have been missed if anyone had been so much as breathing in the room.

"She did," Locan replied.

"I will prepare for your arrival," Carini said, then the line clicked off.

"You're Carini's daughter?" Leda and Traylon shouted at the same time.

"Yes, she is. Now prepare the ship for landing," Locan ordered.

Leda and Traylon rushed to do as Locan ordered, even the other girls left the room as if they had a job to do, probably just to get out of the tense environment.

L cornered Leda moments before landing. "Tell me what you know of my father."

Leda pursed her lips. "He's pretty sexy for an old guy, nice enough. He never treated me as someone who doesn't deserve to exist, I guess now I know why." She shrugged. "You'll see soon enough."

L moved to the window which was now showing a jungle-like terrain and people rushing about. She spotted a few animals she didn't recognize, and tent structures set up. Locan had explained to her that the group moved often to stay hidden, and this particular spot had a space large enough to land the ship, which was good because it was easier to hide the ship on the ground than in the air.

She was excited for so many things, meeting her father, her people and getting her feet on solid ground. Fresh food and fresh air! She wondered if they would sleep in one of those tents or stay on the ship, it didn't seem reasonable to give up a comfortable room for a tent, but she'd be okay with whatever Locan wanted. For the last week they'd been sharing his room, but her things were still stacked up in hers.

"Brace yourselves," Traylon shouted out as the ground drew nearer.

L could see one man standing a bit apart from the crowd. He was tall and wide, long grey hair and even from this distance she felt certain it was her father. So intrigued by the possibility, she didn't notice anyone else who was gathering, and it wasn't until they touched the ground that she realized how many people were there, it looked to be about fifty! Old, young, and in between. No children though and L worried.

"When's the last time someone gave birth here?" she asked Locan.

"Years, I was one of the last. When people first got together here outside the city, a few babies were born, everyone was overjoyed, but the luck ran out quickly and I think the last baby born is only a few years younger than me. Rylin is the first breeder-born female to give birth that we've seen. Are you ready to greet your people, Princess?" Locan said, putting a hand on her back.

"Don't leave my side," she ordered.

"Yes, Ma'am," he teased, but she could feel he was as nervous as she was.

"What are *you* nervous about, you're a damn princess," Leda huffed beside her, gaining a sharp look from Locan.

The airlock door opened with a dramatic whoosh and the wet, hot air from outside rushed in and slapped her in the face. Along with it she was assaulted by the sweet smell of flowering foliage. Overall, it was pleasant and relaxing after a moment of getting used to it, not familiar, but somehow comforting.

"Home," she whispered, "And so many people."

"All waiting to see their new Princess," Leda said with a grunt.

"Shut up, Leda," Traylon hissed.

"Everyone shut it," Locan growled and stepped forward, pushing gently on L's back.

"Welcome home, Locan!" the grey-haired man called, stepping forward through the crowd.

"Carini, may I present L?" Locan said, pushing her forward slightly.

Murmurs went through the crowd as they realized that the Princess L had returned to Prias, but L barely registered the awe, she was consumed by the realization that she was looking into the face of her father. His eyes were green, reminding her of Locan's and although he was aged, he was still handsome and had a look of power about him, no doubt he was in control here.

"L," he breathed her name, coming forward and putting his hands on her shoulders. "You look like your mother," he said, pulling her in for a hug. She was certain she felt him shudder in her arms and when he pulled away, his eyes were glistening with unshed tears.

"Father," she said, a little unsure.

"It would seem so. I see Cerulean has chosen you as her hero." He touched the stars that marked half her face.

"I'm not sure why, but yeah, it seems so," she said with a nervous laugh.

"I hope your trip was enjoyable, Locan can be surly company," he said with a half-smile.

"It was great, actually."

"Come, meet your people, we have much to discuss." Carini grabbed her arm and pulled her into the waiting crowd, leaving Locan and the others behind.

L looked back, pleading in her eyes, she wanted Locan with her, she needed his support. He only nodded. This was something she'd have to get through on her own.

It was overwhelming, everyone wanted to touch her, greet her, and tell her how thankful they were that she was here, how they believed she was going to save them all. With each passing vote of confidence, she felt her nerves tighten, her anxiety ratchet up and her fear grow. There was no way she was all the things these people needed her to be, not alone anyway. Some of the men looked like Locan, and she assumed they were Warriors, that was good, they'd need the help if they decided on a full attack—something she never imagined would cross her mind. She was a doctor, not some kind of warlord.

After meeting so many people she couldn't remember a single name, Carini led her on a walk through the small settlement. She noticed Traylon trailing behind and wondered if Locan had ordered him to stick near just in case she needed help. She appreciated the thought, but was disappointed it wasn't Locan sticking near, what could he possibly be doing that was more important?

Carini showed her tents where people had made their homes, and where they kept supplies, a central cooking area and shared food supplies. There was no farming going on but gathering was abundant, and hunting, too, apparently; she saw dried meat, and someone was skinning something fresh that looked like a very large and very hairy pig.

"We will feast tonight in your honor, Daughter."

The way he called her daughter filled her with joy, she felt like she was dreaming, to be with her father! It was enough, she didn't need anything more to celebrate the occasion and certainly didn't want to be the center of attention any longer than necessary. "They shouldn't go to any trouble for me."

"The people want to honor you, their Princess. You can't imagine what your just being here means to them."

"I am not sure I can do much, but I hope to."

"You will, I am certain." His confidence made her nervous, what if she weren't everything they'd been waiting for?

When Carini finally led her to his private tent where they could talk, she hoped Locan would respond to her feelings of anxiety, she knew he could feel it, but where was he? Traylon stationed himself outside, giving them privacy, which she appreciated. The way he avoided catching her eye prickled her nerves all the more though and she felt like she might lose it soon if Locan didn't show up.

"So, tell me of your life, L, what do you know of your mother?"

"Where's Locan?" she asked, instead of answering.

"Oh, who knows, he usually seeks out the company of a lady when he returns to Prias," Carini said with a laugh, then frowned. "Sorry, I'm not used to the company of a princess, I suppose I should watch what I say."

"No, not at all," she gritted between clenched teeth. Anger and hurt replacing everything else she'd been feeling. She pushed it aside and told him of her life on Earth and her mother's letter, which he asked to see someday.

He told her his version of the events with her mother and how he'd run when Temis' guards had come to kill him. He'd barely made it out of the city alive and wandered for a month before finding the others. He'd heard rumors of what was happening in the city but never held out any real hope of finding his daughter again if she even actually existed.

"I assure you I exist," she laughed.

"I can see that, I am overjoyed! We will make plans tomorrow; we must move before your presence here gets back to the city."

"It may be too late for that. Jabon knows of my existence, and he could have easily beat us back here." L told him about their adventures getting here and why the small girl, Sansorin was so important. No one wanted to piss off a Goddess, even a half mortal one.

"It sounds like you are already proving the predictions right, you are a fierce protector, and you are unafraid of danger to yourself."

"I don't know if unafraid is the right word, but I certainly don't want to save myself over others. I want to help my people."

"You will, your presence alone will energize the cause."

L hoped it was true. Her stomach rumbled then, reminding her she hadn't eaten since breakfast.

"Oh my, I bet it's well past time to eat, the sun will set soon. I can show you to a tent that has been prepared for you and you can freshen up before dinner."

"Actually, we'll be returning to the ship, no need to take someone's tent from them," Locan said, walking in.

L gave him a sharp look, "Will we?"

Locan cocked his head curious to her harsh reply.

"You think to speak for the Princess?" Carini said with shock.

"I think to speak for my soul-wife," Locan said, standing a little straighter and notching his chin up.

Carini gasped and glared at Locan. "How dare you! You had no right!"

"I did everything I could to resist," Locan admitted quietly but he held his head high as if daring Carini to challenge him.

"And where the hell have you been all day?" L demanded, ignoring their argument.

"Making sure the other females had safe places to be and answering a million questions about what it means now that the Princess is back on the planet. Did you know that Jabon was spotted nearby in the last few days?" Locan glared at Carini.

L gasped and spun to look at her father. "Are we in danger? Did you know?"

"I heard the rumor, but often the Enforcers are seen in the jungle, never have they found our encampment, it is shielded by the blessings of the Goddesses."

"Oh," L said, relaxing a bit. "Still, this isn't good, they are looking for *me!*"

"We will keep you safe, you know that," Locan growled and his eyes flashed blue momentarily. "Even if it means leaving Prias."

"That is unacceptable," Carini insisted.

L crossed the space and hugged Locan, "I would not leave these people to suffer if there's something I can do to help, but thank you for the offer."

Carini watched them embrace and shook his head. "I should have expected this, I always knew there was something special about Locan and I can see that he's finally accepted every part of himself, that has to be your doing."

"I might have nudged him a bit," L admitted.

"You are your mother's daughter," he said, surprising L with a laugh. "She pursued me endlessly until I gave in against my better judgment." He reached out and tucked the streak of white hair behind L's ear. "I sometimes wish I'd been stronger, then she might still be here. But then you wouldn't be, I suppose."

"She might have been more help than I will be," L said quietly.

"*You*, my child, are what the God promised me when I was about to give up." Carini pushed up his sleeve and revealed a spattering of orange stars. "The God Titan came to me when I felt your mother die. We were soul-tied and I knew when hers left our reality to join the ancestors. I was going to join her, take my own life and be done with the horror that this planet had become. Titan stopped me. He promised that one day a Warrior woman would return to me and lead us in victory. I believe that is you, L."

"I don't know about the Warrior part, but here I am."

"I just can't believe that you already belong to someone else," Carini said with a hint of sadness in his voice.

L frowned, "I don't know about the belonging part."

Carini looked curiously at Locan. "Does she not understand what's happened?"

"She knows," Locan growled.

Carini pushed L behind him and growled back at Locan. Both men started to puff up as their Warriors began to surface.

"Oh, come on! You two are ridiculous. I am Locan's partner and lover, we shared pieces of our souls with each other, I still belong to myself, but everyone needs to take a couple of deep breaths."

Neither male moved.

L pushed between them, a hand on each chest. "Can we at least all agree that it's dinner time, I'm starving."

Locan broke first, looking at her with concern. "You should eat, you'll need your strength." His eyes were full blue, showing his Warrior.

"Feed me, my Warrior," she said with a wink. He growled at her and it warmed her.

"I believe a feast has been prepared to celebrate your arrival, and apparently we are celebrating a union as well." He looked at her with seriousness. "As long as this is truly your chosen path, you want to be one with this Warrior?"

"I do," L agreed, with a smile for her father.

The people had indeed prepared a feast. Tables were set up around a firepit with enough food to feed twice as many and it was all unrecognizable, but it smelled good. L was reintroduced to too many people to remember and when she sat down next to her father with Locan on her other side, she really did feel a bit like a princess.

"Where's Leda and the other women from the ship?" Traylon was next to Locan, but her other friends were missing.

"They are probably with the others," Carini said as he accepted a plate of some kind of meat dish.

"Others?" she questioned.

"The breeder babies, they don't usually join us," Carini explained.

"What?" L demanded; sure she couldn't have heard that right.

"It's just that they are more comfortable with each other," Carini explained.

"Are you fucking kidding me right now?" L had been warned, but she didn't think it would bother her this much. She kind of liked Leda, she felt nothing but sorrow for the things Tanea and Rylin had gone through, and none of them deserved to be treated with disrespect, to be cast out by the rebels because of the way they were conceived. She stood up and glared around the table. "Fuck you all, you think you're better because you know your parents, because you were created consensually?" she looked over at her father. "I refuse to be a part of this."

L walked away from the silent table, she knew Locan followed, not because she heard his movements, but because her soul was crying out for his support, and she could feel his answering.

"Where the hell are they?" she hissed, not wanting to look stupid wandering in the wrong direction but also not wanting to go back and ask.

"Take a left," Locan whispered.

"If I'm here to change things, let's start with this," she said, taking a sharp turn.

Locan put a hand on her arm and gently led her. When they got near the other group, the chatter and laughter was loud and warming. It was a small table set modestly with twenty men and women around it, laughing and eating, all with white-blonde hair and deep blue eyes.

"Wow," L gasped, she knew there was a passing resemblance between Tanea, Rylin, and Leda but this obvious similarity was surprising.

The group froze and looked at her, most just curious, Leda looked pissed.

"Princess L," a tall lean female stood and offered her hand.

L took it happily. "Sorry, I don't remember the names I got earlier."

"Oh, most of us weren't part of the welcome committee," she said with a laugh. "My name is Therin."

"Therin, may we join your table?"

"Of course! All are welcome here," Therin said quickly, and everyone shuffled a bit.

Leda gave an approving smile as L and Locan sat. A short time later, Traylon walked over and forced space next to Tanea who pretended to ignore him, L didn't miss the small smile that touched her lips though, and it warmed her heart. She was rooting for those two.

"So, you're here to save us?" Therin asked as they ate.

"I'm here to figure out where I came from, and yeah, if I can do something about the situation on this planet I will."

"Cerulean believes you will," Therin said, motioning to her face.

"Yeah, I guess so."

"The Goddesses don't appear to us halflings," Therin said with a shrug. "But we believe they are looking out for us too."

"That's not true," L said quickly, then she felt her face heat as she realized how her words could be taken. "I mean, that they don't appear to the babies born of breeders," she quickly corrected. "Leda, tell them."

Leda glared at L. "Amber has come to me; she has gifted me, and I know that L is loyal and true. If we were going to follow anyone into battle against that horrid city, it would be her. *If* she could convince her father to treat us like equals. We won't fight beside people who think we are less than they are."

Therin nodded agreement and L wondered if Leda was some kind of leader here too. At the very least, L could tell that Leda's opinion was respected.

L took a deep breath and met eyes around the table as she spoke. "I was born on Earth, birthed from a mother who escaped the Hospital and Temis. I may have been conceived differently than most of you, but I feel no more connected to the city than any of you do. *They* have every reason to want to take the city that they left and grew up dreaming of, but for us, we have other options. I respect whatever decision you all want to make; I think we'll be more successful together, both halves of this beast taking back from those who should never have been there in the first place. I don't know if the others would attempt it without you, and I think they need to be made to admit that they are not strong enough without you." L felt confident in her words and when she felt Locan squeeze her leg gently, she knew he agreed with her words too.

"And live as servants there instead of here? No thanks," a man huffed, and a few others murmured agreement.

"Absolutely not, I am the rightful ruler, right?" L couldn't even believe she was saying it, but it was true, and she needed to project some serious attitude here. "I would never allow anyone to be forced into any position they didn't choose."

"And you support her in this?" Therin asked Locan. "It's obvious you two are in some kind of relationship beyond protection. I assume that's why Sorlyn is pouting in her tent tonight instead of here with us."

L ignored the flare of jealousy and forced herself not to look at Locan with hurt and accusation, she let their soul-tie tell him, flooding him with it. She felt his hand grip her leg firmly and she knew he was feeling it.

"Yes, she is my soul-wife and I support her fully. I haven't spent my life retrieving all of you, just to see you dumped off to a life of servitude," Locan said firmly.

"And I support any decision my daughter makes. I will make sure there is no Prian who doesn't understand that we must work together, or we will all fail."

L turned to see her father standing behind her looking embarrassed. "Just because things are easier one way, doesn't make it right, I should have stepped in from the beginning when the first of you were brought here and treated poorly. I owe you all an apology."

Therin winked at Carini. "We accept, Carini, you've always been kind. None of us thought you agreed, but we were disappointed when you didn't stop it."

Carini nodded, "I never wanted to be in charge, it's not what *I* was born to do. I see the error I've let pass for too long. It will go on no longer, come, let us join tables and eat as one."

The group moved quickly, picking up whole tables and moving them to join the main group. They were welcomed cautiously, but it was a start.

"Here one day and already making demands, Princess," Traylon teased after dinner.

"Maybe just valid suggestions," she said with a smile.

TWENTY-FIVE

Locan sent L to the ship with Traylon and Leda after the meal was over and cleaned up. He was going to seek out Carini, but first, he needed to speak with Therin.

"You had to bring up Sorlyn?" Locan hissed at her.

"I don't think it's fair to Sorlyn and I don't think it's fair to L, to keep the relationship in the dark."

"I don't think it's your business to bring up."

"Did she think you were pure before you bedded her?"

"No," he gritted out.

"Then she would have to be stupid to assume you had never engaged in relations with another member of this small tribe."

"I never made promises to Sorlyn."

"No, you didn't. But she did, didn't she?"

Locan glared at the woman. Why was she trying to cause trouble? "What is it you are after?"

Therin crossed the short distance and poked a finger to Locan's chest. "I am not willing to put myself or my people at risk if that princess is the type to throw a fit and make a stink because of something as dumb as sex. If she can't handle your ex-girlfriend existing in the same space as her, I know she isn't the savior we've been waiting for."

Locan was surprised by Therin's thinking, it made sense. She was testing L's loyalty to the people over her personal desire.

"Therin, you are a great leader, I hope that you join us tomorrow as we begin discussions, we will need a good plan before we make a move."

"Accepted," she said with a curt nod. "And Locan," she called as he was about to leave her tent.

"Yes?"

"For what it's worth, I like her, and I *do* think she's what we have been waiting for."

Locan looked back at the woman and smiled. "Me too, I'll talk to Sorlyn again and make sure the two meet tomorrow, there's no place for jealousy when we have a battle to fight."

Therin nodded approvingly.

Locan went to the tent he'd visited earlier in the day. He found Sorlyn pouting on a cushion, petting a small beast with sharp teeth and claws, her little pet that hated him and had more than once bitten into his flesh for being in what he deemed his personal space.

"What do you want? Have I been banished?" Sorlyn hissed.

"Your pouting is childish and unexpected, Sorlyn."

"*Unexpected!* You return with a soul-wife and *my* reaction is unexpected?"

"You know I never promised you anything, we were only having fun."

"I offered you my soul many times," she hissed and the beast in her lap hissed as well.

"I told you every time that I wasn't interested in that kind of thing. I should have left you when you offered the first time, I realize that now. It wasn't fair that I continued to see you when I knew you had feelings beyond mine."

"No, it wasn't fair."

"I'm sorry, Sorlyn, I never meant to hurt you."

She gave a heavy sigh and looked at him with glistening eyes. "I guess I know that, and it makes me mad that I can't really hate you for it."

"Will you meet her tomorrow?"

"I will consider it."

"Thank you."

Locan left her tent feeling slightly better, but knew he was going to have to have a similar conversation with L and that felt daunting, so first he sought out Carini.

"What do you know of the Jabon sightings?"

"You were just seen coming from Sorlyn's tent, am I to trust you have not decided to step out on your relationship with my daughter?"

"Your spies work fast," Locan grumbled.

"Answer the question, Locan. I am her father, and I will not allow you to hurt or embarrass her."

"I was only setting things straight with the woman, I don't want her pouting to get in the way of our mission."

Carini nodded, satisfied with that answer. "Jabon started showing up on the outskirts about a week ago. So far, he's been unable to break through our field of protection, but it has made hunting difficult, we have to wait for an animal to wander inside the circle. We can't risk moving camp while he's so close, because we would lose that protection until we set up again somewhere new."

Locan frowned. "He is searching for L; I expected that."

"She's safe as long as she stays within the circle."

"I'll explain the boundaries to her, and I *will* keep her safe," Locan promised, then hugged his leader and friend.

When he got back to the ship, he found L curled up on his bed, fast asleep, their discussions would have to wait until morning. He smiled down at her as he undressed.

She is perfection, his Warrior purred in his mind.

"Yes, and all ours," Locan whispered as he laid down next to her and pulled her body against his own. He inhaled her scent and closed his eyes, delighting in this perfect moment. He was home on Prias with his soul-wife, the Princess was on the planet, and she was already bringing its people together. Their future was unsure, but the outlook was better than he'd ever seen it.

L was surprised to wake up alone, she'd felt Locan join her on the bed last night, but she'd been too tired to say anything, even though she'd felt like they needed a little air-clearing conversation. A lot had happened yesterday, and it had exhausted her body and mind.

She showered and dressed in shorts and a t-shirt; the weather was balmy here. She didn't find anyone else on the ship when she left the room, so she decided to venture out. Hoping she'd run into Locan or her father right off.

The white-haired girl who was hanging out around the entrance to the ship was not someone she remembered meeting yesterday, but she also knew that she had met and forgot a lot of people yesterday, so she couldn't be sure.

"Princess L," the girl called with a friendly wave and smile.

"Good morning," L called back.

"I was thinking I could show you how to do some gathering this morning," the girl held up a couple of baskets. "My name is Sor."

Something tingled the back of L's brain, but she couldn't put a finger on it. Her eyes darted around, but she didn't see anyone familiar enough to reassure her. "I should find Locan," L muttered.

"It's important for everyone to pitch in, Princess," Sor said, and L immediately felt challenged. Was this some kind of a test, to see if she thought she was too good for menial tasks?

"Of course, let's go."

Sor's eyes lit up and the smile on her face didn't quite match.

L followed Sor in the opposite direction of the camp, through thick jungle that look surprisingly similar to Earth foliage, except for the scent. It was something she'd never encountered, but she liked a lot.

"What sorts of things are we looking for?" she finally asked when they had been walking for a few minutes.

"Something special. Berries that are sweet and ripe this time of year, but they are a little bit of a trek. The others will really appreciate our effort though."

L was regretting her decision not to eat breakfast by the time Sor stopped and pointed. They were at a little clearing covered in what resembled thick pink moss, and in the middle like a little island, was a huge green bush covered in plump orange berries. A furry white animal raced through the clearing as they walked. It resembled a small dog but had a tail similar to a raccoon and short tusks hung from a wide mouth.

"Tanscat," Sor said, indicating the animal. "They are not friendly."

"Thanks for the warning," L laughed, she had been debating trying to pet the thing, it looked so soft. "What are the berries called?" L realized that although she'd learned the Prian language, she didn't automatically know what words went with what things, like when Sor said Tanscat she immediately recognized the word as being a Prian animal, but until she saw what it was, the word had meant nothing to her mind.

"Belbins, they are extremely sweet and pop in the mouth. Try one," Sor held out a handful of berries.

L took one and threw it into her mouth, it did pop between her teeth and the taste was sweet. Quite unexpectedly, her head fuzzed, her stomach clenched, and when she finished throwing up, she was surrounded by some very satisfied-looking men.

"Shit," she whispered, her eyelids heavy and her limbs numb.

"Such language for a princess," a man with a long, jagged scar on his cheek sneered. "Allow me to introduce myself, I am Jabon, and I am going to get you safely back to your uncle."

"Locan," she tried to scream but a sharp pain hit her neck and her world went black.

When consciousness returned to L, she found herself lying on a cot in a very sterile environment. She sat up slowly, rubbing at a painful bruise on her neck.

"Sorry, we had to knock you out, if you hadn't puked up the berries it wouldn't have been necessary, they would have knocked you out for long enough to transport without added help."

L spun around and nearly fell off the bed. The man who spoke was not the one she'd seen briefly in the clearing. This man was elderly; deep wrinkles marked his skin, and he was bald. He wore black robes that hung off a bony body and he leaned heavily on a cane. Nothing about his physical form seemed intimidating but his eyes were deep, black and soulless, and she wondered if he'd sold that soul some time ago.

"Uncle Temis," she gasped, somehow knowing this was the face of evil that had haunted her mother and everyone else on this planet. Her eyes darted around the room, assessing again. She was in a windowless room and the only doorway was the one he currently stood in. She thought she might be able to get past him, but she doubted there weren't strong young men nearby ready to help him if needed.

"I'm impressed, you recognize your kin."

"I recognize evil when I see it," she retorted, and he laughed.

"Spunky, like your mother; too bad she couldn't see my vision. I am hoping you'll show more shrewdness." He offered her his arm. "Walk with me, let me explain myself before you judge."

She shuddered at the thought of touching him; but saw no reason to not get as much information as she possibly could. She stepped forward and grabbed his elbow. Her arm immediately flared painfully, her stars warning her that this was not a good man. *Where the hell were you when I was entering that damn clearing?* She thought harshly.

They walked out of the room and emerged into a long hallway and as she'd suspected, there were three large men waiting there, Warriors, she recognized them immediately and glared at each one. How dare they abandon their people for Temis and his insanity. Temis talked as they went past door after door, all closed.

"I saw our people suffering greatly and I sought help, like a good brother and Prian. I went far and wide, looking for a planet that might hold an answer to our reproductive problems. I found it with guidance from the God Coal. I brought back the Doctors, Saval and Raval from the planet Unbree. They held the key; they knew how to manipulate the body to produce a child."

"Artificial insemination?" L asked.

"Yes, the Earth term fits. I offered a way for our species to survive and have delivered on that promise."

"Did you sell your soul for power?"

Temis laughed and pulled up a sleeve, revealing a spattering of black circles. "Nothing is without a price, though I have given up on that sort of thing. It's really a young man's game and Jabon has proven himself a worthy successor. Everything I do, is for the good of the Prian people."

"You kidnapped my mother, locked her in the Hospital," L accused. "You tried to force her to marry you!"

Temis opened a door and led her into a large area that looked like it might be a common living space, still no windows and very sterile, that's when L knew, she was already inside the Hospital.

"I only brought her here to keep her safe, as I wish to do for you, child. I would have kept you both safe and happy."

"You took her away from the man she loved and tried to have him killed!"

Temis frowned, "Yes, a shame I wasn't able to remove that blight, it is terribly unseemly for a princess to give a piece of her soul to a member of her guard. It was never allowed when Achromic was around, I do think that's one thing she did right."

L pursed her lips and resisted the urge to tell him she'd done the same. She didn't think it would aid her in the moment. "So now what, you have me locked up here, do you plan to inseminate me?"

"No child, you are no doubt perfectly fertile, as was your mother, somehow. I plan to guide you in choosing a proper mate, someone who will help you to rule Prias properly."

"Great, let me rule, I'll start with sending the Doctors back to the hell-hole planet they came from."

"Oh no, that would never do. In fact," Temis motioned to his right, and she turned to see a man standing there, he was tall, white-blonde hair and deep blue eyes, he looked no older than her, but something told her she wasn't seeing something. "Dr. Raval has agreed to be your husband."

"Fuck you!" L hissed and stepped away from Temis, putting as much distance as she could between herself and the two men.

Her back hit the chest of one of the guards and she stopped moving.

"Don't you see, it is the only thing that will heal our people. The Doctors have a special type of power, not only can they inseminate our infertile females, but they have managed to retain their youth all this time. We can breed a people here on Prias impervious to age and more fertile than any other."

"No way. The children of breeders who escaped and are now living with the rebels have not given birth, the Doctor's children are no more immune to whatever is affecting this world than the rest of us."

Temis laughed quietly. "That's because they were not given the injection after they were born, those who were born here and kept in the city have received the proper injections, they are able to breed bountifully! Your people, *our* people are flourishing here."

L shook her head, none of this made sense, and there was no way she was marrying some ancient old doctor, no matter how young he looked.

"I'm already someone's soul-wife," she revealed, hoping to dislodge their plan.

Temis hissed and Dr. Raval glared. "That is unfortunate, we will have to ascertain if you are pregnant before we complete the ceremony."

"How about fuck no," L hissed and jabbed her elbow into the rock-hard stomach behind her, then bolted for the door.

No one followed her or tried to stop her, she flung the door open and found herself on a balcony about thirty stories in the air. Her stomach hit the railing and she latched onto it desperately as she stared down to the ground. Below her, a sheer cliff of steel surrounded by small, brightly colored buildings, and bustling people. In the distance she saw a river that ran green and brilliant, shining with reflected sunlight and even farther, the beginning of the jungle where Locan must be. She closed her eyes and felt for him, and a bit of comfort surrounded her. He was alive, she felt their connection and his fear, his anger and his Warrior's desire to kill and destroy. They were coming for her, she just had to live long enough for them to get here.

"The crown is the key," a voice whispered and although she couldn't see it, she knew it was coming from Cerulean.

L wanted to ignore the Goddess, she should have been around earlier when L was getting kidnapped, why the hell was she showing up with advice now? But L knew, her arm tingled as things started to piece together in her mind and a plan formed, she just hoped Locan was making the same connections.

"Take me back to my room," she demanded when she returned to the room.

"Of course, you must be very confused and worried. I want you to feel safe, I am your uncle, and I am only looking out for your best interest."

L resisted rolling her eyes. She did notice that Dr. Raval was no longer in the room, for that she was grateful. "Where are the other women?"

"They are resting, I didn't want to overwhelm you with lots of people. They will be so excited to meet their new queen, we must have a crowning ceremony soon too, it's been far too long since Prias has had a queen in command."

"Actually, I want to eat, and I want to be shown to my mother's palace." Her plan solidifying in her mind. "I am the Princess; I want to be treated like one and living here is not it. Take me to the palace and I want a feast. Crown me tonight, I would take over immediately, with your blessing of course." L nearly gagged on the sweetness of her last words, he bought it though, so it was worthwhile.

His grin was wide and his eyes bright. "Of course, you should be treated well, I only want you to be safe."

"These men will keep me safe, I have no doubt," L indicated the guards. "I will *not* remain here like a common breeder!" She pouted and stamped a foot, playing the part of spoiled princess.

"Of course, of course. Let us go to the palace and tonight, my niece, you will be Queen." He held out his arm again and she took it quickly, hiding the disdain from her face.

TWENTY-SIX

Locan knew as soon as she was in trouble. Every part of him had reacted and the Warrior had exploded out so fast he knew he'd scared those around them. Everything was black except the bright blue dots in his vision that told them where she was. They ran, fast and hard; it wasn't enough. They arrived in the clearing, and she was gone, the only thing that had kept them from killing Sorlyn right then and there was the knowledge that she was the only one who knew what had happened to their L.

Now Locan was landing his ship as near to the city as he dared. It was full of their people and weapons, and they still wanted to kill Sorlyn. For now, having her locked in the ship's prison cell was enough to temporarily satisfy the Warrior.

"You need to think clearly, Locan, we can't just pour into the city screaming for a fight," Carini was saying for the hundredth time.

"Maybe *you* can't," Locan grumbled, and his Warrior agreed heartily.

"My plan makes sense, and you know it," Carini continued. "Therin will take a group through the city and find out what they can, if we know where she is then we will be much more capable of rescuing her."

"You want me to wait while she's in there?"

"Yes," Carini said simply with a heavy sigh. "I know what you are going through, it tore me apart to know that K was in there without me to protect her, but I knew she was alive and that was enough. You know L is alive, feel her soul in yours, she is alive and as long as she is alive, we have a chance to save her. If we go in and get killed, then she can't be saved."

Locan hated that Carini was right, he could feel that she was alive, but he could also feel that she was frightened. He wanted to run through the city destroying anything in the path to her. It wasn't a well thought out plan.

"Fine, send Therin," Locan hissed and stalked back to his office. He couldn't talk to anyone right now, not while he was sitting around waiting and L was suffering.

"Dude, you could really mess this shit up." Violaceous and Verduous appeared in his office, and he was tempted to throw something at them.

"What the hell do you two want? Why didn't you stop this from happening?"

"You know we can't interfere like that, besides, the path that we are on is destiny. But Mom did send us with a message," Violaceous said with a smile.

"She said that you need to let her take the crown, only then will she have the power to take full control," Verduous said giddily.

"Oh, very helpful," he grumbled.

They giggled and disappeared.

Locan poured himself a drink and settled in to wallow until Therin's group returned with information.

"The crown," he grumbled.

The crown will give her control over the Royal Guard, his Warrior said thoughtfully.

"Not without Achromic it won't."

So go find her.

"Right, if I knew where she was—" Locan froze, remembering a line from K's letter.

K had heard the rumors, but it was too late for her.

"Shit," Locan growled.

By the time Therin's group returned, Locan was dying to get their plan underway, and the group's information confirmed it.

"They are having a coronation ceremony tonight," Therin reported. "The Princess has been taken to the palace to wait, and after that," she looked at Locan quickly then away. "There will be a marriage, L and Dr. Raval."

Kill everyone! His Warrior roared, and his vision turned red, but something pricked at him and he looked down to see a purple and green star appear on his hand as it gripped his knife.

"We have to let the ceremony take place," Locan growled.

Everyone turned to look at him with shock. He hadn't shared their plan yet.

"Not the marriage, obviously, not that it would matter, she's ours," he growled, "but the crowning. She must be Queen. That's the only way she'll have the power she needs."

"What power?" Traylon asked.

"Achromic abandoned us, power over the Guards means nothing anymore," Carini said.

"But I know where Achromic is."

Carini's eyes lit up with excitement. "Dear Goddess, yes, if she wears the crown and Achromic is there to empower her, she will be able to order the Guards. Locan, does she know? Do we have time?"

"I hope so," he hissed down at his shimmering hand.

· · ·

L stood in a room that had been her mother's. It had been recently dusted but otherwise it looked like nothing had been touched in many years and she relished the knowledge that she was seeing something so personal to her mother. The warmth of being close to her things was overwhelming and she embraced the comfort of it for a moment, letting her worry ease a bit.

"Your mother would love to know you are here in her personal space after all this time."

L spun at the familiar voice.

Verduous floated near the window with a satisfied smirk on her face. "Princess L, always getting into trouble."

"More like always getting pushed into danger."

"Same thing," Verduous said with a giggle. "I am here to make sure you understand the significance of the crown."

"It'll give me the power to control the Royal Guard, as long as Achromic is there to give me her blessing."

"The Royal Guard members cannot deny the Queen. If your Warrior succeeds in freeing my grandmother, they will be the weapon you need to take out Temis, but Jabon is something else. He holds a lot of my grandfather's power, and he will not be easily killed." She disappeared then and L sat on the bed.

The plan was good, but it was full of holes and what-ifs, and she had no idea if it would be enough to take down Jabon full of Coal's power.

Over the next few hours, she was waited on by silent and frightened servants, all of whom were obviously born of breeders. She was brought food, that she had to admit was delicious. Then she was led to a bathing chamber and given clothes to wear. A brilliant red and gold tunic and pants that were soft as silk and light as air. She felt truly royal as her hair was braided delicately and her makeup done with a finesse she'd never have managed on her own. The result was breathtaking, and she twirled in front of a mirror, delighting in this fairytale moment. The orphan child was about to be crowned Queen! Too bad it was under duress and supposed to be followed by a wedding to a man who was possibly hundreds of years old and very much not her type.

"You look ravishing," Temis said when he came to collect her from her room.

"Thanks," she said without feeling.

"Are you excited for the ceremony, my niece?"

"I am," and she meant it.

Temis led her into a ballroom full of people dressed in bright colors and fancy fabrics. These were not servants or workers, and most were older, and not breeder-born. There were some who were obviously breeder-born there too, dressed just as nicely, these must be the children Temis was selling to his contemporaries, raised in wealthy families.

"Where's the Royal Guard? I demand to be protected at all times," L hissed.

"Of course, my dear, they are near." Temis pointed out several large-bodied men wearing black uniforms. She noted each one—ten in all—they were integral to her plan.

"Tell me, how is it that more Guard members were born?"

"Magic of the Doctors, they managed to breed some Prians naturally, specifically to produce them."

This meant they were untouched by whatever alien material the Doctors were injecting into the others. She hoped it was true, because it would mean they truly were bound to the crown and Achromic. She had a momentary thought about how her power would affect Locan, would she be able to control him, would she want to? Would their love be lost, their bond broken? Fear filled her but she had to ignore it, if she lost everything with Locan but managed to save the planet, it was what she had to do.

Murmurs followed them through the room as she was led to

a stage and a throne. The Doctors were there, and so was Jabon.

"I prefer to be alone on the stage," L pouted and stuck out her lip, really putting herself into the part.

"My dear, you must have support and protection, the people must see that you have the backing of not only me, but the Doctors and Jabon. He's become an important part of our city."

"I don't like his face," she said honestly.

Temis laughed, "A princess always has a delicate eye. I will send him to the back, so you don't have to look at him."

She sighed, it would have to be enough, she didn't trust him not to interfere.

The ceremony began as soon as she stepped on the stage. Temis addressed the crowd, introduced her to a roaring round of applause and then the crown was brought out on a black pillow. The crown itself was simple, a silver filigree with diamond-like stones covering it. It caught the light brilliantly. When it was lifted onto her head, she felt a shiver run through her and a brightness exploded in her mind, she knew what it was immediately, Achromic, the mother Goddess, her white-hot power filled L, and she felt like she was invincible for a second. It faded quickly and she was back to feeling herself, only more confident.

A gasp filled the room and even Temis stammered. "My d-dear, look at your face."

L turned to the window, and the side of her face that wasn't covered in blue stars, now held a bright white sunburst.

"You've been marked by Achromic," he gasped.

A hiss behind her drew her attention and she saw Jabon's eyes flare black and narrow on her. He was dangerous, the light in her recognized it.

'Coal,' a voice in her head whispered and L didn't even question it.

"Royal Guard!" L commanded with a voice that was layered

with power.

"No!" Jabon yelled and leaped forward, knocking Temis to the ground in his haste to get to her.

The old man groaned and rolled to safety; L managed to sidestep the incoming threat but ended up backed right into the arms of Dr. Raval.

"My bride," he sneered.

"Guards!" L called again and they were there, swords drawn and pointing at the men.

"Kill them all," she said before she could stop herself.

Chaos ensued. The guests scattered, none willing to risk their lives for this coup. Temis was the first to die. Dr. Raval was next, a sword to the throat while his arms still held L.

"I wasn't sure you understood," one of the Guard members said with a smile and a wink as he offered her his hand. Around them, swords clashed, and a dark fog filled the room.

"I understand enough," L laughed and let the man drag her toward a door.

She caught sight of Dr. Saval getting a sword to the chest and that only left one.

"This isn't possible!" Jabon shouted, black smoke billowing out around him. "She can't give you her power, she's contained!"

Jabon was suddenly there, between her and the door. The Guard held up his sword to defend her, but she knew it wouldn't be enough.

"We made sure to release her in time."

Locan's voice hit her and every muscle in her body relaxed, everything was going to be all right.

"It's not possible," Jabon hissed.

"Isn't it?" a voice filled the room but there was no body to contain it.

"K had heard of the soul of the Prian people being under the city," Locan said. "She left those words in a letter to L. It wasn't hard to figure out if it was true."

"You read it!" L was momentarily offended, then quickly got over it. This wasn't the time.

"Coal contained his wife there for years, making the Prian people weak and infertile."

"I deserved my time!" A booming voice answered and this time it was male, Coal. Jabon shivered at the sound and took a step back.

"And you sold your soul to be a part of it," Locan growled at Jabon. "Guard, take her to safety, I've got this."

L was pulled away as Locan moved toward Jabon who was ready to fight, sword up and anger in his eyes.

"Come, my Queen," The Guard said as he pulled her to the door.

She was joined by Traylon and Leda, but she didn't want to go, she was safe, her people were safe, she was sure. "I can't leave Locan." She looked at Traylon. "He can't do this on his own."

"He's not alone," Leda said.

L turned and saw a white figure floating behind Locan. She was amazing, huge, and blindingly bright. L had to squint as she looked at her. White hair flowed around a black, naked body, her eyes were shining like two suns, and her lips were the color of blood. She was a horrifying sight, but L knew, she was on their side.

Coal was equally terrifying as he appeared behind Jabon. Just as large as his wife, his body was a red so deep it was almost black and his hair was black with highlights of gold, his eyes were bright red and he looked like something even her nightmares wouldn't be able to imagine.

The two watched each other with hatred burning between them, reflecting the look Locan and Jabon were giving each other.

Death was in the air, waiting to take some or all of these people, and L felt her throat close, so much fear for her love and her people.

Coal made the first move and Jabon imitated it, throwing out a hand, and a black bolt of power shot from his palm, hitting Achromic in the chest and knocking her back a step.

Locan got a dagger to the chest and fell back a step. L screamed and tried to rush forward. Leda and Traylon held her arms as she struggled.

Achromic roared and lifted two hands, shooting fiery light out of her palms at Coal. They landed at his neck and his roar of pain was satisfying.

Locan pulled the dagger from his chest at the same time and flung it at Jabon's neck, slicing deep and a shower of crimson blood sprayed. He screamed and covered the wound with his hands, but it didn't do any good, the blood seeped from between fingers, and he fell to his knees.

Locan was the clear winner and he stepped forward, sword drawn, ready to take the head off this terrible foe.

Achromic launched her body across the space and tackled Coal. They exploded in a fiery explosion and disappeared.

Locan swung hard and Jabon's head rolled across the now silent room.

It was over.

L looked at Locan with her mouth hanging open. They were both bloody and breathing hard, but she didn't care, she flung herself into his arms and held on tight, showering his face with kisses.

"Locan, I didn't know if you would come."

"Nothing could have kept me away, you have a piece of my soul, remember."

"Oh my God! Locan, can we, are we still?" She couldn't make her thoughts stabilize enough to express her worry.

"L, settle down, it's all fine now."

"But Achromic's power," she whispered, her hands on his face and staring up into his blue eyes, this was the Warrior she was talking to. "Warrior, has anything changed?" She trusted him to tell her the truth no matter what. Locan would spare her feelings, not the Warrior.

"Nothing," he growled and crushed his mouth to hers in a possessing kiss.

She sighed when he finally pulled away, her knees weak. "Good, because I have a lot of work to do and I am hoping I can find a good man to be my King," she teased.

"How about a strong man who makes plenty of mistakes but loves you endlessly?" he said, his eyes now their brilliant green.

"That works too."

A white light filled the room, stopping all conversation. Achromic appeared with blood in her hair and a sadness in her eyes.

"I have destroyed him, let the Prian people rejoice and worship me once again," Achromic proclaimed.

L wasn't sure she liked the sound of that, but she knew better than to argue with an all-powerful Goddess.

"Achromic, we are forever grateful. I hope to do you proud in my rule of these people," L said, not sure where exactly the words were coming from, but they felt right.

The smile on Achromic's face told her she'd hit it right.

"My daughter will continue to watch you closely to see that you do," she said ominously and disappeared.

It was more than a year before things settled into a comfortable rhythm within the city; Prians and those who had been born from the Hospital tentatively working together and learning to respect each other. Traylon finally convinced Tanea to marry him, and Leda settled down with Rylin happily raising Ferlin and Sansorin together.

Two more years passed before L and Locan welcomed their own princess into the world. Achromic was there to bless M, and L couldn't imagine a happier existence though at times she still missed Aunt Sarah and Katherine. Perhaps someday she'd convince Locan to take them back to Earth for a visit, to let M see where her mother had grown up. L knew that the experience of seeing where her own mother had grown up had changed her, she thought M might feel the same way. Of course, there would have to be something done about her face, L would never be able to walk down the street looking the way she did now, even if it was a great sign of importance on Prias, the marks of the Goddesses would cause a stir on the streets of North Idaho.

A SPIDER IN THE GARDEN

We hope that you enjoyed this release from 5 Prince Publishing. Here is an excerpt from Courtney Davis', A Spider in the Garden.

A SPIDER IN THE GARDEN

CHAPTER ONE

Aranha walked through the shadows of the city, same as every night, dressed in ripped up black jeans, a black tank top, and black boots. Her long silver hair was braided down her back and although a passerby might not notice, she had three knives tucked strategically into her outfit. Her black eyes darted around, assessing those she passed, wondering if they had left anything in her web, wondering if she would be seeking them out later. She was vigilant as ever for danger, knowing how quickly the tables could turn, how swiftly she could become the hunted. She knew which parts of the city to avoid and she was a master at hiding when she needed to. She hadn't survived two hundred years alone without learning a few tricks.

She strode into an alley where she often found what she was looking for. A web hung nearly invisible between a broken light and a brick wall. She stepped close and reached up, a small brown spider darted away quickly, heading back to the shadows. She smiled at it.

"Don't worry, little friend," she crooned and it stepped out, peering at her curiously with its many black eyes. "I'm only here for the web."

She swept the thin silk into her palm and watched as it glistened on her skin, she loved this part. Her mind filled with images and words, memories and thoughts. She sifted through them, threw out the mundane, the boring and the happy. She was looking for misery, she was looking for lust and she was looking for the perverse.

She wasn't disappointed.

"You could have told me he just passed by," she scolded the spider and turned.

She saw his face clearly in her mind, it was attached to the memory he'd left on the web. Memories were funny things, a person remembered not only what happened or what they did; they often remembered what they thought they looked like while they did it. Sometimes it was more of a third person experience, not always completely accurate, but she'd had lots of practice sorting out what was real and what was fictional in memories. So not only did Aranha get to see the deed that was done, but the face of the perpetrator as well, or at least a personal approximation of their face. People were terrible judges of their own look most of the time. Luckily, she'd been at this for quite a few years and she was able to reconcile the memory of a face with reality, with sufficient accuracy.

The face she saw this time, she recognized passing only moments before. She moved quickly to follow, sliding through the thin crowds. She formed a web between her fingers, sifting as she went, looking for thoughts from him. Brains were as unique as fingerprints and their patterns were marked on the thoughts the webs caught. Even without a face in it, she could match a thought or memory to a person if she'd already found their fingerprint before.

"Hey baby, you lost?" A boy of maybe twenty called from where he was crouched on a stoop. He was dressed in low slung, baggy jeans and a tight white tank top. His dyed-blond hair was cut short and he had a sly smile on his face. His thoughts drifted into the web; *Sexy thing, I wish she would come sit on my lap. I bet she's a firecracker in the sack. She could handle this dick.* He got up to follow her quick pace. "Hey, I'm talking to you. I can help you. I can get you where you need to be." He gave a dark laugh.

Aranha crushed the web in her hand and spun around, she didn't need him to follow her. "Go home, boy. I'm not interested in your little dick."

"Whoa, you got quite the mouth on you! Sounds like you need someone to teach you some manners." He sauntered closer.

She didn't have time to lure him away and teach him a lesson on respecting women, she had a mission. The fact that he was inhibiting her right now was irritating, but she knew he was harmless. His thoughts had been lecherous, not violent. He thought of himself as a Don Juan and couldn't imagine a woman resisting his advances. Of course, if she were to respond to them, he would likely not know how to take things to the next level. He looked like an idiot and probably lived in his mother's basement while telling people she was just his roommate. She let him stare at her for a moment, taking in her fully black eyes, they never passed for human. Then she opened her mouth and let her long black fangs extend.

That did the trick. She could smell the urine as he pissed his pants, standing frozen to his spot. He wasn't even man enough to run for his life, he'd stand there and let her eat him. "Stupid boy," she hissed and turned, rushing now to try and catch up to the man she'd been tracking.

Aranha spun another web in her hand and sifted once again, irritated that the stupid boy may have ruined her chances. She didn't always succeed in finding the owner of thoughts she decided to pursue, but she rarely failed, and this was a situation she refused to give up on.

She wasn't sure why she was here, but she knew she could do something about the other monsters out there. She'd seen that he had a small boy in his basement, chained up like a goddamn animal! She let the anger fill her and sharpen her senses; this kind of disgusting being didn't deserve to walk the earth. This wasn't someone she could let slip through her web.

Aranha hurried through the streets, passing people who hardly registered her existence. Thoughts flowed through her web and she looked for the pattern she'd felt from the monster she was chasing. As always, she was also watching for scent or thought from any other night creatures. She could never let her guard down, couldn't risk a run in with one of them. A shudder ran through her at the thought of what would happen if she did. She ignored the part of her that wished for it, the release from this loneliness and pain. Death. The end to all of the darkness and filth, the horror that was this place. It could stop... she could stop...

She shook the dark thoughts away and hurried on, more determined than before. A purpose was driving her. As long as she continued to attend to that purpose, she could keep the suicidal thoughts away. Someday she wouldn't be able to stop it, she knew she would present herself to the beasts that could take her down and she would welcome the release. Not today, not as long as there was a helpless soul cowering in chains that she could help.

"Shit," she grumbled as she caught the familiar scent of vampire nearby. She rushed into an alley and shifted, scrambling out of her pile of clothes and up the side of the brick, backing herself into a tiny hole.

She peered out of the darkness, eight unblinking eyes watching for the enemy. A tall woman with long red hair and pale skin, dressed casually in jeans and a t-shirt, stopped at the entrance to the alley. She sniffed the air delicately and peered with narrowed eyes into the darkness. There was nothing to see, just garbage and stray cats. Aranha had hid her clothes and weapons behind a dumpster but if the vampire decided to walk further in to investigate, she might find them, she might find her.

Aranha was confident in her ability to take out a vampire, especially if it was alone, but they rarely were. They tended to travel in pairs, sometimes flanked by werewolf guards. She would have a hell of a time against a group of more than two, it wasn't worth the risk if she could avoid it. One of the only reasons she survived was because they didn't expect to find her, and if they ran across her scent, they were not likely to know what it was they were smelling. Being the last of a presumed extinct species had its benefits.

Another vampire joined the woman, this man was short and round with a deceptively kind face. He put a hand on the woman's back and she motioned to the alley. He turned with a curious eye and sniffed the air.

Death was right there, staring into the alley, eyes searching the walls, the fire escapes, and the roofline. They stood for a long time and Aranha waited. She was on a mission—tonight was not the night to meet her end.

Tomorrow might feel vastly different, perhaps tomorrow she would kneel in front of those two and present her neck, close her eyes and let the final darkness seep into her soul. It would sweep her off this earth and she would find herself in another place, or nowhere at all.

The vampires eventually continued on, but Aranha didn't move for another ten minutes just to be sure. A spider crawled over to investigate who had intruded on her home. They looked at each other and Aranha tapped one of her feet to communicate that she was friendly, and would be leaving soon. The spider was satisfied with that and moved along.

Aranha crawled to the ground and shifted back to human, then dressed as quickly as she could. She headed out to the street, scanning for danger, then turned in the opposite direction that the vampires had gone. She knew she had lost the human for sure now, but she had an idea of where to head. The memory showed a basement, no doubt it was a house and not an apartment because he would need privacy. Since the man was walking, it was likely he lived close and there was only one small neighborhood of houses within reasonable walking distance. She had a destination in mind and set off with determined steps.

The neighborhood street was quiet when she got there, it was quite late and most humans would be settled in for the night. Houses in disrepair lined both sides of the street along with cars in a similar state. It wasn't a nice neighborhood. Maybe it had been once, thirty or more years ago, but now it was a smear of decaying humanity.

She was going to have to get close to the houses one at a time to search properly, she couldn't risk missing the boy. She took a deep breath, resigned to the search, even if it took all night. She would never allow a helpless being to be treated like what she'd seen. Sometimes she wondered if humans didn't deserve their place as food for the supernaturals, the way they treated each other was horrendous.

Aranha started with the first house, moving close, sticking to shadows. She knew she was looking for someone in a basement, so she concentrated on basement windows. She crouched and peered, holding out a webbed hand to try and catch anything alive down there.

House after house was blank. Even a sleeping brain gives off waves of dreaming she would have caught. The poor thing wasn't in any of those, or... she was too late. She wasn't giving up though, not until she'd checked every basement, so she carried on. Catching the mundane thoughts of humans going about their life, or dreaming of better things. Some were drunk, and raging in their minds about how they could have been great, if only this or if it weren't for that. Humans were always blaming others for their situations, not knowing how easily they could just make a different choice, how it wasn't too late to take themselves out of whatever hell they'd made. Often the only thing holding them back was an addiction; drugs, alcohol, or sex that they refused to give up. Humans too often chose those addictions over their own wellbeing or happiness. Self-destruction seemed to be ingrained in humanity. The drug brains were the worst, just dark pits of despair. They reminded Aranha of her own darkness and the pit she often slipped into where she wanted to seek out an end to all of it. Crawling out of that tar pit was a hell of its own. So far, she didn't regret that she had made the journey over and over, but it never completely left her; as if she always had one foot stuck in the cloying black pit, ready to overtake her if she just let go a little more.

Perhaps these humans felt the same way, maybe it was why so many of them didn't run away when faced with a creature who wanted them for dinner, why their instincts froze them or drew them closer rather than told them to run. They were deep in that pit and their escape was standing in front of them in the form of sharp teeth and claws. Perhaps their predilection to addictions was why humans were prey, not predators. A predator's instinct was survival above all else, a predator would never give themselves over to something that would dull the senses and leave them open to harm, no addiction would get in the way of a predator's desire for what they wanted.

What did all predators want? Prey and power; to be fair, these were probably just other forms of addictions. Things that pulled and prodded the being in one direction or another, kept them from seeing themselves for the harmful beings they were.

Aranha shook herself out of the familiar dark train of thought. She wasn't sure where she fit, she knew she wasn't prey, knew her instincts were for survival, but power wasn't something she desired either. The only thing that came close to being a desire, was purpose, she wanted a purpose and that kept her going out every night in search of those who most deserved their place at the bottom of the food chain. Because she also needed prey to survive, and until she could let herself die, she was forced to survive.

She wasn't instinctually prey; she wasn't fully predator... she was other and that suited her just fine.

As her mind flipped through the meaning of her own existence, and whether or not she deserved to continue it, she kept looking and finally she found something in a small grey house. She bent down to a window that was barred, that was her first clue that this might be the place, none of the other houses had barred basement windows. She pushed her hand close, web strung between each finger. There was a curtain on the inside of the window but a crack told her it was dark in there and as far as she could tell, the whole house was quiet, not a light or noise anywhere within.

She didn't have to wait long; she got a stream of random images. Someone was down there, dreaming, and it wasn't her perpetrator, but it might be his victim. Now she needed to know if it was someone's teenage son, or if it was a prisoner in chains. She straightened and walked around the back of the house, slinking smoothly through the shadows. She tried the back door, locked. She could take care of that easy enough though. She listened carefully at the door for a moment hearing nothing, then picked the lock and slipped inside. She was still sifting for thoughts but she couldn't get anything, if there was someone else in the house, they weren't close.

She slunk through the darkness without issue, her eyes saw well without much light. She'd come into the kitchen from a back porch and spied a door that had a heavy lock on it that was far too excessive for an indoor basement. Excitement filled her, this was definitely a sign she'd found the right place. She didn't want to waste time trying to pick the lock now that she was so sure. With a small bit of effort, she was able to rip the lock off the door, splintering the cheap wood. She froze after the cracking noise reverberated around the house. If someone was asleep upstairs or in the next room, they would have definitely heard that, and she was prepared to fight. She had a hand on a knife and was crouched in an attack ready position, waiting.

She heard a groan in the basement but nothing else. After a moment she went down. She kept the knife ready, in case she was wrong about what she was about to encounter. The smell that hit her mid stairway was intense and she knew the poor boy had been down there for a long time. When she reached the bottom of the steps, she saw him and she had to bite her lip to keep from crying out in rage.

He looked like a pile of rags thrown on a dirty pad on the floor. He was shivering and shaking and she wasn't sure if he was awake or dreaming still; his thought pattern was erratic. She put the knife away after her web caught no other thoughts in the room.

"Can you hear me?" she whispered. "My name is Aranha, and I mean you no harm." She held out her hands to show that they were empty.

"Get out of here, he will come back, he'll take you too," the boy croaked out. He sounded like the words were painful to say and he didn't move from his fetal position as he spoke.

Aranha was vibrating with rage, how could anyone be

treated like this, why were there people on earth who would do such a thing to another, it made no sense! She knelt by him, afraid to touch him, afraid she would hurt him while she tried to help.

"I am going to get those chains off you. I could rip them off but I don't want to harm you, do you know where the key is?" She knew it would be faster to rip them off, but it wouldn't be gentle.

"He keeps it in his pocket."

"Is he here?"

"I don't think you would have gotten this far if he was, Ma'am."

"What's your name?"

"Jonah."

"Okay, Jonah I am going to go see if I can find the key."

"You should get out of the house before he comes back, he's going to be so angry if he knows you were here, he'll—"

"He won't hurt you ever again, and I *will* get you out of here." She touched his head gently and he jerked as if she'd slapped him. "I won't harm you, Jonah, I swear it. No one is going to harm you ever again," she said fiercely. Every instinct in her was crying out to help the boy, tears of anger stung the backs of her eyes and her fangs extended, wanting nothing more than to tear apart the monster who had done this.

"Please, Ma'am, it is better for us both if you get out while you can." He moved his head slightly and she saw he had deep blue eyes in a dirty face, sunken cheeks, and cracked lips.

He looked starved and weak. She wondered when the last time he'd had any water or food was. What would be the point of this torture? Aranha's hands fisted and she must have had a terrifying look on her face because Jonah scrambled away, groaning with every movement.

"He will die this night," she vowed. "I am going up to find a key. If I don't find it, I will be back and I will rip those off you as carefully as I can. I won't leave the house without you." She hoped her words were reassuring but his eyes closed and he just sighed sadly.

As she walked away, she heard him sobbing behind her and she couldn't stop herself from punching the wall as she went up the stairs. This was why she was here, this was why she was on earth, to stop this kind of atrocity from going unpunished. A bit of the darkness lifted from her soul; she had a purpose in this moment.

She started in the kitchen, searching for a key, then found the bedroom upstairs and rummaged through drawers. No luck. She was about to just go rip the chains off him when she heard the front door open. She pulled out a knife and smiled, her fangs descended and she waited. She would have been upset to miss out on the punishment part of this rescue mission. She would have come back the next night for it if she'd had to, but waiting was always so frustrating.

The man didn't turn on any lights as he fumbled through the house, he was likely drunk, and on his way to abuse Jonah. Aranha crept out of the bedroom and down the stairs. She was fast and stealthy; the human wouldn't detect her until it was too late. She was in the kitchen doorway when he got to the now ripped open basement door. He was staring at it, dumbfounded, weaving slightly; definitely drunk.

"What the hell?" he slurred.

"Sorry, I didn't have a key," she said casually.

He spun around and faced her with surprise that turned quickly to lustful hope. "Well, hello there, is it Christmas? You look like an angel wrapped in a bow."

"I am your death, dear. You've been a very bad boy." She held her voice steady, conversational, as she spoke to him.

His face slowly registered surprise then turned angry. "Get out of my house, bitch. My son is no concern of yours."

"Your son? This is how you treat your son?" She spoke carefully, trying to keep from lashing out immediately.

"He's not what you think, he's an animal!"

"The only animal I see here is you." She stepped forward and he stepped back, moonlight slid in through a window and she knew he must be finally registering the inhuman blackness of her eyes. She smiled, letting him see her fangs.

"You're one of them!" he gasped.

"No one else on earth is like me, but there are far too many like you," she said simply and shoved him down the stairs.

He tumbled and rolled, in his drunken stupor he was unable to steady himself and he landed with a satisfying thud at the bottom. He groaned but didn't get up. She was a little disappointed as she walked down the stairs. He deserved torture, but he obviously wasn't going to stay conscious long enough for much of it.

"Where's the key?" she hissed.

"Fuck you," he groaned.

She let her black fangs out, dripping venom on his face as she hissed. His eyes widened with fear and he clutched his chest, his body convulsed, he gasped for air, and his eyes rolled back in his head as his heart beat erratically then stopped.

"Shit... that was disappointing," she sighed. "Not going to waste a meal though."

She turned to look at Jonah, he was crouching now, looking at her with fear and shock.

"Don't watch," she said and turned back to the disgusting man on the floor. She bit into his neck and filled him with enough venom to liquefy his insides in a matter of days. Then she shoved him out of the way. No need to wrap him in a web, he was already dead.

PLEASE REVIEW

We hope you enjoyed Princess of Prias by Courtney Davis. If you did, we would ask that you please rate and review this title. Every review helps our authors.

Rate and Review: Princess of Prias

5 Prince Publishing
Arvada, Colorado, USA

MEET THE AUTHOR

Courtney Davis is an author of fantasy with a little romance and humor thrown in. She loves creating worlds and exploring human, and inhuman, interaction. This is her second book with 5 Prince Publishing and her first attempt at a sci-fi base for her fantasy. Creating the different planets and species was a new and fun challenge for her. She resides in North Idaho with her husband and children–teaching, reading, writing and soaking up sunshine. She hopes you find some joy in her writing. Currently she is working hard on more Urban Fantasies to delight her readers.